Marcus Fedder was born in Hanover, Germany, and studied Politics, English and International Relations at the FU Berlin, LSE and Cambridge. As well as writing he is a partner in a hedge fund and previously worked for investment banks and the World Bank and the European Bank for Reconstruction and Development. He wrote *Sarabande* while working as a banker in the City of London. His interest in Sarajevo was kindled during work travel there. He lives in London, plays the cello and paints, selling his paintings in support of children's charities Unicef and FLAME.

MARCUS FEDDER

dexter
haven
PUBLISHING

Published in 2008 by Dexter Haven Ltd
Curtain House
134–146 Curtain Road
London EC2A 3AR

Printed and bound in the UK by
CPI Mackays, Chatham ME5 8TD

J.S. Bach, Suite no 2 in D minor for solo violoncello

SARABANDE

Preface

Twelve years have passed since the war in Sarajevo finished in early 1996. The town is back to normal: tourists visit, Djemal's café is busy, people walk in the hills and pick berries and mushrooms. It is hard to believe that only a decade ago the city was besieged and bombarded daily. Shells were lobbed, snipers killed innocent kids. The siege lasted for four years, or, in other words, it took the international community until 1995 to intervene and stop the bloodshed.

I finished writing *Sarabande* in the autumn of 1994. I typed it up and went to the local bookbinder and had it bound in black cloth. For years it was left alone on a shelf in my study. Then one day it was gone. I discovered it at four o'clock the next morning, when I saw a light in my daughter's room. She was thirteen. She had just finished reading it and was sitting in her bed, looking at me as I knocked and opened her door. I saw tears in her eyes. She moved aside and asked me to sit down, putting her hand on my arm.

'You've never told me the full story, Dad. Now I think I finally start to understand…'

'Understand what?' I asked.

'You, Dad. And Mum. Grandpa. Grandma. Everything. Sarajevo.' She looked at me, thinking. 'When did you publish this?' she asked.

'I haven't, Darling…I couldn't.'

'Why not?'

'It's too personal,' I replied.

She looked down again and then, lifting her head, at me with great seriousness.

'Dad. You've got to publish this!' she said. 'Everyone has to read this book!'

'Why?'

'If everyone in this world read this book, those wars would never happen again.'

She looked at me as if exhausted from this outburst and added quietly, 'If it only made one single person a pacifist, it would have been worth the effort.'

'But I'm not a pacifist, Camille,' I said.

'I know. But you're my Dad and you would never start a war.' She smiled. 'So, please, Dad, promise you will publish it!'

I promised.

Prologue

I am back. I thought I would never return. But here I am, drawn to this one place, that is destroyed, desolate and barren. I play, Bach, D minor, and listen to the cello as its sound fills the air before fading into the distance towards the minarets, and then towards the hills. I open my eyes and look around, and see the rows of graves. Row after row. Yes, here she is, for ever.

Janna.

I play again and close my eyes and see the pictures. Pictures I have been seeing without interruption the last year, the last seventeen months. I see them clearly, some are still, others full of fast and furious motion, three-dimensional. I also hear the sound, smell the smell, and sense the warmth and coldness of those days.

I was hoping to overcome by coming back, by seeing Sarajevo again, now in fragile peace, or rather in an interruption from the shelling, from the war that still ravages the countryside around the town. But no, the intensity of pain increases even further, numbing my senses.

What does it take to understand?

I stop, having finished the Sarabande, and get up to find Djemal and Leila re-joining me. They put their arms around my shoulder, holding on to me as if for support. I feel they know and understand the pain.

'Why don't you write things down?' Leila asks.

I had told her when I arrived about the pictures, like a film, tormenting my days and nights. But I cannot capture all dimensions: space, feelings, smell, noise, laughter, music, time, the time that refuses to pass, or time that flies. I try to tell her this as we walk towards the jeep that will take me back to the airport soon.

'Or write a book and sell your book together with a disc,' she continues. 'And tell the readers to listen to it whenever they are reading. A CD attached to every book. A suite or a sonata to go with every chapter.' She smiles and pauses and looks at Djemal, her husband.

'You've got to get over it,' he insists. 'It's over a year now, and I'm just worried how fazed you still are, living in another world. As if in another time zone.' He smiles. I give him back his cello, which he puts into its case. Its wood is dark. The darkest cello I have ever played, almost like ebony – like his eyes.

'Maybe you could paint a picture,' he continues, picking up our conversation at the edge of the cemetery.

'A series. And write your own music – "Pictures at an Exhibition". All in D minor.'

He smiles again, offering me one of his cigars as we sit down in a little café with a view of the minaret spires. I light it carefully and watch the rising smoke. I look at the label and have to smile: Montecristo. Why does a cigar taste of melancholy dreams? I observe Djemal and Leila through the mellow smoke as I try to gather my thoughts. Djemal looks, lost in thought, at his cigar and then at me.

'But I don't feel things like a picture,' I say to him. 'A painting is a process and then a finished product, static in time and space. In two dimensions, without music, smells or words. It's too difficult, and I'm not Chagall or de Kooning.'

'I think I should write things like a film, maybe a film that runs backwards in time,' I continue after a while. 'A film captures almost all dimensions: you have movement and expressions, and everyone can feel the joy, suspense and sadness. And you have music…but you don't have smells.'

We sit and puff and watch the glow of the burning tobacco turn into smoke and ashes.

It has been seventeen months of living in the past, with pictures from the past. But yes, I realise now, this is the film, my film, that still unfolds each day, each night. Above all at night, when darkness is the screen and silence lets me listen to the life that plays inside my head.

We hug good bye and the jeep rushes me back to Sarajevo

airport where the UN plane is waiting. I feel their tears and they feel mine, blurring my vision.

Five hours of Sarajevo and I am exhausted and drained.

In the plane I close my eyes and see the images that make the film. I order the random and chaotic sequence of the pictures, slow it down, turn it to black and white and back to colour, right back to the beginning. And stop. There I was, playing as I used to do so often on a hazy Sunday afternoon.

I realise now I want to show this film, to share the feelings, to relive the life that was, and show emotions that have passed and yet still hurt.

Out of the window, the Adriatic stretches far until the horizon. We are safe again, returning to France, where I shall be tonight, back in Lujeron, in our garden in the Pyrenees. I get out paper and try to hold it on my knees, gazing at the whiteness of the empty pages. How do you start a film? I will have time to write the first scene on the plane and then continue writing when I am back. I start sketching my thoughts, my recollections of the past, of that one summer day that changed my life with such resolution.

The film

A black screen. Cello music sets in, the Sarabande of the second suite by Bach. After ten seconds white-framed letters appear on the screen:

June 1992

The letters fade slowly and a cemetery is shown.

London, Highgate Cemetery. Ext.

It is June, an early afternoon, a beautiful warm day, blue skies with high-flying swallows. The sun stands almost vertically above, casting short shadows. The graves are marked with white stones and decorated with freshly planted flowers. Tall trees can be seen on the horizon. The camera wanders slowly over the graves of the cemetery, focusing down a gravel path between the graves, where at a distance Dan is sitting, playing the cello. The camera slowly moves towards him. Dan is in his thirties, tall, with a serious face, lightly tanned with black hair.

Dan is playing the Bach suite by heart, his eyes closed, his face in the sun. The camera is getting closer, until it rests on the cello, then on his face. Dan is dressed in black jeans, a black polo shirt and a black pullover.

The focus changes, moving away from Dan while he continues playing, going over the graves, up to the wall of the cemetery, where it focuses up the road. On the road Janna is walking towards the cemetery.

Janna is a woman in her late twenties, with a fine face, black eyes, dark shoulder-length hair, tanned, tall and slim. She is wearing blue jeans and a blue polo shirt. Over her shoulders she carries a green pullover. She walks past the cemetery, the camera following her around, resting on her back. Janna slows down and turns around, trying to find out where the music is coming from. She realises that it comes from the cemetery and puts her hands on its wall to look inquisitively over it.

Point-of-view Janna. The cemetery can be seen; she looks around, at the graves, the flowers and the sky.

Focus on Janna. She pauses, thinking, then climbs over the wall and heads towards the music. The music gets gradually louder as she approaches Dan.

Point-of-view Janna. Janna goes up the gravel path and turns into the lane at the end of which Dan is sitting. He is facing the other way so she can see only his back. She walks up to Dan and around him, quietly in order not to disturb him.

Focus on Dan. His eyes are closed. Janna stops and sits down on one of the stones. Dan finishes the suite and waits for a while with eyes still closed, and then opens them.

I remember this moment as if it was yesterday. Yes, I was wearing black. Black says a lot, though different things to different people. My black was meant to be the black you see in Italy, worn by old people even on hot summer days, not the designer black, which has a different meaning. And people in designer black do not understand the true significance of black, the monotonality of feelings when expressed as black on black.

I was playing, and all the while I was feeling a presence I could not explain, but yet I did not want to open my eyes. When I finally did, after the Gigue, I saw her sitting directly opposite me, motionless, with a fine ethereal smile on her tanned face. I was stunned and closed my eyes again, trying to smile, but for some reason could not smile or speak. She, however, broke the silence, looking at me with sparkling and inquisitive eyes. I looked into those eyes, which were deep, sincere and penetrating.

Point-of-view Dan. Dan looks at Janna sitting on the stone. She smiles. Point-of-view Janna. Dan smiles, coyly. He is surprised and embarrassed.

JANNA: I'm sorry. I didn't mean to disturb you. *She pauses and looks at him, waiting for a reaction, but he remains silent, so she continues.* I love listening to cello music. It sounds so beautiful, and yet so sad. *She looks at him, evidently trying to find something to say.* Your playing reminds me of my father. He plays the cello too. He used to play the same suite. I recognised it. *Focus on Dan, sitting numb behind his cello. Janna continues in a different voice*: Sorry, I disturbed you. But what a place to play!

DAN: I know. *His face starts to thaw as he smiles at her.* I like to play outside or in big places, like cathedrals, or here in a cemetery. *He puts his bow down on the ground.*

JANNA: Oh, do continue and let me just sit here and listen for a while. *Dan smiles in reluctant agreement and continues playing, starting with the Courante of the fourth suite. He stops in the middle of the second of the Bourrées and gets up slowly, but then sits down again as her eyes open. He turns towards her.*

DAN: I … I can't play any more … I'd rather stop. *Silence. They both look in different directions. Then Janna glances at him with a laughing eye.*

JANNA: My father always played on the loo. You know, because of resonance. A cello played on the loo has at least double the sound. *Both laugh. Dan starts packing his cello.*

I looked at her and was wondering what she was thinking of while I was playing. Her father? The places where he played? Why did my solitude have to be broken? Through the haze we could hear the noise of traffic at Highgate, hear the taxis, feel the early summer sky and smell the plants, the blossoms. Janna was still staring at me, unsure of what she should say, yet smiling this eternal smile with serious eyes. What sort of person was she? What does a woman with such eyes do? Unanswered questions were shooting through my head.

'You really shouldn't stop, and I shouldn't be bothering you.' She smiled, walking over to a tree, leaning against it.

I had wanted to stop anyway, I told her. 'I still wanted to read a bit out here on the Heath. It's such a beautiful day.'

She remained standing at the tree, showing no intention of leaving, whilst I packed up my cello.

'Do you mind if we go? I guess you're not staying...?' I asked.

I picked up my cello and waited for her. We could hear the gravel underneath our feet as we walked down the path together in silence. The door of the cemetery was locked.

'How did you get in?'

'I jumped,' she said, laughing innocently.

'Oh well...OK. You go first.'

I helped her over the wall, holding her foot and lifting her up. She was surprisingly light. On the top she looked back, smiling. I smelled her perfume, which was strangely mixed with some other smells that I could not decipher. I have a pretty good nose: this was certainly not pure Chanel, but a mixture of Annik Goutal with smells of disinfected corridors. I tried to savour the smell, but it vanished in the air. She jumped.

'Well done. Can you take it?'

I handed her the cello and jumped over the wall myself.

'You wonder sometimes why they bother about gates,' she said.

We walked in silence, side by side, not looking at each other.

I cannot let this moment pass too fast, and so I leave my script to join my parents in the garden of their old Château of Lujeron. The plane ride from Sarajevo was too bumpy. I couldn't write, and only started once I had arrived back in my room, in the quietness of this château, the solitude of the thick walls behind the honeysuckle growing towards the roof. The garden has enormous trees, which stop the wind that comes from Spain over the Pyrenees. Evenings over here bring almost total silence. Silence from nature, which is rare: no birds, no bees, no barking; even the steady humming of the river seems to be dying down. This is the silence I needed to live again. I often play the cello: Bach, Britten, cello concertos without the accompanying orchestra, sonatas without the piano, and hear the music as if from a distance, peculiar both in space and time. The evenings I often spend alone, smoking cigars, puffing to watch the bitter smoke rising, following imaginary patterns in the motionless air. This is the time I see the film and write.

And, thinking back to Highgate Cemetery, I still ask myself today why one meets the one in a billion person, what is the special gravitational force pulling two people together.

'What is the statistical probability of a comet hitting another comet in their random flights through space?' I ask my parents, sitting down, taking the cup of tea they had left for me in both hands.

My father pours himself another cup of tea and gets up to pluck some weeds from between the flowers. He looks at me at some length. He does research into DNA, a subject too complicated for bankers.

'What are the chances that you meet a close friend by chance in the Guggenheim?' he asks, looking at the weeds. 'It happened to me,' he continues. 'What are the chances that you meet someone who is thinking the same as you do at exactly the same time? It happens to your Mum and me all the time.'

He pauses with a clump of weeds in his hand.

'And comets do collide,' he adds.

I get up and go back to my room to write, but cannot think. I light a candle and look past the flickering flame of the burning match into the stillness of the garden and on to the pages I am slowly filling. I close my eyes again and recall the moments of our first encounter, see the film slowly passing, slower than reality.

JANNA *hesitantly*: May I ask you a question? *Dan looks at her inquisitively. Janna looks at her feet. Her feet are filmed as they pass over the ground – tanned, slim feet in dark-blue leather sandals.* Why do you play in graveyards?

Dan continues down the road, looking straight ahead. Both are shown from the front, walking side by side. Dan answers quietly, feeling uneasy at having to answer the question.

DAN: Not sure. Maybe because it's so beautiful. And quiet. He adds after a pause to reflect: and ultimately peaceful.

The moment I had said it, I felt it sounded trite. But it was right at the same time. Cemeteries are the ultimate peace. I sensed that Janna was still looking for something else. No, not something else, but for the real reason, which she expected to be deeper, buried under layers of past time. But yet I was not capable of thinking ahead or of what to say, as the moments, though they were passing slowly in reality, seemed to be rushing by. She looked at me for some time, trying to find out what I was really thinking. Fine lines were furrowing her forehead, her eyebrows moving closer, almost connecting.

JANNA *in a very soft voice*: Just because of that? *They walk in silence side by side for some time. One can see the ground passing underneath their feet.*
DAN: No. *He shakes his head, still looking down.*

I stopped. Janna also stopped. I put my cello down and leaned on its case and looked for some time into her eyes, recollecting my thoughts. Finally I spoke.

DAN: Well, as you ask: I can tell you why I play the cello, in cemeteries. *Dan pauses for a long time and looks into her eyes, which remain serious, withstanding his glance.* I play to remember some people I loved, who are dead now – so maybe I play from sadness. *She smiles.* And because I simply like playing the cello. It sounds very melancholic, and beautiful. I love playing Bach, you know – he wrote a number of suites for solo cello

which really are great music. *She smiles.* But I also play
other stuff – Britten wrote great music for the cello,
Dvorak, Haydn, whatever…*He slowly continues walking,
she catches up with him. They reach Hampstead Heath.
They walk across the grass in silence, each looking just in
front of them. Then Dan pauses and looks into the
distance, where the skyline of the City of London is visible.*
DAN: Shall we sit down? *Janna nods. They sit down, close to
each other, almost touching shoulders.*

I looked into her eyes. They were dark, black and changed over
time. They changed when she was laughing or when she was
irritated, furious or sad. But then, they also changed over months
– that is their basic tone, their deep reflection, expressing curiosity,
intensity, conviction and always urgency.

DAN: Ever since I was nine I've been playing with friends –
duos, quartets, and also in orchestras. And then I've
also been playing on my own. I had one particular
friend who played the organ. But he's dead. He died in
a car accident. He was my closest friend and a fantastic
organist – I played with him in churches. *They look at
each other. Neither smiles. He stares into the distance and
lowers his head.* After his death I often played for him.
Dan looks at her from the side. And…well, it doesn't
matter. *He looks at her, studying her face.* I don't know
whether I should be telling you this. *He pauses for a
long time.* Maybe it's better to…*They remain silent for
a while.*
JANNA *quietly*: I can imagine how you felt. It's rare to find
someone who's faced death at our age, unless he's from
Africa or Cambodia…or Yugoslavia.
DAN *smiling at her*: Well, I guess it would be a bit much to
compare myself with someone from those countries.
Particularly from Yugoslavia, if you think about what's
happening over there today.

JANNA: I know. *She glances at him and nods her head and lies down on the grass.*

DAN: It's just awful. *Janna raises her head, preparing to change the subject.*

JANNA: Do you live here in London? Or are you just visiting graveyards?

DAN *smiling*: Actually, I do live here. I don't believe in graveyard tourism. And you? Do you live nearby?

JANNA: Not far from here. *She pauses and looks at him.* But what do you do? I mean, when you're not playing music?

DAN *laughing*: Don't know. Sometimes I think I'm a plumber…

JANNA *interrupts him, laughing too*: You look more like a priest or a lawyer.

DAN *laughing*: Close. Pretty close. How did you guess?

JANNA: The way you talk, the way you dress.

DAN: In fact, I'm in investment banking, or rather in something called private equity. Well, it's a bit of private equity, a bit of M&A… *She looks at him with a frown and then into the distance. Dan glances over and adds*: I buy companies and sell them.

JANNA *looking at Dan*: M-n-A – what's that?

DAN: Mergers and acquisitions. Buying and selling. Companies instead of cars.

JANNA: Sounds fascinating. Can you just buy and sell companies like that?

DAN: Well, not quite like apples and oranges.

JANNA: So?

DAN: I think plumbing is probably more fun… *smiling again.* Well, actually, it's pretty similar.

JANNA: I thought banking is so boring.

DAN: I actually enjoy work. It's quite varied and challenging and I get to travel a lot, which is fun. *He pauses a while.* But then again, sometimes, when I'm alone, I feel it's pretty senseless, you know? It's all about making money, not really about building things or making this world a better place.

JANNA: Oh, come on, not everyone can be that saintly. And look at what the world is like today, despite the fact that so many people get paid to make it a better place.

DAN: Yeah, I guess a lot of people have different opinions about what a better world should look like.

JANNA *sits up, shivering*: It's getting cold…*Dan slowly gets up and holds his hand out to Janna to help her up. She looks at the sky*…and late too.

DAN *looking at his watch*: I think I've got to go…I hadn't realised…*He shrugs his shoulders.*

JANNA *hesitating, shyly*: Hmm…Do you want to meet again?

DAN *smiling*: I'd love to. Are you free tomorrow?

JANNA: Sure. In the afternoon.

DAN *pausing to think*: How about in Hyde Park? *Looking into the distance.* Actually, do you know the Orangerie in Kensington Gardens?

JANNA: Yes, I think so. You mean the one that's a café?

DAN: Yes, right at the end, near Notting Hill Gate. Do you want to meet there?

JANNA *nods, smiling*: Sure.

DAN: Is half past four OK?

JANNA: Could we make it four?

DAN: Actually I'll still be playing tennis. But if you haven't got much time, I'll cancel.

JANNA: No. Half past four should be fine.

DAN *watching her for some time*: Take care.

JANNA: See you then. *She hesitates, stretching out her hand towards him.* I'm Janna…by the way.

DAN: Oh sorry. *He takes her hand.* My name is Daniel. *He gazes for some time into her eyes. She returns the direct look, smiling warmly.*

JANNA: You will come tomorrow, won't you?

DAN: Absolutely.

JANNA: Bye then.

DAN: Take care. *He briefly touches her shoulder and retreats. They walk off in different directions. Shot widens to show how both are walking away from each other over the Heath, fading.*

I probably slept less than an hour that night. Too much was going on in my head. Who was this person who had entered into my life, shaking my fragile equilibrium? I felt like the victim of a spell, unable to escape. I went to my study early in the morning, but could not concentrate on work and played on my computer, counting the hours until the afternoon. In the end I asked my friend Tom whether he wanted to play tennis earlier, and we met up straight after lunch to play.

Contradictions

Hyde Park Tennis Courts. Ext.

The courts are in the middle of Hyde Park, surrounded by high trees and bushes. There is a bowling green, and people are sitting on benches next to the tennis courts. Dan is playing tennis with Tom, a colleague and friend about the same age as Dan. While the focus is on Dan and Tom, Janna can be seen coming across the park from the distance. She recognises Dan. She changes her direction to walk towards the courts. Dan and Tom stop playing and start packing their stuff. Dan changes his polo shirt and puts on a light pullover. Tom and Dan are seen approaching the exit. They part, shaking hands. Dan turns round and sees Janna. She is waving her hand, smiling. Dan walks up to her.

DAN *smiling*: I hadn't expected you here.

JANNA *face very happy*: I just walked past and saw you playing. Hi.

DAN: Hello. *They shake hands and look into each other's eyes for some time, standing close to each other.* It's good to see you.

JANNA *laughing*: Did you doubt I'd come?

DAN *protesting*: No. Absolutely not.

JANNA *smiling at him*: So, who won?

DAN: My friend Tom, of course. I'm crap.

JANNA: You weren't that bad from what I could see.

DAN: Do you play yourself?

JANNA: Yes. Not very well, though.

They set off and walk next to each other in silence. Dan, while walking, turns and looks at her.

DAN: Do you know what? I spoke only about myself yesterday. Sorry.

JANNA: Don't worry. We didn't have that much time.

DAN: Let me ask you: what do you actually do? Are you studying?

JANNA: No. I'm a doctor.

DAN: A GP?

JANNA: No. I work in a hospital; with children.

DAN: Hmm…That must be fun.

I think back. My first thought was Janna in the surroundings of a hospital, with little children running around, smiling, kids playing happily. I could see her in her element, taking them into her arms, happy about their recovery. Able to help, fulfilled. I glanced at her and saw that she had turned quiet, and her face had become serious. We walked in silence while Janna gazed down at her feet. She gradually slowed and then stopped, looking at me with dark and serious eyes.

'Actually, it's fun, but it's also often quite depressing.' She looked down, pausing for a moment, and then at me again.

'It can be quite sad. I work with children, but it's not measles, rubella or broken arms. I work in a ward that's special in a way. It's a cancer ward – you can imagine what that means.' Again she paused and her gaze became more intense.

'Cancer is an amazing illness. It strikes and we don't know why. The kids don't know what's happening to them. You know, if you fall and break an arm, it's easy. You were an idiot, fell off a ladder and ended up in hospital. But how do you explain to a little one what is happening inside his body? About cells? How do you explain radiotherapy or chemotherapy? Why does his hair fall out? Why should he have this treatment that afterwards makes him feel nauseous and makes him vomit all the time? It's tough.' She sighed and we both walked silently across the park, looking at black crows circling in the air before landing next to an enormous oak tree.

'And then, my work involves death. All the time. Life and death. That's why what you said touched me yesterday. I see death every month, sometimes every week.' She shook her head.

Suddenly a group of noisy kids crossed our way, tearing us out of our thoughts, forcing us to laugh. She smiled at me, all of a sudden, and said, 'Come on. Let's change the topic. I don't want to talk about this now. Another day. It's just too pathetic to talk about death each time we meet.' We walked on in silence, Janna taking my hand.

'You know, my job is actually very fulfilling, and often quite a lot of fun. Besides, I love children. They really are wonderful. And it's not all that bad all the time, as most of them actually do make it and get cured.'

Orangerie. Int.

The Orangerie is a beautiful Victorian building, part of Kensington Palace, at the end of the Palace Gardens, red brick, surrounded by perfectly manicured lawns, flowers, bushes and trees. Inside, the Orangerie is painted all in white. There are people sitting at the tables, drinking tea, eating cakes and ice cream. Janna and Dan too are sitting at a table, drinking tea, eating scones. Dan is looking pensively out of the window, through which the warm sun is shining, and then at her.

DAN: I was wondering. Why did you climb across the cemetery wall? I mean, were you attracted by the graves or by the music?

JANNA: What do you mean 'by the graves'? It doesn't happen every day that someone plays music there, and I pass by almost every day... No, I was surprised to hear someone play Bach.

DAN: Did you know it was Bach?

JANNA: Of course. I told you I recognised the piece – my father used to play it.

DAN: Sorry. Of course. *He looks at her.* Do you play any music yourself?

JANNA: Yeah. The radio...and the flute.

DAN: I love the flute. It's funny, had you asked me to guess, I would have guessed piano or flute. *He turns around, changing the subject, with a different voice.* I'm actually puzzled by your accent. Where are you from?

JANNA: From Yugoslavia. Or rather, from what's left of it. But I've been living in England for a long time.

DAN: Since when?

JANNA: I came here right after high school to study medicine, and now I work here. And even have a British passport...and my uncle lives in Edinburgh. You know, when one doesn't have a home country any more, one has to adopt one. I think I've adopted Britain. I really like living here.

DAN: And where in Yugoslavia are you from?

JANNA: Bosnia. In fact from Sarajevo. But we also lived in Belgrade for some time.

DAN: Sarajevo? That's a war zone.

JANNA: Oh, Sarajevo is one of the most beautiful places on earth. At least it was. The summers are beautiful and warm. The hills around have deep forests with flowers and mushrooms, which we used to go and pick. The town is so lively, multicultural. I love the churches and mosques.

DAN: Why are there mosques?

JANNA: Well, the remains of the Ottoman Empire. The bigger part of the population is Muslim. But there are also Christians, Jews, everything...a very tolerant society...at least it used to be.

DAN: Hmm. Well. I guess no longer...

She dreams into the distance, not looking at Dan, slowly drinking her tea. Then suddenly she pulls herself together, waking up, smiling at him.

JANNA: No. It's grim. Ghastly. War since April. Constant shelling by this fascist Mladic and his Serbian troops. But the Croats aren't much better.

DAN: I know. I've actually read a lot about it. I mean about all of Yugoslavia, the breaking up of the country, the ethnic hatred that's come back after all those years.

JANNA: It's frightening.

DAN: Initially I thought that Tudjman was a relatively decent guy, but he is just as bad as Milosevic or Karadzic.

JANNA: Agree. But it shouldn't be like this. I mean, one thing I cannot understand is how you can have a siege of a whole town when the UN is right in the middle of it.

DAN: What?

JANNA: Yes. It's pretty unbelievable. They are right in the middle of town, and war is going on around them. I mean, it's not the United Nations, but these Unprofor units have had their Balkan headquarters in Sarajevo since February this year.

DAN: And they don't do anything to stop the war?

JANNA: It's a joke. *Raising her voice, turning her head to look at him.* They do nothing. Nothing. Most people in Sarajevo hate them. The shelling goes on, every day and they drive around town in their Humvees or armoured personnel carriers. In the meantime, shells kill some people here and there – and then, bang, sixteen people killed in May when they deliberately shelled a bread queue.

DAN: I read about it. It's not only the sixteen dead, but probably hundreds injured...

JANNA: And you know what 'injured' means. You can imagine: hands blown off, feet ripped up, eyes blasted out, shrapnel splinters deep in the body. *She quietens down again and adds with a low voice, almost whispering*: It's awful. *She pauses.* And then the concentration camps.

DAN: I know. It's like in the forties.

JANNA: And what does the world do? The EU does nothing. And the US? Well, Clinton stated with his

sickening twitching mouth – here let me read it to
you... *Janna gets a newspaper out of her bag.* 'If the
horrors of the holocaust taught us anything, it is the
high cost of remaining silent and paralysed in the face
of genocide.'

DAN: Yeah... and the UN impose sanctions on Belgrade, as
if that would do anything.

JANNA: It's sickening.

Dan nods silently.

JANNA *pauses and adds between sips of tea*: I really do hope
that Owen and Vance finally carve up the place and
bring peace. Once there's peace, you can reunite what
they carved up, but for now this would bring peace
and stop the slaughter. *They sit in silence, Janna looking
at Dan.* Actually, I don't want to talk about Sarajevo
now. Not now. Another time, maybe. Why do we
always talk about death? *She smiles at him, sipping her
tea.* How about you? You aren't very English either,
I guess.

DAN: Well, no. Only sort of. My parents came originally
from Germany. You know, in the thirties. They are
Jewish. They came over as kids, met here in Britain
and then moved to the States.

JANNA: Hmm.

DAN: But I was born in Switzerland, where we also lived
for a while. *He looks into the distance.* In the seventies
we also lived in Germany.

JANNA: Are they here or in the US now?

DAN: No. They decided to live in France. In the south.

JANNA: At the sea?

DAN: No, they prefer the poverty and solitude of the
Ariège.

JANNA: Where's that?

DAN: About an hour south of Toulouse.

JANNA: And there they play music in cemeteries?

DAN: Ha ha... No, that's just me.

JANNA: Let me guess: are you the only child?

DAN: Yes and no.

JANNA: What do you mean?

DAN: My brother died some years ago. In Israel. He was quite a bit older than me, so I basically grew up as an only child.

JANNA: I'm sorry.

DAN: No, don't worry, that's OK.

JANNA: And have you ever played for him?

DAN *looking into her eyes*: Yes. Well, in fact, whenever I play in a cemetery I also play for him. *He pauses and then smiles disarmingly at her.* You really have the knack of getting straight at the heart of things, don't you...

JANNA: Hmm. Have I? *She pauses, turning her head away.* And your brother lived in Israel?

DAN: Yes. He decided to go back to the promised land, to help build it up. That was a bit self-righteous, I guess.

JANNA *interrupting*: Why self-righteous?

DAN *laughing*: He was a lawyer. And lawyers are the last thing you need when you want to build something. You normally ship them in when things don't work out. *He pours her some more tea.* And then he was also an officer in the army, like everyone over there. *Pausing.* He was a bit of a paradox. He was also a pacifist.

JANNA *mocking*: And an officer in the army in Israel? Driving around in a tank? The one country where they'll guarantee you a war every three years?

DAN: Yes. And he fought in the war.

JANNA *leaning on her elbow and gazing into the distance, playing with her food*: I can't quite make him out. You say he was a pacifist. And at the same time he fought in the war. Even as an officer. That means killing a hell of a lot of people. *She stops and thinks. She looks at him with serious eyes.* If you're working as a doctor and face death in your work the way I do...*she pauses*...you wouldn't be able to kill. *Dan looks at her with serious eyes, ignoring the waiter who wants to offer them more scones. Janna adds quietly*: I certainly couldn't kill anyone. Not even in war. *After a pause, reflective*: Not even in Sarajevo.

DAN: Not even in Yugoslavia today? What happens if you're attacked?

JANNA *with a determined voice*: I'd surrender. Full stop.

DAN *protesting*: And get killed?

JANNA: Yes, rather than having to kill myself. And having to live with murder on my conscience. *Slightly aggressive*: Do you know what it means to take someone's life?

DAN *quietly*: Absolutely.

JANNA: Could you cope with it?

DAN *reflective, looking far into the distance, then down to the floor, then into her eyes*: I'd never go out to kill the way killing takes place in Bosnia today. Never. I wouldn't kill to take revenge either. We have no right to do that. But I would certainly defend my life, if there was some loony out to kill me or my family or my friends. No one has the right to kill. That's a commandment. Thou shalt not kill. But if someone wrongly assumes the right to kill me, I'd shoot first. And if there's a group of people shooting and killing like today in Yugoslavia, I'd certainly support a military intervention. Like in Kuwait. Or rather, like against Hitler in the forties.

JANNA: But that would be horrible. And incredibly bloody. *Very quietly, shaking her head*: And it wouldn't stop the war. The situation today in 1992 is not as clear-cut as in the forties.

DAN: Why not? It's a matter of superiority of arms. Nothing else. After all, there were decades of peace under Tito. Peace by suppression of all this idiotic nationalistic nonsense.

JANNA: But you can't kill to stop the killing. *Quietly*: You've got to stick to the commandments: thou shalt not kill. You can't simply interpret them whichever way you like.

DAN *shaking his head, slightly annoyed, but smiling*: I think that's bullshit. Just look back some fifty years. Had Hitler been killed twenty years earlier, six million Jews wouldn't have ended up in gas chambers. Tens of millions wouldn't have died in that fucking war.

JANNA: Dan, please don't swear.

DAN: OK. OK. I'm sorry I get emotional about this. *He quietens down.* We lost family in Auschwitz. Certainly for my parents this is still a reality that hurts. All I wanted to say is that one could have got rid of Nazism, and with that also Stalinism and Communism fifty years earlier.

JANNA: But who gives you the right to kill? Where's the moral justification?

DAN: Aren't there basic human rights? Human values? Do they not imply that you must act to stop killing?

JANNA: No. I think you're wrong. *Very serious*: Incredibly wrong. *She realises that this conversation is not moving in the right direction. Both are quiet for some time. Then she smiles, caresses his hand and laughingly adds*: That's not to say I don't love James Bond. He does things with style, which is quite different. *Both smile.*
Cut.

Hyde Park. Leaving the Orangerie. Ext.

Janna and Dan are leaving the Orangerie together. They are walking next to one another in silence. Dan lays his arm around her shoulder. Janna smiles at him and puts her arm around his waist. They continue walking for some while. Then Janna stops and turns round and puts both her arms around his neck. He caresses her head, kissing her cheek. They continue walking.

DAN *turning to her*: Do you want to come round for dinner
   tonight?

JANNA: I'd love to, but I've got night duty.

DAN: *hesitantly*: How about tomorrow?

JANNA *smiling slightly embarrassed*: I'm actually going to
   the theatre with some colleagues. How about Tuesday?

DAN: Tuesday is OK. Shall we say eight o'clock?

JANNA *smiling*: Eight is fine. You just have to tell me where
   you live.

*They are seen walking arm in arm, slowly through the
park. They are stopping, holding each other's hands,
talking, smiling. Then Janna holds Dan's shoulders while
kissing him goodbye on his cheeks. They part, each walking
off in a different direction.*
Fading.

She kissed me when we parted and we hugged. But we had been
bickering all afternoon about killing, the right to kill to defend.
My alarm bells should have gone off: here was someone pretty
stubborn and extremely opinionated – well, probably just as
stubborn and opinionated as me. This was the second meeting in
our lives and we were arguing. Slowly, as I was walking home
across the park, I reviewed the last hours, wondering above all
what she was thinking. Despite the bickering, I had this longing
feeling, a bitter sweetness that kept me awake at night.

Even today, I am still puzzled. What a conversation! Why did
we end up talking about the right to kill? About war?

Almost all of my girlfriends had been easy-going – but then I
did not really get that close to any of them. The only exception
may have been Tania, Tom's sister, who was a journalist with the
Wall Street Journal during the day and a great pianist in her free
time. I deeply loved her and we lived together for two years and
played music through the nights. In the end, we separated,
though we keep in touch and I still go to her recitals and she
always spots me in the audience, wherever I am sitting. I stopped
playing Beethoven sonatas for a while when we split up. Tania

became close, very close to me. We played music together, which to me means experiencing feelings together – if you play well – and she played extremely well, both technically and with amazing passion. Tania was the only one to whom I had told the story of my brother – and I knew that at some stage I would be able to share this story with Janna. When Tania had heard it, she insisted on playing in churches with me. We played wherever we travelled to, in Reims, Rome and in small villages in southern France. Once she was invited to give a concert in Jerusalem and we spent the weekend at the King David Hotel together, visiting the places where I had played many years before. And yet, although we were close, she always seemed somewhat distant, far away. There was always something – neither of us could manage to define it – that separated us. It was not the fact that she was so Catholic and could not accept my religion. We could have lived with that. It was something different, a distance I could not bridge, a crucial part of her she did not want me to discover. We left each other, though we still loved each other deeply, platonically. Tania said it was as if we were like wind and water, never able to unite truly.

Returning from the park, I opened my door and reached for my cello and played for a long while in order to be able to think again. Who was Janna? She was about to take the place Tania had vacated, and with her I sensed that there would be no final barrier I could not breach, no part I would not discover.

Death was the factor that had shaped my life, and had led me to focus on important things, despite the banal fact that I spent most of my days making money buying, restructuring and selling companies. And death was the determinant in her life. Here and every day. And then at home, where it had the additional other dimension that it was intentional. Killing. Sarajevo meant death. Death because man killed. And she was standing in between, fighting death she understood at hospital but incapable of understanding the killing in Sarajevo.

Sarajevo. I had a vague idea about the place, not only since I had watched the Winter Olympics and remembered beautiful pictures of a beautiful town with friendly people. From my book-shelves I dug out the old *Encyclopaedia Britannica*, a 1929 edition, and read:

> Sarajevo, capital of Bosnia, Yugoslavia. Pop. (1921) 66,337, chiefly Serbo-Croatians. It lies in a fine situation in a valley 1,800 ft above sea level.
>
> Though it is still half oriental, and wholly beautiful with its hundred mosques, its ancient Turkish bazaar, picturesque wooden houses, and cypress groves, it was largely rebuilt after western fashion in 1878. Sarajevo is the seat of a Roman Catholic bishop, an Orthodox metropolitan, the highest Muslim ecclesiastical authority, and the supreme court.

After the war, Sarajevo remained a melting-pot of cultures. No, more a pressure cooker whose lid had blown off once Tito had died. This was the place where people lived peacefully together as long as there was someone keeping the lid on the pressure. A potentially lethal mix of religion, nationalism, a clash in cultures, history.

It was her place.

Dan's bank. Meeting room. Int.

Old-style furniture, two blue and white antique Chinese vases stand on a Victorian mahogany mantlepiece. Yellow-golden wallpaper and old master oil paintings decorate the walls. The windows are framed with thick, red velvet curtains. A long dining-room-type table stands in the middle of the room.

Six of Dan's colleagues are sitting around the table. Dan is sitting at one end of the table. Everyone is wearing dark suits, drinking coffee. On the table are masses of documents. Deal-related discussion can be heard while the camera is moving around the room. The discussion seems unstructured, with everyone in the group participating, all talking at the same time. Two of the bankers are searching through documents. Dan's face looks tense. He sips a glass of mineral water and leans over to Tom, who is sitting at his side, exchanging some words, whispering. Tom laughs, elbowing Dan, who laughs too.

TOM *addressing everyone*: OK, guys. I guess we all agree. Let me just summarise. *Pausing. Then quietly and determined*: First, over the next week, we'll buy five per cent in the market. Quietly. Then we'll announce our holding. Clear intention: minority stake. We won't say yet whether we'll actually have any takeover intentions at this juncture. Let's leave things deliberately blurred. We can't say that we will or we won't swallow up the whole shop.

DAN *looking down, speaking almost to himself*: We'll tell the full truth – no lies.

TOM *smiling and forceful again*: At the same time, you, James, talk to Medifondo, Adriatico and Sienna Paschi to get them to reveal their positions and intentions. Be frank with them. We need to work with them. Then we'll build up to ten per cent. That should give us indirectly forty.

DAN: IFW fund is hostile.

TOM: Yes, but they are ruthless. They'll sell their friends.

ALI: It's just a question of cash.

JAMES: What do we do with all the retail? They probably still hold thirty per cent?

TOM: That's phase three. Public bid. Thirty thousand lire per share. Anything below forty-five is pure gold for us.

ALI: And thirty is about twenty per cent above today's price.

DAN: Retail will love us. *He sips his water, thinking.*

ALI: And, I guess, so will IFW by then.

TOM: Quite. *Adding after a pause, shifting through the papers*: Ali, please take care of all the agreements. Just go over them one last time. I know we've read them more often than the Pope has read the Bible…

DAN: But still, in contrast to the Bible, we always find last-minute glitches.

ALI: Sure.

Silence. Dan collects his papers and stuffs them into a grey rucksack, smiling at everyone.

TOM: This time they're ours. *He gets up, looking around.* Did I miss anything? *The others shake their heads. Packing their papers, they get up too, except for Dan, who remains seated.* OK. Keep me posted. *All leave except for Dan and Tom. Tom sits down next to him again, loosening his tie. He smiles.* Looks like we'll get them.

DAN: Pretty cool.

TOM: But then the real work starts. We either build value or...

DAN *interrupting with a laugh*: Well, we'll fire the CEO, send the President to Bosnia instead of Siberia, and asset-strip the bloody shop. *He pauses, thinking, pouring himself more coffee.* And then? Once again it's like buying a cow from the herd and selling the pieces of meat. It's all so pointless.

TOM: Well, let's go next time for something different. Let's keep things together, merge them with one of their competitors, create value, something big. Real big.

DAN: Naa – that's just as pointless, and all very well, but (a) the amount of work we'd have to put in is horrific and (b) the return we'd get sucks. I think I'd rather continue doing what we're doing, even though it's so bloody repetitive.

TOM: Come on. We do have fun.

DAN: Hmm...Fast and destructive fun, which brings in loads of dosh.

TOM: But you're just hoarding the bloody dosh.

DAN: So what? I buy art. But, honestly Tom, all the intellectual fun is long gone. It's just a bloody routine.

TOM: As I said, we should try something different. *He pours himself and Dan more coffee and both sip, thinking.*

Something paying a bigger margin. Like buying a country: buy bloody Kazakhstan, sell off the oil reserves to Russia, merge it with Turkey, sell the missiles to Iran.

DAN: Hmm...

TOM *mocking*: Do you ever play the cello when you've killed a company? *Silence, both are brooding, looking into the distance.*

DAN *changing the subject and the tone*: Tom. I must ask you something. I've met someone...

TOM *evidently bored by the subject*: Any good in bed?

DAN *serious*: No – be serious. I think it's hit me. Pretty badly. She's different. I don't know how to say it, just special. In a way I've never been hit before.

TOM: Didn't you say the same about Tania and...?

DAN *interrupting, smiling wryly*: Well, yeah, OK. I did, and you know I meant it. I've never said this about the others, though.

TOM: No. But there you said they were fun. And anyway, it was my sister who dumped you...

DAN *sips his coffee and gets up, walking over to the window, looking out into the distance*: Besides, I'm in a really awkward situation. I asked her for dinner... to my place.

TOM *savouring the situation and smiling with an ironic grin*: And you can't even cook. *Dan nods, coming back to the table, sitting down again.* Great. Then you serve up your disgusting muesli and she bolts one hour later. Remember how Tania hated it. *He pauses and thinks.* Why don't you ship in something from the Ritz. Ritz takeaway. Ritz burgers. The ultimate decadence for the spoilt investment banker. What's her name, anyway?

DAN: Janna.

TOM: And how did you meet her?

DAN: At a graveyard.

TOM: Oh! How very romantic! *He walks around the table so as to face Dan directly.* Would she pass your ultimate

test? Would you let her stay for breakfast? Or would
you chuck her out before midnight?

DAN: You're revolting.

TOM *shouting, protesting*: Why am I revolting? You're the
one who chucks them out before the night is over
because the sight of them at breakfast is too much.
That's you. Not me. Toi, pas moi.

DAN: OK. OK. You sound like Oscar Wilde...Hmm...
Maybe you're right. *He gets up too, smiling, defeated.* I've
got to get going. Got to cook.

TOM: I mean, let's be practical. Um, I could stand in the
kitchen and do the cooking.

DAN: Maybe next time.

Cut.

Dinner, at Dan's home. Int.

*A big living room with a dining room attached. It is a
bright room with modern art, an oil painting by Poliakoff
and a litho by Miro are hanging on the walls. A Calder
mobile is hanging from the ceiling. A mix of modern and
antique furniture. Bookshelves with many books on the
walls, rows of art books. Few plants. Minimalist in terms of
furniture and decoration. Dan's cello is standing in the
corner.*

*In the dining room, which is decorated in a similar
style, with modern paintings and modern furniture, Dan is
seen laying the table. He spreads a dark blue tablecloth on
the table. He has changed, now wearing the same clothes
as in the cemetery. He places candles on the table and
walks across the living room to his stereo, putting a disc
into the CD player. It is Mstislav Rostropovich playing the
Boccherini B minor cello concerto.*

*He opens a bottle of wine, choosing from three bottles.
The doorbell rings. He presses the buzzer and opens the
door to his apartment. He puts on an apron and a pair of*

shoes and goes into the kitchen, which is bright and spacious, with pans, utensils and a Michelin doll hanging from the walls.

After a short time Janna appears at the front door, knocks and, as no one answers, enters.

Janna is wearing blue jeans and a white shirt, and carries a green pullover loosely over her shoulders. She is wearing brown loafers. She looks inquisitively around.

JANNA: Hello?

DAN *from the kitchen*: Hi. Come in. Welcome. *He walks up to her and embraces her, kissing her cheeks.*

JANNA: This smells wonderful. Gosh. I hope it wasn't too much trouble.

DAN: No. Don't worry, I love cooking. Or rather eating. It's Thai food today. Do you like Thai food?

JANNA *delighted*: I love it. *Pause. She smiles at him*: Look. I've brought you something. Flowers for the militant bachelor. *She gives him a beautiful cactus. Dan is evidently surprised.*

DAN: Thanks. How delightful! *He laughs and kisses her cheeks, caressing her hair.*

DAN *moving back into the kitchen*: Well, I think it should be ready by now.

Janna *follows him into the kitchen. She puts her arm around him as he stands at the stove. He stirs a bit and then tries it. He smiles at her with a connoisseur's face.*

DAN: Perfect.

He empties the pots into big dishes, brings them into the dining room. They sit down and he starts serving.

DAN: Would you like some wine? *She nods, smiling. He pours her some wine.*

JANNA: Can I see it? *She looks at the bottle.* Hmm. 1978 Château Talbot. My father would love it. He collects wine. *Reflectively*: Well, no, he doesn't actually collect at the moment. I think he just enjoys his collection.

DAN: Well, bon appétit! And welcome. *They start eating. Then they sip the wine, both smiling.*

JANNA: Wow. This is great. You're a fantastic cook.

DAN: Goes with the job. It's all M&A. Today it was a buyout.

JANNA *looking puzzled*: I'm not quite sure I understand.

DAN *laughing*: Doesn't matter. I'll explain my kitchen M&A another day.

JANNA: Tell me about your job. What is M&A and all that? You don't trade, do you? Or do arbitrage…er…like the guy in *Nine and a Half Weeks*?

DAN *laughing*: No. It's not that cool. In fact, as I told you, I buy and sell companies – it's more like being a used-car salesman.

JANNA *looking around*: But, looking at the way you live, it seems to be a slightly better business to be in. But, how does it actually work? *She looks at him puzzled.*

DAN: Let me explain, it works like this: at the moment we're buying an Alfa Romeo in Italy. A stretch-Alfa.

JANNA: Who's we?

DAN: Tom, some other friends and I.

JANNA: Hmm…

DAN: Anyway, we're buying this Alpha, not only with our own money but with money some other investors have put into a fund which we manage. We just haven't got enough cash ourselves, and we'll also have to borrow some more money too. *He stops and looks at her.* Anyway, as soon as it's ours, we'll send the driver off to Eboli as we know he's useless. Next we empty the boot and sell it. Sell the back seats. Sell the middle section to a scrap-metal dealer. We beef up the motor by adding a few cylinders. Cut the back off and sell it to someone needing an Alfa back. We weld a BMW back to the Alfa front in a way that people don't really notice.

JANNA: Why the back of a BMW? That doesn't make sense.

DAN: We still had it in the back of our garage and we

couldn't sell it on its own. So we simply attach it, and, as it turns out, there's what we call a lot of 'synergy', and it works. Bingo. We've got a brand new car. Faster, better looking. New paint job. We then find a new driver and sell it on, for a big profit. All of that takes about two years. Often longer.

JANNA *definitely confused*: Sounds exciting to me. But also a bit like a mixture between alchemy and fraud.

DAN: Well, it's not that exciting, and we are all much too cowardly to commit fraud. *In a less excited voice*: But when I think about it, I'm sometimes actually pretty bored. I've done it so many times. It becomes routine, without any new challenges. It certainly isn't very fulfilling. I really would like to do something else. Something completely different.

JANNA: Like what?

DAN: Don't know. Open a kindergarten. Work for Unicef. Maybe that's what I'll do next. Do something more meaningful. Like you. *He looks at her and adds after a pause, during which both take long sips of wine*: Or just play the cello.

JANNA: At cemeteries?

DAN: You're smiling, but I mean it. I'd like to play, in churches around the world. Big ones, like – I don't know – St Paul's or the Grossmünster in Zürich, or maybe also in a big mosque like in Casablanca, or the Blue Mosque in Istanbul...

JANNA *smiling disarmingly at him*: You know, if I didn't know you a bit and if I hadn't promised myself not to swear, I'd probably say you sound 'full of shit'... *She laughs.*

DAN: Yeah. I guess you're right. *He gulps down the wine and pours himself some more.* But when you play in places with such amazing acoustics, you sound much better than you actually are... and I'm just not that good...

JANNA: What? I heard you play Bach, and you said you
can play Britten and Walton, and you're saying you're
not that good?

DAN: No. It's true. Well, yes, I can play Bach suites, but
not the sixth one. It's just too damn difficult. And I
can play Boccherini, but not really the third
movement. I get stuck. I can't play Dvorak. When I see
Rostropovich leisurely sitting behind his cello playing
that concerto, I'm just jealous.

JANNA: Oh, come on.

DAN: You think I'm better than I actually am. But, I tell
you, I'm crap. I even wanted to give up at one stage...

JANNA: Hmm. *Quietly*: I actually had to give up for a while.
I wasn't allowed to play the flute for a number of years.

DAN: How come?

JANNA: At our school we had our version of Mao's cultural
revolution – just about when theirs ended, and our
director banned all musical instruments and classical
music and declared them decadent, capitalist and
bourgeois.

DAN: That's silly.

JANNA: Well, yeah. But it was for real. My parents were too
afraid of the consequences, and wouldn't let me play.
They even hid their piano when teachers came to visit,
till that guy got removed and things got more or less
back to normal again. But for two years I wasn't
allowed to play. *She pauses.*

DAN: And then?

JANNA: Then? Then it was too late. Up till then I'd always
wanted to become a professional flautist, but...*She
picks up the glass of wine and takes a long sip*...then I
refused and was more concerned with everything that
was bourgeois, capitalist and decadent for a while. I
smoked, hung out with boys, read trashy magazines
from the West and was not really interested in classical
music till much later.

DAN: But you picked it up again.

JANNA: Well, yes, eventually. But it was too late to become a professional musician. I missed the boat. And once I became a student, I got over my capitalist phase and became left-wing again.

DAN: After what you'd experienced in socialist Sarajevo as a kid?

JANNA: Well, yes. That was not left-wing, though. Those were just bloody bureaucrats, tyrants, who used left-wing ideology to justify their privileged decadent lifestyle. *She pauses again and looks around.* And now it's sort of funny that I'm having dinner with you (*she caresses his hand*) who so obviously loves and lives a capitalist lifestyle. *She laughs, but then turns serious again, taking the glass, sipping the wine.* This really is most delicious, as is the food by the way. *She pauses again and continues eating.* Hmm...*She stops and looks at Dan*: But Daniel, let me ask you this question: is making money not important to you?

DAN *thinking*: Well, I'd be lying if I said it wasn't. After all, I spend my working life making money, rather than living according to my convictions. *He pauses and drinks and looks into the glass.* But what are my convictions? I think if I knew that, I'd do something else. In the meantime, tomorrow morning, I'll be going back to the office to work on my deal in order to make money, whereas you're off to work to help your kids.
Janna does not answer, but looks into her glass, drinking the wine.

JANNA: I actually don't really know either what my convictions are.

DAN: Well, you are very pacifist.

JANNA: Yeah, but that's not the reason why I am a doctor.

DAN: So, why did you want to become a doctor?

JANNA: I guess when I started studying medicine, I thought being a doctor would be an interesting job, and medicine an interesting subject to study. I couldn't have done law or economics or history for that matter. Let alone maths. That's far too abstract and I can't study abstract things. And then, when you're a doctor, there's the altruistic element. I mean, it's great to help people. *She pauses, reflecting.* But then again, a friend of mine pointed out to me that ultimately people are altruistic only because it makes them feel good doing something good. And I had to realise that was the case with me too. I love living a simple life and doing good, because it makes me feel good. *She smiles.* I guess that's pretty egoistic and not very noble.

DAN: It's very human. I mean, not everyone can be Mother Theresa. *She finishes her plate and looks into the dish standing in the middle of the table.* By the way, would you like some more?

JANNA *nodding*: Yes please. It's delish. *Dan serves her some more food and wine.*

DAN *looking silently into his glass*: Tell me, you said that your father also plays the cello?

JANNA: Yes. And he is – or rather was – pretty good. But he never wanted to play in public. When he was young, he and Mum often played together, chamber music with friends. But I think in recent years he played less and less. Sometimes he and Mum still play together, Beethoven sonatas.

DAN: What does he actually do?

JANNA: He's unemployed. Like everyone else.

DAN: And before the war?

JANNA: I don't quite know. I know this sounds silly. He was working at some economics research institute, but also ran some sort of import–export business on the side.

DAN: Sounds to me like he was a spy or something…

JANNA *smiling*: He used to be a Marxist when he was young. But later he changed his views, without changing his job, which was a bit difficult. And he also got involved in local politics – hence he knows everyone in Sarajevo, and in fact in the whole of Bosnia, even in Belgrade.

DAN: Also Serbs?

JANNA *glancing up, surprised*: Well of course.

DAN: Hmm...

JANNA: We all used to live together. It didn't matter whether you were a Serb, a Croat or a Bosniak; a Muslim, a Jew or a Christian. We have a lot of friends who are Serbs.

DAN: Still today?

JANNA *looking down thoughtfully.* No. Not all of them are still our friends...It's amazing to see what happens to people in war.

DAN *pensively*: I guess I know what you mean. My parents also experienced that when they and their parents had to leave Germany. Not all of my grandparents' friends and business partners remained friends. *He pauses, sipping his wine.* Are you in contact with your parents?

JANNA: Sure. That is, if I can get through to them. The lines are dead, so I write to them and they write back. They always manage to smuggle letters out of Sarajevo. *She pauses and sips the wine, holding the glass against the candlelight, thinking.* I really love my father and I'm even closer to him than to my mother. He is the most wonderful father you could ask for.

DAN: That's a nice thing to say...

JANNA: Well, he's patient, tolerant, supportive, and yet at the same time challenging and interested. He always pushed us kids to have a great education, with the view that we should be able to contribute something to this world. Although he turned away from Marxism, he always kept his altruism, enthusiasm and idealism. *She pauses and looks at Dan, who smiles back at her.*

DAN: Sounds like you were very close to him.

JANNA: Of course. I mean, we did so many things together. He taught me to ride, to swim, to pick mushrooms, to ski. And I remember when I was small, he took me to the fair that came every year to town and we went straight to the stall where you could win a teddy bear or other toy on the shooting range with an old gun. He always hit right in the middle and won teddies and other stuff…much to the annoyance of the stall keepers. *She pauses again and smiles sarcastically.* He would have made a superb sniper…
They continue eating in silence. Janna picks up the bottle of wine, looking at the label.

DAN: By the way, where did he get his wine from?

JANNA: Most of it from his father and from his grandfather, who were wine merchants. All pre-1970 Bordeaux wines, I think. Maybe some Burgundy.

DAN: And how has the war changed…I mean, how are things now?

JANNA: I'm not sure. On the one hand everyone is pretending to have some sort of normality, and he deliberately tries to give his life a degree of that. On the other hand, this normality is surreal, as everyone is suffering. Friends are getting killed. They haven't seen my brother Milutin for ages. He's trapped, or fighting. I don't even know, as Dad doesn't want to talk about it. There's nothing to eat.

DAN: Yes, I saw on television, how the place is surrounded by tanks and artillery. But aren't the hills part of Sarajevo?

JANNA: Well, yes and no. I mean, there was never any barrier or anything. Sarajevo is in the valley and the Serbs are on the hills. And they're shooting down at us. The front line is on the hills, except for one part, where it comes right down into town, down to the river. In fact at the same bridge where Archduke Franz Ferdinand got shot.

DAN: That's a bit ironic...

JANNA *sighs*: You live face to face with the other side...I cannot even call them enemy. *She pauses and looks into the distance.* So, yes, things are really grim. No jobs. No money. No hope. Imagine, daily shelling since April. Imagine what that does to you. To society. Friends, neighbours turning into enemies...*She sighs again, shaking her head.* But, then again, they are fine.

DAN: And you also have a sister?

JANNA: Yes. She's called Jasminka. She is sweet, and I should really try to get her out so that she can go to school in England. But it's damn difficult to get an exit visa nowadays.

DAN: Hmm. When did you actually leave Sarajevo?

JANNA: I came here for my studies, and stayed on.

DAN: Yeah, you told me...

They sit in silence for a long time, finishing their wine. Her hands move across the table, touching his.

JANNA: You know, Sarajevo is so far away. I've moved on. And I wish I could forget all about it. And I would, were it not for my parents and Jasminka. *She looks into his eyes and beyond.* And my brother, who I used to be very close to.

DAN: I know. Sometimes you have to move on in life, even if it's difficult. *He pours some more wine into her glass and then tops up his own. Both sit back and sip.* My parents moved on, forgetting in a way what their friends and relatives had suffered. But I'm not sure in what way this changed their lives...changed them. Made them more distant when I was young. *Looking at her:* My parents were very different from yours; they were very distant and cold when I was a child. They would have never taught me to swim or to ride. I hardly ever saw them – they were so busy doing their research and stuff. *He stops and sips the wine, looking up at the clock.* Gosh, it's already eleven o'clock. When does your shift start tomorrow?

JANNA: Six...a.m.

DAN: That's uncivilised.

They get up, having finished. Dan takes the dishes into the kitchen.

JANNA: Can I help you with the washing up?

DAN *from the kitchen*: No. Don't worry. My cleaner will take care of that tomorrow.

Janna is about to take the bottle of wine into the kitchen.

DAN *laughing*: Oh, just leave it on the table. She normally takes care of that first.

JANNA: You're such a spoiled brat. *They move out of the dining room into the living room.* That was fabulous. Thank you so much. *There is a moment of silence, when neither knows what to say. Janna then turns round to Dan, smiling coyly*: I think I'd better go.

She takes a step forward towards Dan, holding up her cheek. He puts his arms around her. Slowly, they embrace and then kiss, slowly, carefully; he is caressing her head and hair. They pause, looking for a long time silently into each other's eyes, smiling, then kiss again.

DAN: Can't you stay a bit longer?

JANNA *sighing, in between two long kisses*: I think I might consider that.

Fading.

When we went to the bedroom it was dark with the full moon shining through the windows, casting powerful shadows and a silvery light. I saw her naked the first time in black and white, or rather silver and shadow, a tender and graceful silhouette. We kissed and loved each other, and afterwards lay silent, each in our thoughts. I must have fallen asleep before her, as I do not remember her resetting the alarm, which tore us brutally out of our dreams.

Dan's bedroom. Int.

Furnished in minimalist Japanese style. Futon on the floor, tatami mats, a Japanese painting and calligraphy on the wall. A low Japanese table with a teapot and teacups, a Japanese cupboard, a bookshelf with books and a widescreen Sony television. It is dark inside and just getting light outside. An alarm clock rings. Dan and Janna are heard moving around in the bed, reaching for the alarm, then stopping it.

DAN: God it's early. What time is it?

JANNA: Five a.m. Sorry.

  Silence. The room is dark. He is lying on his back with Janna on her stomach across him. Both are covered by a blanket. Janna props herself up and they look into each other's eyes.

JANNA: It's too dark to see your eyes. They are completely black.

DAN: Like yours.

JANNA: I had a really weird dream. I've got to tell you about it. I was flying over a stream, which was sort of meandering through fields. It seemed like late summer or autumn. I remember thinking while I was flying that this was incredible, that flying can't be possible, though I'd love to fly in my normal life. I was dreaming that I should bite my arm to check whether I'm awake, or just dreaming. I did, and continued flying, to my utter amazement. Underneath me were miles of harvested fields, some of them burning. A valley that was incredibly long. I didn't manage to reach the end, as much as I tried. At the end of the valley there was a town with factories, an airport, churches and minarets. I had no idea where I was going or why. I looked at the sun, which was lying low, ready to disappear, casting long shadows. And then, all of a sudden, I realised this must be Sarajevo – but why could I not reach it? And then the alarm went off. I was shattered and had difficulty getting back to reality, and then…*She pauses and turns over to look into his eyes*…I remembered that reality had moved on and had become a dream.

Janna gets out of bed. She is naked and her slim silhouette is visible against the faint light from outside. She walks to the bathroom, switching on the light, closing the door behind her. Dan slowly sits up in bed, then gets out of bed too, going to the other bathroom. They can be heard taking a shower. He returns and dresses in a suit and a white shirt.

DAN *shouting over to her*: Can I get you something to eat? Or do you have breakfast at work?

JANNA *shouting back*: What do you have?

DAN: Er…Only muesli. Sorry, no croissants. Not even bread. *She comes out wrapped in a towel, drying her hair.*

JANNA: I'm not sure. Well, let me try it. Have you got tea?

DAN: Sure. Coffee. Orange juice. Vodka. Everything.

Cut.

Outside Dan's house. Ext.

They are seen coming out of the house. The street is now bright, but empty. Most of the cars are Mercedes, Jaguars or BMWs. They walk along the pavement and approach Dan's Land Rover. It is an oldish, green, hard-top short-wheelbase model, not washed, dents on the side. He opens the unlocked door for her. She looks at the car in disbelief.

JANNA : And I thought an investment banker would drive a Porsche or something else tacky.

DAN: Sorry.

JANNA : I'm deeply disappointed. Had I known that, I would have gone by black cab. What an embarrassment to arrive at hospital in a cattle transporter!

Cut.

Why me?

We laughed. For a second I thought she had really meant it, probably because it was too early in the morning for me to appreciate her sense of humour.

My Land Rover was old and rugged, with simple, reliable technology without all this electronics stuff. And it drove like a truck, without power-steering. I had had it for ages, having bought it second hand from a farmer who must have transported his cows on the front bench. It needed a certain amount of cleaning and redoing, a thought I objected to at first, as I preferred it in its original state, with straw on the floor. All my colleagues were driving around in flashy Porsches, and Tom had an Aston Martin, and no one understood why I stuck to this car.

When we arrived at her hospital, I stayed only for a few minutes as she showed me the ward, the rooms with her little patients, the common room. She loved the place. It was full of hope and optimism, full of paintings on all the walls, full of smiles. Everyone smiled – the nurses, the doctors, the cleaning staff.

We kissed a shy good-bye before I left through the swinging doors and walked down to my car. I drove straight to work – I needed to occupy my mind. I was not able to deal with all the impressions of the last ten hours simultaneously.

Janna's hospital. Int.

A children's ward, twelve beds in a big room. There are pictures on the walls, toys on the floor. Ten beds are occupied by children. Two are empty. The children, some of whom are bald, are playing, quite happily, some in their beds, some on the floor. Some are running around, appearing quite healthy. From the outside, the sun is shining into the room.

Janna is seen doing her morning round from bed to bed. She is accompanied by two other young doctors and two nurses, who are wearing casual green uniforms, the type worn in an operating theatre. Janna, however, is wearing blue jeans and a white hospital jacket. She has a stethoscope around her neck. The nurses carry files, into which Janna looks from time to time and in which she makes notes. She is moving from bed to bed. She crouches down to be nearer to the children when she talks to them, she smiles and cuddles them; they are happy, smiling back.

Janna has a warm smile on her face and treats each child individually with warmth and attention. Yet she is efficient, examining the wounds of those who have bandages. She gives quiet instructions to the nurses and to junior doctors. Exactly what she is saying cannot be heard because of the background noise. Finally she turns to one bed with a little girl, Christina, a six-year-old, blonde, angelic little girl, small for her age and very fragile. She is evidently in bad shape, but despite her pain tries to keep happy.

JANNA *cheerfully*: So, how are you, my little one? Did you sleep well? *Janna lifts Christina carefully out of the bed and holds her in her arms, searching her face.*

CHRISTINA: Not really. It's hurting so much.

JANNA *with the same positive voice*: It will soon get better. It's already much better than last week. *Christina is nodding, holding on to Janna's shoulders, looking into her eyes.*

CHRISTINA: When can I go back to my Mummy?

JANNA: Just a few more days. How is your tummy? *She carefully puts Christina back down into her bed. She is sitting at first, but then collapses. The nurses help her to lie down properly, laying her little head on a pillow for support.* Is your tummy still sore here? *Janna gently presses her stomach. Christina makes a brave face.*

CHRISTINA: No. *Janna caresses her.*

JANNA *quietly and comforting*: I'll come back to you later. Let me first take care of the other kids next door. Today you'll get the surprise I promised you. Remember?

CHRISTINA: Sure.

JANNA: OK. I'll be back a bit later.

The group is leaving the room and the noise subsides. Christina is trying to sit up again, but is too weak and collapses back onto her bed. Tears come into her eyes. She starts sobbing quietly, holding her teddy bear.

Doctor's room. Int.

Janna and her colleagues are sitting around the table. The room is sparsely furnished with a big table in the middle and chairs around. Two of Janna's large abstract paintings are hanging on the walls. Of Janna's colleagues, there are two doctors, Dr Annan and Dr Khan, as well as three nurses, Anne, Funmi and Angela. Everyone is wearing blue uniforms. Dr Khan pours coffee for everyone, and then walks over to the CD player to switch it on: Chopin. They lean back, holding the big mugs in their hands. Janna looks around at their faces.

JANNA *sighing*: What a morning! Everyone's got a brave face. I'm glad to see that Tom is so much better. And Jim. Did you see how he's climbing around in his bed? What a bundle of energy! *She pauses, and then looks at Anne.* Anne, completely forgot…is little Riccardo…?

ANNE *looking down*: No, Janna…he is…*Shaking her head.*

JANNA: Oh. No. No! I thought he'd make it if he got through the night.

ANNE: He didn't. He passed away in the early hours this morning. In his sleep. *Anne rubs her right eye, and looks*

down. *Janna puts her hand on Anne's hand to comfort her.
The door opens.*

JANNA *continuing after a pause*: And Joseph?
*Professor Douglas, an elderly professor of about sixty,
enters. He has silver hair, is soft-spoken, and wears a dark
suit and black-rimmed sixties-style glasses. He looks around
and smiles at everyone.*

PROFESSOR DOUGLAS: Good morning everyone. Sorry I'm
late, but did I hear you asking about Joseph? I think it
went all right. He'll pull through. I'm pretty positive.
*He pauses and then gazes with a deep and sad look at
Janna.* But I'm concerned about Christina.
*Janna puts her elbows on the table and covers her eyes with
her fingers, putting her chin in her hands.*

JANNA *in a very quiet voice*: Yes, I know. She is the sweetest,
bravest kid.

DR ANNAN: Can you just turn the music down, Angela? It's
really getting on my nerves.

JANNA *looking at Douglas*: And we all have to lie to her.
She'll never get out of here. *Janna pauses.* Never. *She
pauses again in order to reflect.* You know, I normally
don't get involved…at all. But she has really got to
me. *She looks for a long time into her coffee cup, thinking,
and then up and around into each colleague's eyes,
speaking with bitterness*: Why do we bother? Why do we
lie? And let them rot in their little beds? Yes they are
helpless. But so are we! Why can't we be more honest?
*She glances at her colleagues, sighs and sips her coffee. Her
colleagues lower their eyes, feeling uncomfortable. One of
the junior doctors walks over to Janna and lays her hand on
her shoulder, sitting down next to her, comforting her.
Janna continues, in a very quiet voice*: And yet I know
that's not possible.

PROFESSOR DOUGLAS: You know we sometimes have to lie.
He sighs and looks at all of them. But, Janna, is it really
lying? As long as we believe that there's more than a

one per cent chance we've got to be positive. We've got to be hopeful! They'd give up the fight and their will to live but for this little bit of hope that keeps them going. *He pours himself some coffee, and slowly adds two lumps of sugar, stirring the cup.* It would be so cynical to rob them of hope. Like cutting off their oxygen supply. Besides, so many do make it.

JANNA *quietly*: Yes. I know. It's just so goddamn depressing. You know, I spoke with Riccardo before his operation. I cheered him up. Told him he would be out soon, playing with his friends. Travelling to see his grandma in Italy. He believed me. And now he's gone without even waking up. That's what makes me feel so rotten. That's what makes me feel that I've been lying.

PROFESSOR DOUGLAS: But you weren't lying. You and I truly believed that he had a chance to pull through. Just because there's no hundred per cent certainty, it doesn't mean you're lying. *He looks at her for some time and adds*: And yet I know how you feel. You were giving him hope, and couldn't tell him that the chances were 30:70. You couldn't. If you tell someone his chances are 30:70, you effectively reduce them to ten per cent.

JANNA: I know. Of course I know. *Sighing.*
Cut.

Children's ward. Int.

Janna is seen at Christina's bed. It is evening. Christina is smiling at her. It is quieter now. Most children are in their beds; some are sitting around a small table in a corner, building a Lego castle. Two are reading. The nurses Angela and Funmi are with them. Only one bed is empty.

JANNA *whispering to Christina with a cheerful smile*: Come, sweetheart, let's have some fun. *Christina smiles. Janna takes her bed and starts pushing it out of the room, down the corridor. Anne passes by and looks at them.*

ANNE: Hey, where are you off to?

JANNA: Don't worry.

ANNE: Are you still on duty, Janna? *Janna is seen from the back, running down the corridor, pushing the bed.*

JANNA *turning her head with a big smile*: Nope.
Christina and Janna are now seen from the front, running down the corridor. Christina is beaming. Janna stops in front of a door, opens it and pushes the bed into that room. Cut.
Inside the room. Janna positions the bed in front of a video, and switches it on.

CHRISTINA: Yippee! *The Jungle Book*. Can I sit on your lap?

JANNA *smiling and caressing her*: Sure, sweetie. *Janna takes Christina out of her bed and they both sit down in an armchair. Christina's face is shown. She is smiling. Fading out.*
Fading in.
On screen, The Jungle Book *is playing. Mowgli is being abducted by the monkeys. The camera retreats so that the chair with Janna and Christina becomes visible. The camera turns around, showing Janna sleeping in the armchair and Christina sitting on her lap, watching spellbound.*
Cut.

I had to stop writing, as Tania came to visit for dinner. She was in Toulouse on business, and drove down to stay overnight. I was glad to see her. We sat in the garden, talking for hours. My friendship with Tania had become different once we had returned from Sarajevo – it was deeper, as if a new connection had been made. She meets your searching eyes when others prefer to be staring into the distance.

Later, after dinner, we walked the small, dirty path up to the cemetery underneath the poplars. It was completely dark and quiet, bats flying through the air. We sat down on the bench next to the small chapel and smoked, looking over the graves. She had brought me a wonderfully rich and sumptuous Cohiba, which glowed in the darkness. The smoke rose silently, grey before the black sky.

It is 5 a.m., and I have to get up to write. I have this urgency to finish the script, without knowing what comes next. I sit down to capture the dream, the film before my eyes, fearing that it may be gone one day. Fearing that I may wake up one day with emptiness in my memory, incapable of recalling faces, people, moments, conversations or smells.

Alike

We saw each other every free minute, whenever Janna managed to get away from hospital, every day, as June, July passed by. Sometimes we played tennis together. Sometimes we went to the theatre or to see a film, or to a concert. Often we played music together, and the more we played, the more I realised that Janna was amazingly talented. She could sight-read the most difficult scores and play fast, with technical perfection; and yet she played with passion, warmth, or with a certain distance, then with aggression, or an amazing subtlety. But there are not many pieces for flute and cello, so we started to improvise on works of Bach, Haydn, Mozart – she always led off with incredible imagination, and I had difficulty following. When you can improvise together you feel that you are reaching some deeper level of understanding. You must think alike, feel alike, sense alike, dream alike.

I loved listening to Janna playing the flute while I lay on her bed.

But she herself loved painting even more than playing music. I often watched her paint in bold colours and with broad abstract brushstrokes. She painted almost every evening after coming home from hospital. I tried to see her emotions reflected in the colours, in the texture of the oil, in the composition of the picture, but could not yet penetrate the invisible wall. I realised then that if I ever wanted fully to understand her inner self, I would need to understand her paintings.

Almost all of them were abstract, and the less abstract ones were wild landscapes.

'Look, this is the view from our house in Sarajevo,' she once said, digging out a small painting from her huge cupboard. I looked at it, trying to recognise the town.

'It's abstract,' I said, having looked at it for a while.

'I can see the whole town in it. You just have to look. Or maybe I'm just a crap painter,' she smiled.

I looked into her cupboard. It was packed with paintings, probably more than fifty altogether.

'Why don't you exhibit and sell them?'

She paused, and then turned to look at me.

'Never!'

She looked aghast.

'These are my ... I don't know how to express this. My works, no, these pictures are a reflection of myself, of my thinking, my feeling. I could never sell them.' She looked at me with a vague smile.

'You know, Dan, painting is for me like going to a shrink. I paint what I feel when I'm depressed, or when I'm in love, or when I'm hurt. Rather than lying on a couch, I prefer to paint and get things out of my head like that.'

'It's certainly a lot cheaper,' I said.

'Yeah. I hadn't thought of that though. But you understand me now? Each painting has a meaning, has a history, is a part of myself. Even giving them away to family or friends is an effort.' She turned to the window. 'Maybe you will be an exception, but even with you I don't know yet. Sorry to be so blunt. I don't know which picture to give to you, which one you would appreciate and understand. Do you know what I mean?'

The implicit distance hurt.

One day I saw a new painting on her easel. It was black with white, like drops of snow coming teeming down. The oil was still wet. I turned it round and saw the word 'Srebrenica' written on the back of the canvas.

'Why Srebrenica?'

'The last time I heard of my brother, he was there. And you know yourself the situation over there. It's hell. I've no idea how he is, whether he's still there.'

'And your parents can't find out?'

'They are trying to. And trying to get him out, of course. But as far as I know he wants to stay.'

'Why?'

'His girlfriend is there. And he wants to fight. They both want to fight.'

She turned round, searching her own thoughts and became quiet, looking out of the window. In the end she walked out to

SARABANDE

the bathroom and I feared the tears in her eyes. In the door way
she turned around, composed and yet with her teeth clenched.
'You know, Milu's so stubborn. So bloody stubborn. And he always
likes to fight. At school he used to pick fights with his classmates,
and now it's serious.'

She leaned against the window, looking at her paintings and
then moved over to pick up one of the photos of her family. 'You
know, he's older than me, and I always admired him as my older
brother. He was great with me, particularly at school, where he
wouldn't let anyone bully me. And then he taught me so much:
making fires, catching fish, helping me pick mushrooms; and
later he taught me all I know about modern art. And he taught me
one other thing...'

I looked at her.

'Not to give a damn about money,' she continued. 'Or about
those people who care about money.' She smiled and came over
and put her arms around my neck.

'I guess I only see one side in you, and ignore the money-
making side.'

'But I don't care that much about money,' I tried to say.

'Oh yes you do,' she laughed. And then she immediately
turned serious again, and continued, 'But Milu and I also argued
a lot about politics, as I am a pacifist and he is not. When the war
started, our arguments got heated – I strongly disapproved of his
views.'

She paused to search for words, looking into the distance, then
at me. 'Then he became active, and I couldn't approve of his
actions. When the war started and he disappeared from Sarajevo
to join the Bosnian fighters I broke off contact with him. I didn't
want to have a brother who was killing.'

'And what did he do when you broke off contact?'

'He tried to stay in touch. But I was stubborn, even though I
loved him. I loved him for staying in touch even though I rejected
him. I was cruel. Cruel! And then he went silent.'

One day when I found her looking at her photos she sighed
without glancing up. 'I shouldn't have cut him off. It would really

have been better if I'd stayed in touch with both of them. Maybe I could have persuaded them to leave, now that all hope has left that godforsaken dump.'

Most of the time we talked – in restaurants, walking in Hyde Park, at home – we were bursting with things we wanted to tell each other all at once, all at the same time. She longed to tell me about her childhood in Sarajevo, about her work, her feelings as a doctor. And though I got to know her better and better with each minute we spent together, still I felt that I was only scratching the surface, peeling the fine skin off an onion, without getting any deeper.

'You know,' she once said, coming back from work, 'I was four years old when I decided to become a doctor. Isn't that strange? I mean, most people change their views once they mature. It probably means I'll never mature, right?'

And she sat down on a swing in the children's playground opposite her house and started swinging wildly.

'We had a doctor I really admired. He was so wise, so friendly. And whenever I had to go and see him I felt much better when he talked to me and patted my head in his surgery. An amazingly powerful personality.' She paused and reflected. 'I decided I wanted to become a doctor like him.'

We sat down on a bench, and she continued, 'When I was small, Sarajevo was a place full of fun and optimism, and we never noticed that people were different because of their ethnic origins. Ethnic origins – nobody knew what that meant. People either applauded Tito or spat on the television screen when he appeared – that was the only difference. Most of our friends' tellies could have done with windscreen-wipers. Only now that I'm in London do I find out that other things matter – or seem to matter, since for the majority of people in Sarajevo they don't matter at all. We've been living together for centuries: Christians, Jews, Muslims. You should look at the town from the hills, and you'd see those churches and mosques mixed together.'

She paused, looking into the distance, as if at the spires in the valley below her.

'And we all loved culture, culture from the East and from the West. We went to the theatre a lot, to concerts and galleries. Our cinemas were avant-garde in comparison to those in other communist countries. Our Dad took us to the movies all the time, Mum to the theatre, even though we had hardly any money till Dad inherited some when his father died.' She paused and smiled. 'And that's when he also inherited his wine collection – he certainly could have never bought it.'

'But you weren't totally poor. I mean, you managed to study abroad.'

'That's because my uncle sent us money. And he paid for my studies too. The one who lives here in the UK.' She looked at me, and then added, thinking, 'I guess we were pretty poor till my grandfather died. We lived in a very small apartment, where Mum and Dad had to sleep in the living room and we kids shared the bedroom. But I don't remember it as being tough, because my parents were always happy, or at least never showed when they were not. And isn't that what counts?'

In London we spent hours drifting through galleries, Cork Street, the Tate, the National Gallery, the Courtauld. Even though I love art, it wore me down, but Janna was constantly looking for inspiration from other artists. Sometimes she would look at a piece of art, deep in thought, and then smile her slightly sarcastic smile.

'This is such pretentious crap...'

'Why do you stare at it for ages?'

'Just to make sure it really is crap.'

'But it's a Beuys,' I said.

'Do I care? This is not art. This is just pretentious crap. He's such an idiot. Or, rather, people who buy this crap are idiots.'

'I thought you didn't swear...' I interjected.

'But I'm not swearing. I'm just calling things by their name...' Then she dragged me back to look at Rothko, who she could study endlessly.

'Compare Beuys with Rothko, Dan. I think I love Rothko so much because of the simplicity of his paintings and the deep impact his colours have on the viewer – certainly on me.'

'I prefer Mondrian. But can't afford either...'

'Come on, you shouldn't always think about buying and owning art. You are so materialistic.'

Would I ever understand her world, and be part of it? I listened to her stories about her family, her life in Sarajevo that lay in total destruction, her feelings about the country. How can you turn against your neighbour like that? How can you torture the parents of your children's friends? Rape the woman who smiled at you each morning? Shoot the nurse who took care of your sick parents? Janna knew them all, and did not have an answer either, but tried to understand, and explain, where I felt only disgust.

'They got the freedom to build a society in which everyone can prosper, be educated like you, make money, be rich, be healthy, and look what they do. All of them. Well, maybe not all – the Slovenians are an exception.'

'Yes, but making money is not all there is in life,' Janna argued.

'But what else is there that has more value than peace and individual freedom, wealth?'

'Look, don't force me to argue the line of the nationalists. But for a lot of Serbs and Bosnians that is important. National recognition. Justice. Even if it means fighting now for justice, for crimes committed during the Second World War. Or earlier in history.'

'And so they slaughter others to get this?'

'Yes! It's so perverse. They kill the next generation, who have nothing to do with it.'

'Janna. Someone has to stop this nonsense. Bomb them till they stop it!'

'No, Dan. Stopping things by force doesn't work. You just create more violence. This violence has got to stop and it's got to stop from within.'

She looked at me with sad eyes, searching for words, turning towards her medical books as if for help.

'It's like with medicine. You can operate on a tumour but that won't heal the patient. That's why I'm so interested in alternative medicine as a cure for cancer. But I must admit, I've no alternative medicine for peace in Yugoslavia.'

'So operate on them, bomb them, use chemotherapy, radio-therapy to kill the cancer and all those who implant cancers. Once the cancer is dead, you can heal the patient.'

'Stop it Dan. I can't hear it. You cannot kill. It's your Bible that says "Thou shalt not kill"!'

'And "an eye for an eye..."'

'Dan. Can't you see that we've got to stop the cycle of violence and that you cannot stop violence with violence?'

She sat down and buried her face in her hands and stayed silent, looking up after a while, shaking her head. 'Dan, I just cannot understand how someone can have so much hatred to simply kill innocent people, take revenge on others. I think I may be too naïve ever to understand.'

She got up and threw some clothes into her bag. 'I've a night shift. Dan, I'll never understand you and you will never understand me. And still I love you. But now I need to go.'

One Saturday morning she got up early to buy the papers and I found her crouched over *The Independent*, tears in her eyes. She pointed at a picture that went round the world: a little boy lying on the pavement in a street in Sarajevo. Shot in the head. Bleeding to death. His mother, who was coming to help him, got shot in the stomach seconds later. I looked at the picture and felt my throat getting tighter. I sat down next to her on the floor, putting my arm around her shoulders.

'Do you know what goes on in the sick mind of a sniper?' she asked. I shook my head.

'He shot the little boy straight in the head. Nobody will run to help him and pull him to safety, as everyone knows the sniper is still sitting there, aiming. Only his mother can't let him bleed to death, so she dashes forward – and gets shot. Not in the head, but in the stomach!'

'Why the stomach?' I tried to ask, unable to understand a sniper's logic.

'So that she doesn't die straight away. So that she's got enough time to see her son die a gruesome death. And so that she has enough time to realise she can neither help him nor survive herself.'

I took Janna into my arms. She was composed, while I was unable to speak. I did not want her to look at my face, as my eyes were wet with tears. When finally I could speak again I did not want to – I knew she thought differently to me. She would never agree to blow a sniper to pieces, whereas I would kill him, his platoon, his superiors; in fact, I would kill everyone who tolerates his killing.

Janna would offer the other cheek rather than hit back. I am deeply entrenched in the hit-back camp. Hit first, before they can hit you.

In the beginning, she used to call her parents once a week, if she got through. And later, when the post office was blown up and all the phones were dead, she wrote them letters, which she sent to a friend in Budapest, where a courier picked them up and hand-delivered them. That sometimes took up to two weeks.

'I haven't told them about you yet,' she smiled in utmost innocence.

'Why? Don't you believe this will last a bit longer than a week?' I asked.

But she just covered my mouth with her hand.

'Come on, let me read you the letter I got from Dad today. Let me try to translate.' She sat down on her chair, crossing her legs, a frown casting a mild shadow over her tanned forehead.

My Dearest Janna,

Since they blew up the post office no phones are working and there is no way that someone is going to repair the system. What a mess! On the other hand this means that I'm seeing my friends more often. Milas drops by at least once a day and he's trying to find out how he can buy or steal a satellite phone from the UN. What's new? Nothing, really. Shelling every day, but they are hitting the other side of town at the moment. There is not enough to eat, but Mum's carrots have grown and we are enjoying them every day. We all look jaundiced. I've started shooting rabbits so that we can have some meat from time to time, but those little bastards are getting clever and graze on No-Man's-Land. Should we eat the snails in the garden? They look revolting, but the

French love them. So I breed them in the hope of selling them to General Morillon and the French UN officers in the autumn. Well, maybe we'll eat them ourselves after another year of war. I'm thinking of setting up a new business: selling unbreakable glass, i.e. plastic panes. There are so many windows where the glass is missing. People will be freezing in the winter. We won't, as we have masses of wood all chopped up and stacked away. But, you won't believe it, the other day some people tried to steal the apple tree from our garden. I just came back when they were about to swing their axe. Unbelievable. But that is life in Sarajevo. Different crime from your average robbery in London.

Jasminka, who hated school right up to March, now misses it. No school at all this spring or during the summer, and no chance of school unless they stop the shelling. Speaking of which, we are counting. Some nights there are about two hundred plus shells that land somewhere here in Sarajevo. Two hundred shells. Every day people die or get badly hurt. It's awful. I have given our car to the hospital, and they have converted it into an ambulance. Your old cartoon books, Asterix, Lucky Luke and the others, serve as armour plating. A couple of simple cartoon books are often enough to absorb a bullet. They saved me a number of times when I made my way to the airport.

Thank God it's summer and we can enjoy the garden, and the sun has not turned Serb yet.

Love to you from Mum and Jasminka.

Lots of love,
Dad

She paused and looked at me. 'He's never written great letters; he won't get the Booker Prize.'

No word whether her parents had managed to reach her brother, which depressed her.

Sometimes she got a small present from her parents. A leaf from the tree she had planted as a child. Dried flowers. She looked at them and held them against the light.

'These were my flowers. I took care of them, planted them, talked to them. Now Sarajevo doesn't even have enough water to keep them alive. They are dead. Dried. In a way pretty symbolical, if you think about it.'

Janna in turn sent them small parcels – aspirin, vitamin pills, chocolate – and some presents to her sister. When the phone lines went down and she could no longer get through to her parents, Janna told me she was very depressed at first. Later on she seemed relieved, even glad, though she would never have been able to admit it – glad to be cut off from Sarajevo.

As a result, although I followed the war on TV and read about it every day in the papers, Sarajevo for a long time still remained a puzzle to me. She provided pieces of it. I saw the pictures on her walls – saw the houses, her parents, Milas, her family. I saw her skiing, horse riding – a completely normal life. And then I had these fragments of life today, from her, from her parents' letters. News I had previously conveniently ignored suddenly had a meaning. A shell exploding in the Turkish quarter meant something. Janna showed me on a map where it hit. And showed me photos of the houses, how they were before the war. I did not dare raise the question whether she could imagine those houses now. But then she said, 'I'm still amazed that not more people die every day. If you think of the destructive energy a single shell has...'

She dug around in her papers and produced a torn-out page of a newspaper. A photo showed a long-haired middle-aged man playing the cello, sitting on a chair outside, impeccably dressed in black tie.

'Vedran Smailovic. He played Albinoni's Adagio for twenty-two days at the site where twenty-two Sarajevans got killed when a Serbian mortar shell hit a bread queue.' She paused and shook her head. 'His friends got killed, and he just played. Every day. Stoically, ignoring snipers and shelling.'

I remembered his photo going around the world in May after the shelling.

'My father knows him well.'

And she took out her flute and started playing the Adagio, with closed eyes, as if standing there on the street herself.

When she had finished she went over to the window and looked out for a long time.

'I sometimes ask myself, why can't they bail out the town, like they did with Berlin? Why not fly in supplies, build another air bridge?' I said.

'Come on Dan. It's not quite the same. I mean, when Berlin was bailed out there were two superpowers facing each other.'

'And now it could be NATO facing the mickey-mouse power Serbia. Where's the problem?'

'And if the Serbs shoot at the supply planes?' Janna asked.

'Then NATO bombs the Serbs, as simple as that!'

'Oh, God. Dan. Here we go again. Then we would have a major war and it would be horrible,' Janna said.

'No Janna. That's rubbish. They would never attack NATO supplies. It's the same as in Berlin. The Soviets would have never attacked the US supply planes flying into Berlin as they knew what the consequences would have been. Janna, I just don't understand,' I added. 'And I don't understand either why no one wants to strengthen the Bosnian army so that they can defend the country. What's happening?'

We in the West were unwilling to commit NATO forces to protect the civilian population from ethnic cleansing, from concentration camps and genocide. At the same time we were against providing them with weapons to defend their women and children. All my friends felt ashamed about the West's cowardice and understood how the Muslims of this world felt betrayed. For my colleague Ali the situation was very clear: the Christian West would not move a finger to protect Muslims, and while Owen and Vance were feverishly negotiating a peace agreement, carving up the country into cantons, the Serb armies created new realities, ethnically cleansing huge areas.

Janna remained silent. It was evident from the look on her face that she hated this discussion. But she had no answer either, and was even more horrified about the situation.

'But you have to negotiate peace,' Janna insisted in the end.

'Janna! They won't negotiate as long as they are winning in

the field. You have to bomb them to the negotiating table. That's the language the Serbs understand.'

'But then you just have an endless and horrific war that will last for ages. Thousands will be killed. Dan, let's not start again. You have your views, I have mine. Let's just agree to disagree.'

'Don't try to sound like Kissinger, Janna. The difference between you and him is that he would have bombed with napalm and cluster bombs before agreeing to disagree.'

'Oh, just shut up.'

After a while she smiled.

'Oh, by the way, my father called. Milas got a satellite phone!'

'Amazing. Where from?'

'Don't know. I couldn't really talk as I was at work. But he'll call again. Or I'll call him now I have his number.'

Calling

Janna's place. Int.

A studenty, loft-like studio flat – a contrast to Dan's apartment. Sunshine comes through the windows. Instead of bookshelves, Janna has wooden planks on bricks, with rows of medical books, a pile of art books. There are only a few pieces of furniture: a bed, a big, old, dark wooden wardrobe, a chest of drawers, three chairs, a small, old desk, a music stand with music. Her flute case is lying open on the chest of drawers; the whole room looks slightly untidy. There are many flowers in the room, some fresh, some dried; there are candles; two of her bright paintings are hanging on a wall, giving the room a warm and friendly atmosphere. The flat's wooden floor is covered by three rather worn rugs. In one corner is an easel with brushes resting underneath the almost finished abstract painting of Srebrenica. On the shelves and on the walls are numerous photos of her family: her father playing the cello in a garden, her sister on a beach, her brother on horseback, her family all on skis on the hills of Sarajevo, herself playing the flute at a school event, and an aerial shot of Sarajevo.

Janna is sitting on the floor in jeans and T-shirt, barefoot, reading The Independent. *There is a story of the war in Sarajevo.*

JANNA: Oh no! God, no!
She thinks, searching around, scratching her head. Then she looks again at the photo and slowly gets up, searches in her bag and takes out a piece of paper with a telephone number, and walks over to her telephone. She dials and waits. She shouts into the phone.

JANNA: Milas? Milas?

MILAS: Yes. Who is it?

JANNA: It's Janna. Can you let me know when I can speak to Dad, please?

MILAS: He's right next to me. Just hang on a second. Hey, Djemal, it's Janna on the line. *Background crackling.*

JANNA: Daddy? Daddy?

DJEMAL: Hello?

JANNA: Daddy. It's Janna.

DJEMAL: Hello? I can't hear you. Hello?

JANNA: Oh, damn these phones. *Shouting*: Dad! It's Janna.

DJEMAL: Hi, sweetheart. Why are you shouting like this?

JANNA: Daddy, are you OK?

DJEMAL: Sure. Why?

JANNA: And Mummy?

DJEMAL: Sure. Listen. Everyone is OK. Don't worry. You're lucky you're catching me today. I was just about to leave when Milas shouted that you're on the phone.

JANNA: Dad, what about all the shelling yesterday? I just read about it in the papers.

DJEMAL: You get used to that. You know, it happens every day. You in London just read about it from time to time. Don't worry. It's safer than shopping at Harrods.

JANNA: Dad, stop it. This one hit the market. I know you hang out with your friends around there, don't you? Isn't that the place?

DJEMAL: Yes, it is. Glad you remember your Dad's favourite café.

JANNA: God, I'm so glad to hear your voice. I was so worried.

DJEMAL: Janna, don't worry. We weren't there, and now we have to go to the café opposite. The coffee is better over there anyway.

JANNA: Oh, please. *She is silent.* Dad, have you got enough to eat?

DJEMAL: Sure. Plenty of rabbits. I'm still shooting them with my Kalashnikov. Happen to hit some Serb militia men from time to time too.

JANNA: Dad, stop it. Please be serious...

DJEMAL: But the rabbits taste better. Tomorrow I'll fish for alligators in the sewage. That will keep us going for a fortnight, and Mum will make some crock cowboy boots for our UN saviours.

JANNA *has to laugh*: Please Dad. This is not funny. I'm so glad to hear your voice. I was so worried.

DJEMAL: Well, I was worried, since we haven't spoken for ages and I have the feeling that I only get every fifth letter you send.

JANNA: I'm sorry, Dad, there are times I simply cannot write. Not writing means I don't have to think about Sarajevo. Please don't misunderstand me, I'm not trying to wipe you all out of my life. But things look so horrible, I want to forget. I wish you would all leave. Why are you and Mum so bloody stubborn! Why? *There is a long silence on the phone. She finally continues*: I've been trying to call you on Milas's phone since yesterday, but the line was down. I couldn't get through.

DJEMAL: Must have been at your end. British Telecom. Milas's phone works fine. You know it's satellite, don't you? The UN sold it to Milas. There are only two people with satellite phones in the whole town. I don't even hear the clicking of Belgrade's secret police... *Cut, but the conversation continues in voiceover.*

Sarajevo. Ext.

While they are talking the camera shows Sarajevo: scarred houses hit by shrapnel, with broken windows and blackened by fires, houses without roofs, completely

*destroyed, burnt out cars, a burnt-out tram, broken bicycles,
craters in the streets, sawn-off trees, some torn clothes lying
on the ground. This is accompanied by no background
noise; all that can be heard is their telephone conversation.*

DJEMAL *suddenly changing tone*: Janna, I shouldn't be
   joking. I'm sorry. Actually, Mum and I are immensely
   worried. This is getting somewhat like World War II. *He
   pauses.* Some quarters are like Guernica. Janna, it's
   terrible. Terrible! Bombs every day. Shells every day.
   Snipers. They are the worst, killing even children.
JANNA: Why don't you get all the children out of town?
   Let Unicef take care of them.
DJEMAL: What? Janna, you don't understand. Nobody can
   leave the town. The Serbs won't let us out and our own
   people won't allow anyone to leave either. Unicef can't
   do a thing!
JANNA: Dad, that's horrible. *There is a long silence on both
   sides.*
DJEMAL: Janna, I have to tell you, it's grim, and I haven't
   told anyone, not even your mother: I killed two
   snipers the other day, on the 25th of June, to be
   precise. I saw them shooting from a window in an
   apartment block, just beyond the river. They were
   shooting at children running down the street.
JANNA *shouting*: Daddy, please! You shouldn't kill too.
   You're becoming like them!
DJEMAL *quietly*: Janna. I had to. Imagine. They were aiming
   at children, as if for fun. I had to take them out. I just
   couldn't let them go on shooting kids as if they were
   rabbits. Please stop being a bloody moralist. If you
   were here, you would do the same.
JANNA: No. I wouldn't.
DJEMAL: Janna, you can't be a pacifist when they are
   killing innocent children. Can you? I only killed them
   to stop them killing children! I saw them in their

hiding-place, those cowards. And I had to act. *Janna remains quiet.* They are killing anyone. Particularly anyone defenceless.

A long silence, while the camera moves up a street where the body of a dead boy aged about twelve is lying on the ground, uncovered, his shabby clothes torn, his front covered in blood, one foot without a shoe, blood on the street. The boy's eyes are wide open, as if still in shock, his fingers buried in the dirt of the street. The street is completely deserted; the doors of the houses are shut; windows are shattered. The houses are heavily marked by shrapnel. While the conversation continues, the camera moves up the street, focusing through the broken windows into the apartments, showing destroyed living rooms, splintered wood, paintings off the walls, china in pieces on the ground.

JANNA: Dad?

DJEMAL: And then, you know, the problem is that there simply aren't enough doctors to cope. There are a number of them in the State Hospital. But that's not enough. That hospital just can't cope with all the wounded. And those who are around aren't necessarily trained surgeons. Things are really grim. *He pauses.* Constant shelling. You know, they shell the hospitals. Every day. So many patients got killed in the hospitals.

JANNA: How is the State Hospital?

DJEMAL: They're actually doing OK. They get help from the WHO in Geneva, medicine and stuff. They have engineers to repair things. But don't kid yourself, you wouldn't want to be operated on over there either. They sometimes have to do it by candlelight. And they also get shelled.

JANNA: And the Maternity Hospital?

The camera moves to show the bombed-out hospital, the shrapnel-scarred walls, the desolate surroundings.

DJEMAL: Gone. Erased. You know, as it's on the Kosevo Hill it's fully exposed to the artillery on the hills around.

Janna, it's dreadful. It got shelled without mercy. The worst massacre happened right at the beginning, and after that it was moved. I'm amazed that Sarajevo still produces children. But I think it's not so much a matter of love and hope for a brighter future as a lack of condoms.

JANNA: Dad, please don't be so cynical. The war will have to end.

DJEMAL *shouting*: What do you mean, 'cynical'? I see it every day. I hear the shells. See the damage. Smell the dead. This is the life we are all living. *He quietens down again*: Janna, don't misunderstand me. I do have hope. There will be an end. But in the meantime, we have to help. Milas is helping by trading medicine with the UN. And he's smuggling stuff into the city. That's the advantage of corruption: you can actually get things done and you know the price. But still, you cannot buy expertise. You cannot buy hospital experience. Even if we could pay a million bucks a year, no one would come here to operate. That's one of the reasons so many are dying. Not because they are shot dead on the spot, Janna, but because they don't get treated properly! *Pause.* I wish the UN would do something more useful than just drive around in their stupid armoured vehicles. Why can't they ship in doctors, build field hospitals? The only ones who profit from their presence are the dealers and the hookers. *Silence.*

JANNA: Daddy? *Silence.*

DJEMAL: Yes? *Silence.* Janna? *He pauses for some time and then continues*: I know it's crazy. I've been giving this a lot of thought, and it's not easy to ask. We need your help! You should think about coming back to Sarajevo. You're a qualified doctor.
Cut, to Djemal's side of the conversation.

A private house in Sarajevo. In the garden. Ext.

*The camera pans around a garden. The place is shabby,
and a lot of wooden planks, a ladder, some old paint pots
and other rubbish is on the ground. There are two trees, but
no flowers. Leaning against the garden wall, Djemal is
standing, facing the house and talking into a satellite
phone. He is a man of about fifty, dressed in black trousers
and a white shirt. He has a distinct face, slightly tanned,
with a high forehead and clear black eyes. The camera
focuses on his face while he is talking.*

DJEMAL: Please think about it.

JANNA *with desperation in her voice*: Dad, how can I help?
I'm not a surgeon either. I don't operate. My colleagues
do. Not me.

DJEMAL: But you're a doctor at a hospital. So you know
how things work. Or at least how things should work.

JANNA: Yes, but I'm a cancer specialist. I work in a
children's ward. With chemotherapy. Radiation. I'm
fighting cancer. I can't sew people together. I can't
operate to take bullets or shrapnel out of spines.

DJEMAL *interrupting*: But you operated for three years at St
Vincent's.

JANNA: That's years ago! Dad, I told you: I'm starting... we
are starting a completely new treatment for patients
based on homeopathy. The anthroposophical stuff I
told you about. That's my life.

DJEMAL: Janna! Forget your anthroposophical medicine.
That's a luxury you can have after the war.

JANNA: Dad, that's not luxury. We are saving lives. Please.

DJEMAL: But, Janna, now it's war over here and someone
has to operate. It may not be for long. Maybe the war
will be over after the summer. Janna, look. Operating is
like eating spaghetti. Once you know the technique,
you never forget. You said that yourself.

JANNA: Oh, Dad, please. No. No!

DJEMAL *quietly and yet with determination in his voice*: Think about it, please. We really need you. We need someone who has operated before. You worked in casualty wards. *He turns around and looks at the sun.* You told me yourself how you sewed all those road-accident victims together. You even removed two bullets from that bank robber. *Pleading*: Janna, you know you can do it. It's a long time ago, I know, but I'm sure you can do it. *Reflecting*: I could get Milas to pick you up in Vienna or Budapest.

JANNA *sobbing*: No, Daddy. No. No. No! *Silence.*

Cut, to Janna's side of the conversation.

Janna's room. Int.

JANNA *sobbing quietly, trying to suppress her sobs by biting her lip*: Dad, I need time to think about it.

DJEMAL *with a soft voice now*: OK. OK. Maybe you're right. I don't want to pressure you. I'm sorry if I did. *Silence.* Janna, please. We really love you. And miss you. I really do miss you and do think of you. Every day. All the time. *He sighs.* I need to go now, as Milas needs the phone. I shall call you soon. Take care.

JANNA: You too. Please take good care of Jasminka and Mum too. Any news from Milu?

DJEMAL: No. Nothing. Not a word. We don't even know whether he's still in Srebrenica or whether he managed to get out. Please don't ask your mother about him, though. It really kills her to think about him. *Silence. Janna is sobbing. There is a click on the line and it goes dead. She hangs up too. She goes over to the window and gazes out for a long time, then turns round and dries her face and looks at the photos of her family in Sarajevo. She picks up the phone again, hesitates for a moment and dials. The line is ringing and Dan answers.*

DAN: Hello?

JANNA *quietly*: It's me.

DAN *in a joyful voice*: Hi. How are you?

JANNA *composed again*: Fine. *Silence.* Dan, I need to talk to you. I need to see you. Can you come by tonight?

DAN: I've got a dinner with clients. I could come afterwards.

JANNA: Isn't that too late for you?

DAN: I'll finish early. Look, I'll see you then. Need to rush now. *He pauses.* Janna, are you OK? *She does not answer.* Anything wrong? I mean, I could cancel dinner and come straight away.

JANNA: No. Don't worry. Please come after your dinner… I'll explain later.

She goes into the bathroom and the water can be heard as she washes her face. She returns and walks to the easel, looking at the picture. Slowly she takes a new canvas and puts it on to the easel, looking at the empty space. She takes a brush and, checking the texture of the bright red paint, she soaks the brush in it and paints a streak from top to bottom. She takes a step back, looking at the canvas and puts the brush down, shaking her head.
Fading.

Janna's room. Int.

Janna is in bed, sleeping. Her bedside lamp is on. She is wearing a loose T-shirt and boxer shorts. She is lying on her front, eyes closed. The curtains are half closed. The windows are slightly open.

The noise of Dan's old Land Rover approaching the house can be heard. He stops underneath her window. The door slams. His steps can be heard through the open window. The doorbell rings. Janna wakes up slowly, looking around, and then gets up. She leaves the room returning a

*moment later. She waits, standing next to her bed. Dan
enters, wearing a suit. He smiles at her.*

DAN: Did I wake you up? I'm sorry.

JANNA: No. Don't worry. It's not even eleven. I was just
really tired.

DAN *is smiling, studying her outfit*: Let me join you.
*He undresses and goes into the bathroom. The shower
can be heard. She goes over to the bookshelves and
takes out* If Not Now When *by Primo Levi. Looking at
it briefly she throws it with force into the rubbish bin
and walks over to her easel and looks at the painting.
She turns it round, then upside down, and puts it back.
Dan comes out of the bathroom, wearing boxer shorts
and a polo shirt. They embrace and kiss for a long
time. He inspects the painting from over her shoulder,
frowning.*

DAN: New painting? *Janna remains silent. At last she frees
herself from his embrace and looks into his eyes.*

DAN: What was that bang?

JANNA: I threw Primo Levi away.

DAN *laughing*: I gave it to you. Why?

JANNA: I hate novels. Particularly this partisan stuff. You
know I can't stand reading other people's stuff.

DAN: You're weird.

JANNA: Let's go to bed. *They go to bed. She lies down on her
back. He is sitting, facing her.*

DAN: Well?

JANNA *speaking with a very quiet and uncertain voice*: I spoke
to my father today. *Dan looks at her inquisitively.* He
asked me to come back.

DAN: To Sarajevo?

JANNA: Yes.

DAN: And?

JANNA: I said no.

Dan smiles and lies down at her side, taking her into his arms. She does not respond to his tenderness, but frees herself and sits up, putting her arms around her knees.

JANNA: But then again, I don't know. Maybe I ought to go. It's so stupid. Apparently, there aren't enough surgeons in Sarajevo. Too many people are just dying in the hospitals because there aren't enough surgeons. *She pauses, looking at him helplessly.* I just don't know. What do you think? *Dan gets up and walks about. He looks serious and worried.*

DAN: It would be crazy. Absolutely mad.

JANNA: But I am mad.

DAN: Seriously, Janna. Sarajevo is shelled all the time. Anyone walking around gets killed. Almost instantly. You read it every day in the papers, we watch it on television. Those bastards even shell the hospitals. They are out to kill. Without mercy. Bombs. Shells. Snipers. The more innocent the victims, the better, it seems. *He stops opposite her and bends down to study her eyes.* Did your father not tell you what's happening? You can't stay in your bunker all day long if you're a doctor.

JANNA: No. Of course not.

DAN: So?

JANNA: I just don't know. *Dan gets up again, moves towards the window, and opens the curtains to stare into the darkness.* Oh God! I just don't know. I'm at a complete loss. Maybe you're right. I mean, it's certainly crazy. But then, I've done many crazy things. And after all, your brother fought in Israel.

DAN: Yes. And you know what happened! *He walks back to her, holds her shoulders and looks straight into her eyes.* I just don't want the same to happen to you. Besides you aren't a surgeon. *He takes three steps back to the window.*

JANNA: Well, no longer. But I did surgery for three years, and was actually pretty good. Even today, I sometimes

assist in operations, and I've been thinking for a long
time that operating is what I really want to do.

DAN: But there? Besides, you seem to forget what great
things you're doing with all the children in your ward.

JANNA: But I hate chemotherapy and radiotherapy.
Besides, I don't really understand how it works. You
know I was crap at chemistry. *She looks at him and then
at her hands.* But I'm good with my hands and was
good at operating on people. I love that. And I
understand it. It's like plumbing. *She smiles and pauses
and walks over to the easel, taking a brush, adding white to
the canvas. She looks at him with a determined face.* Dan,
do you know what? I have a better idea. I should go
and check out the situation myself. I'll speak with our
friend Milas, and he'll be able to get me into Sarajevo
for a day on a press visa. And then I'll get a better idea.

I looked at her. So that was what the determination in her face
was about! I tried to think about the pros and cons in the seconds
I had before I needed to answer. I could not say no. And by saying
yes, I was hoping that she'd find the place so grim that she would
decide against going to work there.

'Well, why not?' I conceded.

'Oh, come on, be a bit more positive.' She came over and
smiled at me, holding my hand. I felt her warmth, her energy, but
felt cold and hopeless. She let go and sat back on the bed, looking
at me.

'Positive? What do you mean?' I tried to ask. 'What's positive
about parachuting yourself into the middle of a war? I mean for
Heaven's sake, that's just stupid.'

Janna turned around and lay down on her bed, staring at the
ceiling, while I wandered over to her bookshelves, looking at her
medical books. Chemotherapy. Radiology. Paediatrics. No sign of
Practical Surgery in War. Neither of us knew what to say to break
the silence. In the end, Janna got up and walked over to me,
taking my shoulders, turning me round.

'Please, Daniel, try to understand. I need to check this out.'

'I'm going to see my parents tomorrow,' I replied. 'As you have to be on duty over the weekend, I thought I'd fly to France to spend some time with them. I'd love you to come and meet them one day.'

'I promise I will,' she said, hugging me, stroking my hair.

'Promise me first that you won't go off to Sarajevo this weekend.'

'Well, that's easy. Done.' She looked at me, searching my eyes, and then smiled at me with her disarming smile, with her eyes that conveyed so much warmth, that caressed and disarmed you.

'Let's not think about it now.'

She pulled me towards her and we made love, slow and distant, our minds miles apart.

Lujeron

I was glad I could flee. Was this what the distance between us had been about? I now knew what I had not understood. Subconsciously I had feared that something like this could happen, and subconsciously she had known this would come: that she would one day, sooner rather than later, have to decide whether to go back. And despite the fact that she claimed she was undecided, I felt an urge in her to go back, an urge to help, to operate, to save lives. It was built into her nature.

And even if – I tried to think – she left for Sarajevo, the war would not last for years. She would do her bit and come back. Wars in Israel did not last for years. Wars are won and lost. And she would not be sitting in a tank. So why was I worried?

'Because Sarajevo is not Hampstead Heath!' said Tom when I called him to get the confirmation I was looking for. I did not really need to call him, since I knew what he was going to say before I phoned. Years ago, he had been a soldier.

I was glad to be able to see my parents. What thoughts were in their heads when my brother went to Israel? What would they say now? I had not told them about Janna. I was too afraid, in a way. Janna was not Jewish. My parents are. Very.

I landed in Toulouse and drove down the road south, along the fields. The road is lined with high trees on either side, small villages passed by in the distance. Soon the Pyrenees appeared out of the summer haze, first as a faint silhouette against the sky, then as rocks above the green meadows and pine forest. After Boussens I turned off the motorway and drove down the winding country road through sleepy villages. The Ariège is poor, and poverty is reflected in the sad mixture of the architecture. Neon lights, red roofs, low buildings without a lot of charm. Charm you find when you reach the former bishop's town of St Lizier – a mighty palace, two cathedrals on a hill overlooking the valley, signifying the far-reaching power of the church.

I picked up a hitchhiker whose broad accent I hardly understood. He had lived all his life as a carpenter in the village of Mane and was now making the journey to visit his girlfriend in St Lizier. His mother did not understand why he needed to look so far afield to find a girlfriend.

Twenty minutes later we were there. His smile was genuine. His girlfriend will marry him; they will settle either in Mane or St Lizier, and will consider a journey to Toulouse a major event. I felt like telling him about Janna, but then again he would probably understand too well that someone wants to go back home, even if there is war. I drove on in silence, and reached the little village of Lujeron, a village without any great charm – a café, a bar, a baker, a pharmacy, a church. And a graveyard.

I unpacked and went down into the garden to join my parents, who were sipping whisky, each reading a novel.

The same then as now.

I finish writing and close my pen and glance out of the window just to assure myself that I am living in the present, writing in the present, though I'm writing about the past. My parents are sitting in the garden, sipping whisky, each reading a novel. Where is the change wrought by time? Why can I not have the past brought back, just close my eyes and decide that today is yesterday, is last year, and open my eyes and pick up the phone to call Janna? I realise that the present does not exist. It is all either future or past. The moment the future arrives, it is already in the past. And the past is for ever past, even if you relive it in your thoughts, your dreams, your emotions; even if you taste it now in the bitterness of your saliva.

But back to my story. I went down into the garden to join my parents, who were sipping whisky, looking up from reading their novels. It was a beautiful and warm day. The sun was already low, its warm light casting long shadows in the garden from the bushes and the trees. Swallows were flying high in the light blue sky. The whisky shone like amber in the evening sun. My parents were casually dressed, their clothes more than slightly worn. What a change, I noticed then, from their life back in the States, where they used to mix with rather glitzier people than the folks of Lujeron. Not that they were ever part of the glitzy set, but they needed their contributions for their hospital work and research. Now they had retreated to a life they loved. Research, writing, reading, drinking whisky and wine and listening to classical music, going to concerts in St Lizier when the musicians returned each summer.

Yet our tranquillity was not what I had expected it to be. My mother was, as predicted, negative when I told her about Janna. No smile. No encouragement. I looked at her when I had finished, waiting for her approval. She gulped down her whisky and stared at me without a smile.

'And she's a Bosnian Muslim?'

I was getting annoyed. My father withdrew, picking up *The New Yorker*, browsing through the pages.

'Yes. I've told you three times now. Stop looking so glum. She is wonderful, Mum. What does her nationality or religion matter?'

My mother turned her eyes up in disbelief. How I hated that gesture. When I was a child she could drive me crazy with it. I tried to remain positive.

'She is a doctor. And a most amazing person.'

'Dan,' she said with a serious voice. 'We…our family have been Jewish without exception. Since we had to leave Paradise. I don't know of a single exception. Your father's side and your mother's side. None.' She paused, filling up her glass of whisky, taking a sip, adding with angry determination, 'Your brother fought the Muslims. He died fighting the Muslims. He was killed by them. And you want to say that you…'

'Mum!' I shouted. 'She's not a PLO fighter. Neither is she with Abu Nidal. Nor a niece of Saddam Hussein. She is…well…you'll see her.'

'Never.'

'You're horrible.'

It was my father's turn. Until then he had remained quiet, enjoying his whisky and deliberately reading *The New Yorker*.

With an ironic smile he remarked, 'Well, Becks will take the next plane to New York. Just to avoid her.' He got up and poured me some more whisky.

'But I'd like to meet her,' he added.

'Dan, you have never failed in your judgement about women. Whereas I have. See what an awful choice I made.'

We had to laugh. He always managed to break the tension with an ironic remark. My mother sulked and got up and walked over to the house. I feared that this was it, but moments later she came back with matches and lit a long cigarette, and joined in, half smiling.

'Daniel, you've simply got to understand. Our brothers and sisters died in Auschwitz and Dachau. Your brother died in Israel in the war. Where do you think we get the strength to survive? It's religion. Faith. The sharing of a common belief. The sharing of values. And it's the mother who is important in this respect. Religion is the mother's side of the family. What would happen if ever you had children – God forbid.'

'Dan, you know you're our remaining son,' my father said. 'And Becks is just worried how our line of the house of David would survive with a Muslim partner.'

'Her family is fighting genocide in Sarajevo. It's the same situation. What do you think she believes in? In the end we all believe in the same humanistic principles.'

'No Dan!' She interrupted, 'it's more than just humanistic principles.'

'Well, just as an aside, Mum, Jews like Monsieur Sharon slaughtered Arab children. Where are the special principles? Where is the difference to the PLO? Mum, stop being holy.'

We all went to the kitchen and prepared the food, carrying it back out into the garden. My father laid the table and opened the wine. Château Grand Puy Lacoste, 1979.

We ate in silence. My mother was upset, more so than I had thought she would be about a person she did not even know, a person, however, she knew I loved. Why this sentimental religious nonsense? On the one hand, here she was, the modern, cutting-edge scientist. On the other, she was living in seventeenth-century Poland. Maybe that was her charm, but I did not feel like suffering it that evening. But then again I was not a hundred per cent sure whether she was really a hundred per cent negative, or was playing it negative because as a Jewish mother she had to oppose a Muslim girlfriend. We drank a lot of wine, probably three bottles, following our own thoughts as they spun on in silence.

My mother left abruptly, and I stayed on with my father. We smoked, as usual. We both love sitting in silence, following the smoke into the dark, as it drifts away on the light evening wind. Later I told him more about Janna, about her work, her music, about us and what she meant to me. I told him about the phone call with her father and her thoughts about going to work and help in Sarajevo. Although he asked many questions about her, it was difficult to figure out what was going on in his head. He drank silently and continued smoking another cigar, watching the smoke rise gently.

When I came down for breakfast the next morning, both my parents looked tired. To my surprise, my mother came over, put her hand on my arm and said, 'I'm sorry about last night. You must understand. This is the first time you're serious again. It's all a bit much for me.' She sat down, poured herself a cup of coffee and started eating a croissant. 'Seth told me all last night. He woke me up to talk to me and change my mind.'

She sighed. In a way I was moved by my mother's genuine concern, but also annoyed by her attitude.

'I can imagine how hard it is for you if she really wants to go to Sarajevo,' she said while eating her croissant, looking into the distance, sipping her coffee. 'It was in a way the same for us when your brother decided to go to Israel. Though I don't think the situation is quite the same. She'll be in a hospital, not in a tank.'

'You know, in the end, it's her choice,' my father added.

'No one can or should try to take it away from her. You can argue. You can reason.' He paused and looked at both of us. 'But, Daniel, you should support her in her decision. I'll definitely support you. And her.'

To my surprise, my mother said, 'So we'll meet her soon, then. Maybe I won't go to New York after all. But let me tell you,' – she put a hand on my arm and attempted to smile – 'the thought of you having a Muslim girlfriend is grim. You may think she is wonderful, Seth may think you're right, but I really need to be convinced.'

Finally she smiled, and gulping down her coffee she added, 'Allow me to keep my doubts till I meet with her. And if I'm not convinced, you'd better dump her.'

'Becks! You really are mean,' my father shouted over, laughing. 'My mother didn't ask me to dump you!'

I looked at them. I did not know what went on in my mother's head, or in my father's for that matter. How stubborn was she really? Or how tolerant was he? How did they arrive at their views? In our discussions I had asked myself many times whether the horrors of the Second World War were still reflected in their thinking, in their judgements. And how the loss of my brother had affected them. Both smiled at me, and I saw them the way I was used to seeing them.

But then, as I observed them sitting there, I realised that both were looking old – and, in a way, I felt for the first time that they were looking frail, despite all their energy. Both had become old. And yet there was this immensely strong positivity in both of them, which spread to everyone around them. How would this positivity interact with Janna's own immense energy?

I left them after lunch so that I could be back in time for Janna's return from work. We would be back together soon.

Sarajevo

The plane was delayed, and I arrived at Janna's place after midnight. She had been waiting for me, reading comics. I guess that was another side of her I did not understand. Whereas I loved literature and found Primo Levi unbelievably beautiful and sad, she preferred comics.

'We haven't even said hello, and you already have this disapproving look on your face. You are just so intolerant, Dan,' she said, getting out of bed, kissing me nonetheless.

'It's not that…well, I just don't understand why you like reading such crap when there is great literature around,' I tried to argue.

'I just don't like reading stories other people make up,' she said, turning around and picking up one of her comic books. 'But I love Mangas or Lucky Luke. There are real characters, not artificial ones like Anna Karenina or those über-partisans of Primo Levi.'

'Hmm…' I didn't know what to say, so Janna changed the topic.

'I've booked my trip.' She smiled at me. 'I've got it all arranged. I've taken a few days off and will fly to Budapest on Wednesday, and on Thursday morning there will be an early flight into Sarajevo carrying a bunch of reporters, who are staying there. On Friday and Saturday there will be another flight, and I'll take one of them when they fly back in the evening.'

'And where are you going to stay?' I asked.

'With my parents, of course. And then my father will take me to the hospital, and I hope to see some friends too. I'm really quite excited.' She looked at me in a most open and disarming way. I was lost for words, and could only stammer that I did not know what to say. But she just smiled and pulled me closer to her.

'Just don't say anything. I'll be back Sunday at the very latest.'

We stood for a long time in silence. I felt her heartbeat, slow and rhythmical, as she held me tight in her arms. I caressed her hair, her back. Neither of us felt like making love that evening, and we just stayed close to each other in bed, feeling each other's warmth.

Janna had to get up very early the next morning, and I decided to walk to work. The City was close to her home, and my route took me down the dismal, empty streets in the early morning light. London in the morning is depressing when the wind is blowing and it seems that real summer will never come, or that winter will manifest itself not in crisp white silence falling on the roofs, but in dirt and rain and never-ending damp.

In the office I managed to half-forget. Closing my eyes, I saw Janna in her green dress, stethoscope in hand, joking with the kids.

I went home early in the evening and found Janna in a superb mood standing in my kitchen, cooking. Her mood instantly changed my perception of the whole day – her smile was beaming, powerful, convincing.

'Guess what! Did I ever tell you about one of my patients, Joe, a six-year-old? I probably forgot. Anyway, he was operated on less than three weeks ago. Started therapy. And he's ready to go home. It all worked beautifully. That's when you feel great, having achieved something. You should have seen his face.'

I smiled at her, but then again I was plagued by doubts, self-doubts, when confronted with these powerful, convincing feelings. What had I done during the same day? I had analysed a company that we wanted to buy. Spoken to some private equity funds to see whether they were willing to buy part of it, a subsidiary we did not want to keep. I had gone over calculations about how much we would need to invest, how many people we would have to fire in order to cut costs. What if one of those people was Joe's father? Suddenly unemployed, not enough money to make ends meet or to pay for the additional therapy Joe would need to recover fully. I reflected on her last words: 'You should have seen his face.' I felt mean and down. What was I creating?

I shared my thoughts with Janna, but she just brushed them aside.

'But you're building viable companies. Don't be daft. It's not you who's responsible for the job losses. It's the previous management. You need to do the surgery in order to let the patient survive. It's not the surgeon's fault if he has to cut.'

How could I question the words of a doctor who once had been a surgeon, and might be one again.

I walked over to my cello and started playing the second movement of Haydn's cello concerto in C major.

After a while Janna shouted from the kitchen, 'Give me five minutes and dinner will be ready. It's just pasta.'

'Spaghetti Sarajese?'

'Very funny. Actually, for once you're right!'

It was delicious, her Sarajevo recipe with wild mushrooms, tomatoes, garlic and fresh herbs.

'This is how my father used to cook when we came back from the forests in the summer with all the mushrooms and herbs and stolen tomatoes.'

We laughed, kissed and made love, but in the middle of the night I got up and called Tom.

Dan's living room. Int.

DAN: Tom, are you still awake?

TOM: Yeah. Sure. I'm still working. What do you think?

DAN: Look, Tom. I've been trying to reach Tania. But she doesn't answer the phone.

TOM: Probably working on some deadline. You know she doesn't answer when she's got something to finish.

DAN: Tom, can you get hold of her?

TOM: Why?

DAN: I need to ask her for a favour. She needs to get me a press card so that I can go to Sarajevo this week.

TOM: Where? Sarajevo?

DAN: Yep.

TOM: That's fucking crazy. In any event, the *Wall Street Journal* doesn't send reporters to Sarajevo.

DAN: Look Tom, I need to go. Janna is going. I need to go with her, but it's only for reporters and stuff.

TOM: Jesus Christ, you're difficult. OK. Give me a minute,

I'll call her and if I get her, I'll call you right back. But you know what the answer is going to be, Dan. It's a 'No'! Do you really think the *Journal* is just printing guest passes for parties in Sarajevo?

DAN: No. Of course not. But I need one. And Tania is the only hope I have.

TOM: OK. I'll call her.

Dan hangs up and paces up and down the room. After two minutes the telephone rings.

DAN: And?

TOM: She'll know tomorrow. But she'll be bending all the rules. The *Journal* doesn't hire freelance reporters for the day. Anyway. She'll try to get you accredited for the week. But you're crazy, Dan.

DAN: I know. Thanks, Tom. See you tomorrow. *Dan hangs up.*

At four in the morning I heard the fax machine. I rushed down and saw Tania's letter. By eight I was at the office of the *Wall Street Journal*, and by 8.30 an accredited journalist, freelancing for the *Journal* in Bosnia, booked on Janna's flight to Sarajevo from Budapest. At least I knew how to look like a *Journal* reporter.

Thinking back, this really was surreal. A reputable paper sending a banker as a 'journalist' into the middle of a war. But then it was not the *Journal* but Tania, and in the same way I would do everything for her, she would bend every rule for me. I'd bet the *Journal* did not even know they had a reporter out there.

Sarajevo Airport. Ext.

A late summer morning. A UN propeller plane can be seen taxiing to a stand at the airport. Jeeps surround the plane, soldiers jump out, and steps are pushed up to the opening front and back doors. Journalists descend from the plane together with army staff and officials. Janna emerges from the front door of the plane. As she starts down the staircase she looks inquisitively at the neighbouring houses. She descends and walks down the tarmac with the other passengers. The passengers from the back join. Dan, wearing a black beard, sunglasses and a baseball cap pulled low over his head approaches Janna and taps her on the shoulder. She turns round and stares at his face, not recognising him.

DAN *in a deep voice, speaking in Russian*: Dobrej Djen. Vas savut Janna?

JANNA *looking unsure*: Da.

DAN: Menja savut Daniel. Otchen prijatno.
She looks completely puzzled. Dan takes off his baseball cap and slowly pulls off his beard.

JANNA: Daniel! You're crazy. What are you doing here? You're not supposed to be here! Daniel!

DAN: Well, you couldn't expect me to stay behind when you're in a crazy war zone.
They hug for a minute, while other passengers pass.

JANNA: How the heck did you get onto this plane? Don't tell me you want to buy a company here...

DAN: No, I want to buy the country. The market cap of Bosnia is lower than that of an average multinational.

JANNA: One of your targets? You're crazy!...But honestly, are you here as a journalist?

DAN: Yep.
He shows her his Wall Street Journal *pass.*

JANNA: Very impressive. So you're going to write about this dump.

DAN: Let's go. They have this cattle carrier into town. Unless you have arranged for someone to pick you up?

JANNA: No. You can only get through in an armoured personnel carrier, cars are a hit-and-run target.

DAN: More hit than run, I guess.

JANNA: Anyway, let's go.
Cut.

We squeezed ourselves into the Unprofor armoured personnel carrier, the shuttle between the airport and Sarajevo centre. We looked around. People were sitting in silence; reporters with years of war experience were quiet, crouched in their own thoughts. Who were the officials? What were they negotiating? Supplies into town? An end to the war? The partition of the country?

We pulled out of the airport past high fences and soldiers with heavy machine guns, and turned onto the road into town. Outside we saw buildings, bombed, burned out, ugly communist high-rise blocks such as you can find in any suburb of Paris or Moscow. Except that in Moscow and Paris they have window panes and the walls are not marked by soot or damaged by mortar or machine-gun fire. In between the high-rises stood some smaller houses with their own pitiful gardens, bleak, covered with litter, the trees all felled. Smoke drifted out of a window. We sped along the wide road.

'This is it,' Janna said quietly. 'Sniper Alley!'

I looked out again. I had imagined this to be an alley surrounded by houses, but whatever houses there had been were bombed, burned, shelled, destroyed.

'Look at these two towers,' she said, pointing outside. Two huge high-rises, destroyed, the windows gone, cables and curtains still hanging out of some of them. 'And here, look at those houses. This is where the snipers sit.' Janna commented as if she was giving me a tour of Paris, her voice betraying no emotion. We sped on and reached the hospital without being shot at. But why should someone waste valuable ammunition on an armoured personnel carrier?

It looked as if the hospital building had been subjected to very precise shelling. The marks were not the work of some stray shells that had missed other targets. Too many had made direct hits. Janna got out of the carrier and looked around. Pain showed on her face.

'When I was ten years old, I spent a week in here. Look,' she said, pointing up to the top floor. 'That is where my room was. They took my appendix out. I wonder whether the surgeon is still there.'

I looked up. The windows had plastic panes. There was soot above most of the ones on the top floor; the shells must have exploded inside, causing fires to spread. I did not want to imagine the misery of shells exploding in the middle of a ward.

Now it was quiet, too quiet. We could hear no artillery, no shelling, no shots. Some people were hurrying down the street, we looked at them. They were well dressed, the women wearing lipstick, as if they were shopping on Rue St Honore. Janna noticed the surprise on my face and came over, putting her arm around my shoulder.

'They've still got lipstick, I guess that will last through the war,' she said pensively. 'The Serbs want to destroy the people, the way we live, our appearance – and then our will to continue. And the people of Sarajevo resist, and demonstrate their resistance, even if it's only for themselves and for their mirror.'

She smiled again, and her face showed an astonishing serenity as she looked at the hospital. 'I'm going inside. I can't see any sign of Milas anywhere. I hope he'll be here later on to pick us up.'

'Didn't you tell your parents?'

'No, only him. A bit of a surprise.'

'How do you know they're around?'

'Oh, sure. I forgot,' she laughed. 'They may have gone to the beach for the day or picking mushrooms with the Serbs in the hills... Anyway, we need Milas, as I figured he'd get us home. I honestly don't fancy walking to my parents' place, even if you're there to protect me.' She paused, looking at me, waiting. I felt useless.

'What do you want to do?' she asked. 'I mean you can't possibly just walk around as if this were Saragossa or another town in Spain or Italy.'

'I'm just going out to interview a couple of people. I'll meet you back here in three hours' time.'

She laughed.

'God, you really are childish! Look,' she said, 'this is a war. Even if you can't hear anything right now, even if they've stopped shelling for the moment, any second a stray shell can explode in front of your feet and rip you apart.' Her smile had stopped and her dark eyes had turned black and serious. 'Look, Daniel, you're old enough. Be careful, and beware of the snipers. They are everywhere.'

'Please, Janna, I'm not that naïve.'

'Well, coming here demonstrates a huge amount of naïveté. Anyway, just don't cross a street if you can be seen from any of the houses there on the hills or over there.' She pointed at the hills in the distance. 'They are in Serb-held territory, and they are the sniper nests.'

'OK, OK. I'll see you later.'

She kissed me and hugged me silently, and turned abruptly, running towards the doors of the building that had probably been a decent hospital. I looked around. Suddenly I was on my own. I surveyed the buildings across the road. Shrapnel had hit them at the top. There were a lot of holes next to the windows, where bullets aimed at people inside the houses had missed their targets, hitting the walls instead. Black soot stained the walls above most windows also here. I decided to turn right and walk towards the centre. The town was empty, except for the occasional person rushing past, and the occasional Humvee driving unperturbed through town, as if this were California. I was careful before crossing each street, and must have walked for about fifteen minutes when I came to a square and saw a café. I looked inside through the plastic window and saw that it was full. I opened the door, and the conversation died down. It was obviously weird to see a stranger. Few of my fellow journalists would ever venture out of the Holiday Inn, where I too was going to stay for the night. A young waiter came to my table and smiled. He was wearing an impeccably white shirt and black designer jeans; and a longish ponytail. I must have been observing him for some time, and he sat down opposite me.

'The best we have is tea. Lapsang Souchong, Earl Grey, English Breakfast and Peppermint. And home-made cake.'

I opted for the peppermint tea, which he served with style in beautiful china. It was wonderfully dark and aromatic, like the mood in this café. I paid with deutschmarks. Strange, a war zone where the dollar isn't the common denominator. Around me there were only elderly men. Where was Djemal, Janna's father? I think I got him right – a man at the back of the room, with darkish skin. He was staring at me at the same time. Had Janna sent a photo? Did he know by now?

At that moment the door opened and a young woman rushed in and shouted something I did not understand. Three men jumped up and others followed. I gulped down my tea, left a big tip for the waiter and joined them in my new role as a journalist, smelling a story. We ran down the street, back towards the hospital. At a crossing we stopped. In the middle of the crossing lay two children, a little boy and a little girl. The boy seemed motionless at first. Was he already dead? The girl was in shock, her eyes wide open in fear. A puddle of blood had formed under their bodies.

A small group of elderly people had already gathered, looking at the scene, none willing or able to help. More men and women were approaching cautiously. I watched them – grey, ashen faces, without emotion.

Sarajevo street crossing. Ext.

DAN *turning to one of the men in the group*: What's
    happening?
MAN: Snipers. We don't know where they are. But the kids
    got shot.
    *Dan looks around and at the children, whose arms and legs
    are moving slowly. Both of them are whimpering; the little
    girl's dress is covered in blood.*
DAN: We've got to get them. Otherwise they'll die.
MAN: You can't do anything. The snipers are still there to
    shoot the rescuer. We have to wait for a UN car to give
    us cover.
DAN: Look at them! They're bleeding. They'll die unless
    we get them.

MAN: But...

WOMAN: Wait, the UN may come in a few minutes...

DAN: How many?

WOMAN: Don't know. Five? Ten?

DAN: But the kids will be dead by then.

He looks around and sees a large metal rubbish bin. He runs to the bin and grabs the lid. He also takes a large bag of rubbish and makes his way through the group of onlookers. He ducks behind the corner of the house and peers onto the street.

MAN: Don't! No!

DAN: Damn it!

Dan throws the garbage bag into the middle of the crossing as cover, ducks behind the large bin lid, dashes forward, grabs the girl and drags her back. Immediately shots are heard, the first one tearing into the bag, and bullets bounce off the asphalt, hitting his shield. When he is about to reach the corner of the house, a bullet hits its wall and a piece of brick splinters off, hitting Daniel on the forehead, opening a wound that starts bleeding. Dan reaches safety with the girl. He is ashen-faced and panting, and blood runs down his face. Everyone is staring at him. He lays the girl on the ground and a woman crouches down next to her to hold her head. Dan bends over her to check whether the girl is breathing, and notices blood dripping from his head. He straightens up and looks around. At that moment a UN truck drives up and stops between the boy and the sniper. The door opens and a soldier reaches out and pulls the boy into the truck. The truck drives backwards until it reaches the crowd and the girl. Dan gets up and lifts the girl into the truck and gets in himself. The truck drives off.

Cut.

Sarajevo hospital. Ext.

The truck drives up to the hospital and stops in front of the main door. A nurse comes out. The truck doors are opened and Dan gets out, the collar of his shirt by now drenched in blood; he is very pale.

DAN: Quickly, get the kids into hospital. They lost a lot of blood. *Another nurse comes running out with a stretcher and they carry the children into the hospital. The driver of the UN vehicle gets out too and walks over to Dan and looks at his head.*

DRIVER: You need stitching too. Here, take this. *He takes a tissue out of his pocket and hands it to Dan. Dan presses the tissue on his forehead and it is soon soaked and red. Janna comes out of the hospital.*

JANNA *shouting and running towards him*: Daniel! What happened? Oh shit! Shit!

DAN: I'm OK, don't worry. Just bleeding a bit.

JANNA: You need to…Let me have a look. *She examines the wound.* You need stitching. Let's go inside. I'll stitch you up, but it will be painful – they've no anaesthetics. What the heck happened? Tell me!

I felt the needle going through my skin, the pain when the skin was pulled together. I told her what had happened, waiting for her comments, but she remained quiet. At the end she just said, 'It's so typical. No one helped. Everyone just standing around. Why haven't they got shields to protect themselves? It's not the first time they need to rescue someone who got shot by snipers. I just don't understand. People just stare, don't they?'

She was silent for a while, as she poured iodine onto my wound. Then she said with a determined face, 'Let's go. You need a proper hospital; you should have an x-ray done. It isn't just your skin that's damaged. Whatever hit you also knocked your skull.' She turned away, thinking. 'Besides, I don't want to stay here either. I don't want to see my parents or anyone now! I'm so fed up!'

'But Janna…I mean, you've come all the way here, and now you leave without seeing them? Or your sister?' She hesitated for a moment. 'I know it's tough, but I just can't listen to them bombarding me with their arguments why I should stay.'

'Oh come on,' I said. 'Can you imagine how they'd feel if they knew that you were in town and didn't even visit them? I can travel back alone.'

She was looking around, as if for inspiration, and then concluded, 'Look, stuff it. I'm so fed up. Why am I always supposed to be the nice one? I want to go home now. With you. Besides, Milas hasn't turned up.'

So we took the one flight the same evening back to Budapest. We did not stay at the Holiday Inn, the only real hotel in war-torn Sarajevo. I had no chance either to interview Karadzic or meet Janna's parents. On the other hand, we were both glad when the plane had reached a height where we were safe from missiles.

In Budapest Janna slept most of the time, and we talked about everything but Sarajevo. Whenever I tried to steer the conversation towards her departure and her work in Sarajevo, towards the war, she changed the topic or light-heartedly kissed me to shut me up.

On our flight back to London, Janna was unusually quiet. I dropped her off at her hospital when we arrived, and she stayed there overnight. I returned to the office on Monday and found a fax on my machine, sent from the Forum Hotel in Budapest.

Dear Dan,

You are at the hospital and did not want me to wait, so I am sitting here in the luxury of this beautiful hotel. I feel deeply guilty for what happened in Sarajevo a few hours ago. Dan, I am still stunned at how close you came to death. How crazy you were! But then you saved a child. An amazing stunt! Welcome to Sarajevo!

Had this not happened, I might have simply stayed on at the hospital, but you brought the reality of war straight back to me.

I loved the hospital. It was archaic, but genuine. The machines were pre-war, but they worked – well, not all of them. But the real reason I wanted to stay was because I was needed. There was work for me straight away, so I took off my coat and stitched someone up. No, not you, but someone else who had cut himself with broken glass. Not even bullet or shrapnel wounds. And I talked to all the doctors and nurses. This is where my mission is, Dan. That's what I thought until you came in bleeding. Now, I admit that I should not be fazed by the appearance of someone covered in blood in Sarajevo – after all, that is why I want to be there in the first place. But it was you and your head that made the war so much more direct. And all the time I was stitching I had to think of all those people who were standing around. If everyone stands around, the snipers get away with their killing. Why were you, the foreigner, with no attachment to this town, the only one who dared to save the children? Was it because you were the only one who did not act rationally? Were you the only one with guts? To be honest, I felt ashamed more than anything else, and the moment I had finished with the last of the fifteen stitches I wanted to get out as fast as possible. I was so fed up. Now, being out, I am disgusted with myself: I fled when faced with the slightest problem. And I'm torn, as to whether and when I should go back. At least you are alive and safe. Dan, I am immensely proud of your guts, but also stunned at your ruthless stupidity…don't ever dare to go back to Bosnia as long as there is war. War is not the zone for you. You should stay as a predator on Wall Street, not Sniper Alley.

A waiter is bringing me another cognac. I marvel at the beautiful colour. I need Remy Martin XO today as my stomach is still upset. And it's even more upset when I think about the absurd fact that I am sitting here in a five-star hotel, enjoying one of the highlights of French civilisation, while only a few miles away from here people are subjected to the most grotesque bestialities that Europe has witnessed since the fall of Nazi Germany.

Rather than trying to find an explanation, I am going to down the cognac, send off this fax and rush back to your hospital.

Dan, I really do love you. Come home soon when you've read this, so that we can play some music together.

Love,
Janna

News

I went home early. When we met up in the evening, she was once again her usual cheerful self. I was at home, playing the cello, when she arrived. She came rushing up the stairs and smiled and kissed me for a long time.

'Go back to your cello. I'll join you in a minute,' she said.

I started playing the first movement of Haydn's cello concerto in C major. Janna took her flute out of its case and stood behind me, trying to improvise an accompaniment. We played, but after a few bars we got stuck. I stopped, and we started again, but we both got stuck again at the same place.

'This is definitely not for today.'

'Maybe we should go and play tennis instead.' She took her flute apart and put it back into its case.

'Let's go.' She smiled. 'I'm glad you're feeling better.'

I looked out of the window. Outside it was still light, even though the sun was low. It was warm.

'Are you sure? Now? Look, it's already pretty late.'

'So what? We can still play for an hour. And then we can go and have a pizza somewhere.' She came over and examined my head.

'Can you play with all your stitches?' she said, gently lifting the plaster. 'Well, it looks OK. Let's go.'

She walked to the wardrobe to get her tennis shorts and sweatshirt, and started undressing.

Hyde Park tennis courts. Ext.

It is early evening. There are big cumulus clouds in the sky and the sun is low, between the horizon and the clouds, giving a warm and powerful light. The trees cast long shadows over the courts. Janna and Dan are playing tennis together. Janna plays well. It's a fast game. Janna is serving. She focuses in concentration, and serves an ace.

JANNA: 15:30. *They continue. He loses. 30 all.*

DAN: Hey, wait. Not so fast!

JANNA: I'm aiming at your head! *They play, he loses again. 40:30.*

DAN: Sadist! *She serves again and he makes another mistake.* Yours. *As they pick up balls, they come together at the net. She smiles at him, kissing him briefly.*

JANNA *with a grin on her face*: I've got to tell you something.

DAN *smiling too*: Well?

JANNA: I'm pregnant. *She takes his hand and pulls him closer towards her, gazing into his eyes.*

DAN *moving a step back*: Holy smoke! And you went to Sarajevo? Pregnant? How long have you known? *She shrugs her shoulders. He looks at her with a sudden questioning glance.* Are you sure? You're not kidding, are you?

JANNA: No, of course not. That's, well, yes, I mean of course I'm sure. *Nodding*: I guess as a doctor I know these things. *She smiles.* I actually found out last night. I was two weeks overdue and did a test.

DAN: Hmm. *He is smiling at her a bit ironically.* This is all a bit earlier than I guess either of us planned.

JANNA: I know it's a bit ironic that this is happening to a doctor. *She looks down.*

DAN: Well, I'm not quite innocent in this matter. But...*He laughs at her and jumps over the net towards her.* I think this is wonderful. Absolutely fantastic, although I can't quite imagine myself as a father. *He holds her in his arms, caressing her hair.* Remembering my statistics classes from business school, I think the chances of this happening were pretty high, considering we've been making love on average twice a day.

JANNA: Well, not quite...

DAN: OK, OK...*He stares at her.* I guess that means an end to your Sarajevo plans.

JANNA: Let's not discuss this now. I think you're right, but I haven't yet decided, particularly given what I saw, which urged me to go and, then again, it pissed me off so that I want to stay away.
Fading.

Hampstead Heath. Ext.

Janna and Dan are walking slowly arm in arm over the Heath. Both wear casual clothes. It is a warm and sunny day with blue sky; people are lying in the grass.

JANNA: I can't wait to see the place, sit in the garden, go hiking with you. By the way, have you got the tickets?
DAN: Yes. I've got them at home.
JANNA: And you're sure we'll both arrive around the same time?
DAN: I think so. Actually, my plane lands about twenty minutes earlier. If I'm not there, just wait for me. I'm on the Air France from Milan. *He stops to look at her.* How are you feeling in the mornings? As far as I can see you haven't changed.
JANNA: Actually I do feel nauseous. I just try to hide it. And I hate throwing up, so I try not to.
DAN: Any cravings yet?
JANNA *smiling disarmingly*: Only for you.
DAN: That's worrying. *They embrace and kiss.*
JANNA: By the way, my father wrote me another letter. This time a bit more meaningful.
DAN: What do you mean?
JANNA: Well, he explained the situation in the hospitals, the patients, etc. He was seriously pissed off when he heard that we were there.
DAN: Milas told him?
JANNA *nodding her head*: I think so. Anyway to me what he

writes sounds more like they need a good engineer to get all the broken equipment going again. I came to the same conclusion when I was there. Or new machines for that matter, rather than another surgeon. They have doctors, I know. I saw them. And I asked Milas.

DAN: So why did your father ask you to come back?

JANNA: I'm not sure. I guess it's like everywhere. There are enough doctors to deal with the everyday illnesses or births. But when a shell hits a house, you need twenty more to deal with all the wounded. And he sees the shells hitting houses.

DAN: I could see that too.

JANNA: Oh please, Dan! I really have to think hard about this.

DAN: Whenever you think you have to go, just think about the onlookers, who did nothing.

JANNA: Dan, stop it, please.

DAN: Sorry.

JANNA: I'll talk to Milas again, though I think he's biased. He's been getting so many people out of town he doesn't want to ship me in.

DAN: Any news from your brother?

JANNA: Actually, yes. My father wrote that they had heard from him via a friend.

DAN: Is he OK?

JANNA: He seems to be OK, but still stuck in godforsaken Srebrenica. Fighting the Serbs or the United Nations.

DAN: But there's no fighting any more.

JANNA: Well, I think he's now buying medicine and stuff from Milas, who buys it from the Croats, who rob it from the Serbs, who hold up and plunder the relief convoys.

They lie down on the grass, Janna resting her head on Dan's stomach. She turns over to Dan so that she can look into his eyes.

JANNA: You know, right now, when we were walking over there across the Heath, I suddenly remembered our very first meeting, our first conversation. I asked you why you play the cello in cemeteries. Do you remember? And you replied, 'It's because of sadness and death.' And you told me that your friend, the organist, had died. And then you told me that your brother had died, but you just left it at that. So I never could rid myself of the feeling that there was something deeper, yet another dimension related to your brother's death. And I somehow feel that it was this experience, this dimension, that's made you so absolutely opposed to my going to Sarajevo. Not what you saw in Sarajevo yourself, but that experience. Daniel, you have to tell me what other, I mean, what else there is that makes you feel the way you feel. I need to understand.

DAN *sighing and not looking at her*: I've told you. The main story is: my brother died and he meant a lot to me. There isn't that much more to it. *He caresses her face.* I haven't told many people what happened, in fact only one other friend…I was in a way waiting to see whether you'd ask.

JANNA: Well, I have asked.

DAN *sighs, sits up and looks into her face.* It all started ages ago, in fact, when I was five and first played the cello. From that first day on I wanted to become a cellist. On my fifth birthday, my parents took me to a concert by Pablo Casals, you know, the Spanish cellist. We went behind the stage to meet with him after the concert. He looked at me for a long time and told my parents that I should be a good cellist – don't ask me why. And I realised that I wanted to be like him. Big, distant, wise. Living for music. In music. By the time I was eight, I played quite well. But then my life imploded into a big black hole…*He pauses*…when my brother died. He lived in Israel – that much I'd told you – and died in the war. In '67. He was a lieutenant in the army...but still he died. *Reflecting*: Israel was his chosen country. And he wanted to help build it up, rather than live in the set and saturated world of Europe or the States. *Janna nods without turning to him, playing absent-mindedly with the flowers that grow beside her.* In everyday life he was a lawyer, and played the oboe. He always played the oboe. *He smiles at Janna to break the gloom of the story.*

JANNA: Even on his tank. It must have been so annoying.

DAN *pauses and looks down again:* It was strange, if you think about it, that already at my age I could feel the contradictions he was going through. He was not the typical soldier, the Moshe Dayan type or, worse, the Sharon type. My brother was thoughtful, analytical, incredibly grown up, and yet with the great gift of talking to me in my own language, of knowing what I was thinking, what I was feeling, what I wanted to do. My parents never picked up on these things. I think I told you – they always remained distant...*he becomes quiet and looks away from her.*

JANNA: Yes you did. But it's an important part of yourself. *Dan watches her from the side. She glances first ahead and then at him with serious eyes.*

DAN: Well, so he died. *He pauses, staring ahead into the distance, and then down again.* He was not only my brother but also my closest friend. Closer than my parents or anybody else. *He lies down on his back, looking at the sky, the clouds, the birds – swallows – which are circling high above the Heath.*

DAN: Aged eight I understood what war meant. He had explained it to me when we last met during one of his visits. In a way, he believed he was invincible. And as he believed it, I, of course, believed it too. His death meant utter devastation for me. Everything was burnt. Destroyed. I understood what death really meant.

Death is the end of reality, and of dreams. And the end
of dreams is the beginning of all ends. *He pauses again,
glancing up. She has her eyes closed.* I was in a state of
shock and for one full week just cried in bed. I
couldn't eat or go to school. I just cried. And then,
some time after the war was over and things were safe,
we all flew to Israel.

I have to stop writing. Even after all this time I still feel acute bitterness in my throat. I lie down on my bed and have to think again
about those days, which are like centuries away but yet have the
power to evoke emotions, that slowly paralyse my mind. I pour
myself a glass of single malt to stop paralysis. It always works.

I see the flashback passing by – see myself all in black with my
little black cello case, walking about in this foreign town.

Jerusalem, 1967. Ext.

*Aerial view of the town, the olive hills, the wall, then
focusing on the King David Hotel, a palatial building of
massive presence. Dan as a small eight-year-old boy is seen
with his half-sized cello coming out of the main door, the
porters greeting him and smiling. He does not smile but
seems oblivious of his surroundings, turning right and
heading down the road. Next, he is seen walking on top of
the wall, carrying his cello, then passing through the
narrow streets of the Christian quarter, playing in front of
the Church of the Holy Sepulchre with little children
watching him. And then back, going through the narrow
streets, sitting in front of houses, smiling at people who
stare at him somewhat in disbelief. While he is walking
and playing alone, Dan's conversation with Janna is heard
in voiceover.*

DAN: I took my cello along. I had a little cello. Half size –
it really was small. I still have it at my parents' place,
and keep it for if ever I should have a son or a
daughter…And then there was my brother's grave. We
held a ceremony for him as we couldn't be there for
his funeral. There were a lot of people and I knew
nobody…

*A cemetery outside Jerusalem. From above Dan is seen
standing with his parents in a group of people in front of a
grave, holding his mother's hand and grasping his cello-
case in his other hand. When the ceremony is over, he goes
and picks up a chair and sits down to play the cello. He
plays the Sarabande from Bach's second suite while his
audience listens silently, their heads bowed. He is playing
the way a child plays – making mistakes, hitting wrong
notes, but continuing without getting stuck – his eyes
closed. Suddenly he lifts his head.*

DAN: I looked at them. Who were all those people who
had come to my brother's grave? Were they his
friends? How many others of his friends had died?
Where were their parents? *Dan finishes and people leave
silently. Dan remains sitting, and a young woman
approaches him and crouches down next to where Dan is
sitting. She is beautiful, with dark, long hair, covered by a
deep-blue scarf. Her eyes are obscured by sunglasses, which
she slowly takes off as she crouches down next to Dan. Her
eyes are red and full of tears. She wipes the tears away and
caresses his head. They can be seen talking. Dan gets up.* I
only saw my brother's girlfriend once. For some reason
I had felt that my parents did not approve of her.
When she was next to me, I understood: she wasn't
Jewish. She was a Christian, but she had lived all her
life in Israel. She took me into her arms, and I cried
because she cried and because I felt that she was so

much closer to my feelings than my parents, who were not crying, and who then seemed cold and lacking the heart to embrace her at this moment of immense pain for all of us. *The woman crouches down again and Dan sits down on the chair again, and plays the Allemande movement of the first Bach suite.* She looked at me for a long time while I was playing, and then, when I had finished… *The woman gets up and kisses him gently and disappears into the crowd.* I never saw her again. *He pauses. He is seen packing his cello into its case. Slowly he walks away from the cemetery. At the entrance his parents are waiting. His father tries to take him by the hand, but he pulls his hand away, holding on to his cello instead.* I was very bitter about my parents' rejection of my brother's girlfriend. They were cruel. Then my parents basically left me alone. And I discovered Jerusalem on my own, taking my cello with me. But I had no one to talk to. I felt my parents were distant, somehow absorbed in their own sadness, which they seemed unable to share with me. So I felt very alone, despite the fact that everyone at the King David was absolutely charming. You know how children can live in a complete dream-world. I was so lost that I only talked to my cello, and strangely felt that it was the only thing that understood me. So I talked, and played. And I dreamt I heard its answers in the music. *He pauses.* I played on top of the city walls and in the old town – and at his grave. I went there every day to play for him and to talk to him. And it felt as if he talked to me. I guess I was going mad. I lived a life totally separate from my parents. I had my own room in that huge hotel. And played my cello and talked with my cello and my brother. *He pauses for some time, thinking.*

Hampstead Heath. Ext. (continuation)

Dan sits looking at Janna. Dan's voiceover continues as active speech. I became desperate. At this point my parents decided to leave. And I was forced back into the routine of daily life – school, my friends, the whole thing. *He pauses.* So I gradually got over this loss. But I had decided to wear black, just black, and to play for him whenever I could.

JANNA: So that's why you're still today wearing black?

DAN *looking at her and smiling vaguely*: I guess so. *She turns her head and returns the smile.*

JANNA: So what happened then? I mean after you left Israel?

DAN: Getting back to school was like being thrown into cold water. I hated school and wanted to drown. But my friends didn't let me drown. It still took six months after we'd left Jerusalem to accept life as it was. But then I didn't feel like playing the cello any more, and spent every free minute playing football with my friends instead. I was sure I was going to become a professional footballer, and decided then never to become a professional cellist. It was only one evening at Hanukah that I picked up my cello again and felt like playing.

JANNA: And that's why you're still playing for him.

DAN: I guess so. *Janna remains silent for quite some time, then she turns round towards him, though he does not look at her. She caresses his head. Staring past him into the distance, she slowly nods.*

JANNA: I guess I'm starting to understand your feelings, and where you're coming from. Why didn't you tell me earlier?

DAN: You didn't ask...

JANNA: I guess I've always wondered, but never asked. *She looks at him in silence and sighs*: I guess this also explains your opposition to pacifism.

DAN *thinking, without looking at her*: My brother was a
pacifist, but a weird one – at the crucial moment he
did not desert, leave Israel or protest but climbed into
his tank. That's one aspect I've been thinking about a
lot. How can you be a pacifist and then drive a tank? It
was too late – I could never ask him. But you're right,
it was then that I resolved I'd always fight, fight to the
bitter end.

JANNA: But that's horrible, and will never bring peace.
Lasting peace.

DAN: No, I think you misunderstood me. I'd fight for
justice, for the right cause, or if I'm attacked. I
wouldn't go out and fight an offensive war. My
militarism is purely defensive. No 'eye for an eye, a
tooth for a tooth'. I completely reject that. But you
must understand, Janna, had the Jews, had the world
started earlier, the horrors of the Second World War
wouldn't have happened.

JANNA: Had the Germans been pacifist, Hitler would have
never got anywhere.

DAN: But they weren't! So millions had to die, and in my
view that could have been prevented. Janna, can't you
see?

JANNA: I can see where you're coming from, but still I'm a
pacifist. You cannot destroy evil with military force.

DAN *looking at her, then turning away to look into the
distance*: I guess we'll always have different views. I just
hope that things in Bosnia will change and prove you
right. But no, I wouldn't bet on it.
Fading.

Lujeron

Inside Toulouse Airport, arrivals hall. Int.

Dan is studying the arrivals board. The plane from London is shown as having landed. He walks slowly over to the gate. People are seen leaving the customs area. Janna arrives, sees him and runs up to him with a big smile on her face, throwing her arms around his neck. She holds him for a long time before walking off arm in arm. They walk towards the car-rental area and stop at the Hertz counter. A woman hands them a key and a folder. They are leaving the terminal. Cut.

Arriving in Lujeron. Ext.

The car is seen arriving. The night is pitch dark. The car stops. Dan jumps out and opens the gates. Janna drives through into the courtyard. The car stops again and she gets out and opens the boot.

JANNA *whispering*: God, it's so warm. Amazing. In September! *She looks at the house*: Are your parents still up?

DAN: My father probably is. He's still writing a book, and he does it at night, when he's not bothered by my mother. *While he talks, they are taking their bags out of the boot. Janna looks around. Seth comes out of the house, and walks with outstretched arms towards them, welcoming them.*

SETH: Well, greetings, Dan. *They embrace and Seth looks at Dan.* What the heck happened to you? *He examines the wound.* Looks ugly.

DAN: I banged my head. *Seth nods and turns to Janna.* And you must be Janna. *They shake hands.* I'm Seth. Dan's father, as you can see. Welcome. *He pauses, looking at them.* I'm glad you've made it. Mum is already in bed. I guess you've eaten, but would you like a drink?

DAN: Why not? Good idea!

SETH: Well, come on in.

They walk into the house.

Cut.

We stayed only briefly in the living room, where logs were burning in the open fireplace, drinking a glass of Hine Cognac. Janna had been working the last thirty-six hours. My father noticed her yawning and, finishing his Cognac, quickly excused himself, leaving us gazing at the fire. 'Let's go to bed,' Janna said, pulling me out of my chair.

We entered my bedroom, which was huge and dilapidated. Wall paper was hanging off the ceiling and the fireplace was full of ashes. Janna closed the shutters of the two windows and looked at the chest of drawers and three travelling trunks.

'Looks like you're packed to go away. I could use those trunks soon!' She smiled disarmingly before jumping into bed. She looked around again, as if the room had changed from this new perspective.

'So this is where you will retire to one day?'

While I am writing these words, recollecting our conversation, I look up from my computer and gaze around. This was my room then and is my room now. The windows are now open. Warm air is flowing in from the garden and I hear the river in the distance. Our owl is making noises from the attic. My chest of drawers and my travelling trunks are still here, still filled with the same things. 'So this is where you will retire to one day.' I hear her voice and smell her skin, a smell that seems forever engraved into the wood. So this is where I have retired to?

I see her eyes when I close mine, black and yet sparkling. I recollect her breath against my neck as I lay with her on the white sheets in the warmth of the night. Although I've often questioned what I am doing, I never thought I would retire from my job, the fun of London or New York. And still, my answer then was the same as my answer is today, despite the fact that I am sitting here, writing these lines in autumn darkness two years later.

'Probably. Sometime in the future. If I ever retire.'

Janna lay down on her back, I leaned over her, looking into her eyes. 'But there's no hospital with a cancer ward in the neighbourhood.'

'But by then I'll probably be able to operate pretty well.'

'Please, don't start this now. I'm far too tired.'

'Sorry. Just joking.'

I felt her kiss, her hair against my cheeks, the warmth of her delicious tongue. We made love, subtle, wild.

And yet I had to think about her words, while drifting in and out of consciousness: 'But by then I'll probably be able to operate pretty well…Sorry. Just joking.'

Was she joking then? I ask myself today. Or was it her true self, escaping in a second, without thought, in the same way as it was escaping minutes later, expressed as passion in the darkness? Was it deliberate? Did I want to find out, or did I prefer to live in a state of denial as long as possible?

When, hours later, I awoke, feeling her presence next to me, and listened to the mountain air, blowing south, I thought about the following day, dreading the morning, dreading the encounter with my mother. I feared that all her stubborn intentions and resolutions would solidify into a bloc of intolerance the moment she saw Janna walk into her garden, as she could so beautifully nonchalant, with her inquisitive smile. It must have been close to four o'clock when finally I fell asleep again, deciding to worry about tomorrow when the day arrived.

Lujeron. Dan's bedroom. Int.

*It is morning. Dan is alone in bed, sleeping, gradually
waking up. From behind the shutters, sunlight shines into
the room. The clock shows 9.30 a.m. Dan wakes up. He
looks around and then at the clock.*

DAN: Shit! *He gets out of bed. He looks into the en-suite
bathroom.* Janna? *No response. He opens the shutters and
light enters the room. It is a sunny morning. Birds are
singing. He looks out, first at the sky, then across the
garden and down. Underneath the window Janna is sitting
with Rebecca. They are both smiling and relaxed. They stop
talking and look up, waving.*
REBECCA: Good morning, Daniel. How are you? You've
been sleeping a long time. Come down. Join us for
breakfast. *Dan looks puzzled. He turns away from the
window, goes to brush his teeth, wash his face and gets
dressed. Same clothes as usual. He leaves the room.*

Lujeron garden. Ext.

*Janna and Rebecca are sitting outside in armchairs. There
are croissants, orange juice, coffee and tea on the table.
Dan enters the garden through the main door of the house.
He approaches his mother and kisses her cheeks, and,
turning to Janna, kisses her on the lips, caressing her head.
He looks at a loss. His mother is wearing blue corduroys, a
blue shirt and worn-out Nike running shoes. Janna is all in
green, barefoot; her old Adidas shoes are next to the table.*

REBECCA *in a cheerful voice*: You're a lazy bum. We've been
up for more than two hours. Since seven. And you
haven't even brushed your hair. Shame on you. I
found Janna here in the garden, reading. We couldn't

wait for you men to have the grace to come down. You're all spoilt little pashas. Get yourself something to eat. And get something for your father too. But hurry up. Janna and I want to go to St Lizier. I guess you may wish to come along too.

DAN: Yesss Madame. *He imitates a military salute and disappears again without commenting.*

REBECCA *shouting after him*: We'd also love some more cappuccino. *Turning to Janna, trying to be serious and to look grim*: Never let him tell you what to do. He's used to bullying people. He's got the office for that. *Dan reappears and sits down with them. Rebecca examines his head.*

REBECCA: So, how did this happen?

DAN: I banged it.

REBECCA: Where?

DAN: Please, Mum, do I need to...

REBECCA: Anyway, that's not what I wanted to know. But, did you sell the shop in Birmingham?

DAN *gloomily*: Yep. Manchester, by the way.

REBECCA *smiling*: How much did you make this time?

DAN *grim*: Mum. You've never ever talked about money. Don't become nouveau riche at your age!

REBECCA: I was just wondering whether it's enough to buy a hospital in Sarajevo!

DAN *annoyed*: What the hell do you mean?

REBECCA: Well, Janna seems to think about going back there some time. At least, as you would probably express it, 'she is contemplating the notion'. *Rebecca takes her glass of orange juice and, while looking at Dan, slowly takes two sips.* She needs a place to work. You could buy it for her. *Rebecca smiles at him in an overly sweet way*: With anti-aircraft missiles and all. *Dan says nothing and just eats his croissant and pours himself orange juice. He looks at both of them with a slightly annoyed expression. Janna stands up and moves towards the door of the house.*

JANNA: I'll be right back. I'll just go and make the cappuccino. *When she is in the house, Rebecca gets up and hugs Daniel.*

REBECCA: Dan. I've spent all morning trying to fight her. But she won, she beat me. She beat all my resolutions to be hostile, to reject her, to make her dump you.

DAN: Mum, you're worse than I ever thought. You're so horrible.

REBECCA: No wait. This is your fault. Why did you not tell me how she is?

DAN *barking at her*: You didn't want to listen!

REBECCA: But you could have told me nevertheless.

DAN: Look, Mum. If she can change your views over breakfast, then I'm just not that impressed by your convictions!

REBECCA: Oh come on, Dan. Of course I wasn't that hostile. *Looking at him with serious eyes. She walks around the table and sips from her glass of orange juice, smiling at him again.* And she is such a wonderful person...Are you sure she's a Muslim?

DAN: Oh stop it. When will you ever overcome your bloody prejudices?

REBECCA: Dan, what do you mean 'prejudices'? Anyway! She's like one of us. Besides, I'm thrilled to become a grandmother.

DAN: Old bullies say that differently.

REBECCA: Oh sure: 'We've become a grandmother.' But I'll never carry a handbag. But, seriously, why didn't you tell me?

DAN *still pretty grim*: What? That she's pregnant? How could I? It only happened last night.

REBECCA: Rubbish! Stop joking! It's true, though, isn't it? *She turns around and looks into his eyes. Dan nods, still eating. She looks at Daniel seriously and lays her hand on his arm.* You're right. I do owe you an apology for my prejudice. Mind you, I gave her a pretty hard time this morning. I just didn't want to accept that she is…well, just the person she is.

DAN *laughing*: You're so incredibly arrogant and rude and awful!

REBECCA *protesting*: No, no. Well of course I'm arrogant and rude and awful, as you put it. But Dan, I've also changed. I learned the hard way. *Dan looks at her puzzled. Rebecca's face turns serious.* I don't know whether you remember. When your brother died, he had a girlfriend, who was a Christian. We met her only once, in Jerusalem, at his grave. And I rejected her, because she was a Christian. So she turned to you, you were the only one of our family who she could embrace and share her grief with. I was cruel, but I only realised it much later, and then it was too late. *She is silent and looks away, sighing.* But Dan, I did realise it and learned from this cruelty. *She turns to Dan again.* Anyway, I think I like her. She seems so sincere. Her attitude. Her work. Her family. *She adds after a pause, staring into the distance*: And even contemplating the idea of going to help children in Sarajevo. *Looking at Dan again, very pensively*: Maybe she reminds me of your late brother.

DAN *ironical and still somewhat disbelieving*: And I thought you wanted to fly to New York for a bit of conspicuous consumption, rather than meeting a Muslim, PLO and God-knows-what terrorist.

REBECCA *abrasively but smiling*: Oh. Just shut up! *Janna comes out into the garden again.*

JANNA: I couldn't find the espresso machine.

REBECCA: Oh, don't worry. *Rebecca gets up and takes her by the arm.* Come on. Let's go. I want to show you St Lizier. We'll have a cappuccino over there. You'll love the place. It's the most beautiful little town, with a great cathedral, a loony bin where Seth and I will end up in a couple of years, and a fantastic view over the

whole of the Pyrenees. *To Dan*: You're coming along,
my dear, aren't you?
DAN: Can I please finish my breakfast?
Cut.

'How are you getting on with your writing?' asks my mother as I
come down into the garden. 'We hardly see you at all. And we
wanted to go to St Lizier.'

I have to smile. 'It's strange that you say that right now. I'm
just about to write about St Lizier, our visit there with Janna.'

My mother looks at me, but says nothing. Is she unsure of
what to say? I do not know. Instead we eat, each entranced by our
own dreams, listening to the silence. I feel my remark has caused
a shadow to fall over her and Seth, like the shadow of a tree when
the evening sun starts hiding behind it on its way behind the
horizon. They have been active all day long, writing an article;
now they want to go off to a concert. Some Russian pianist is
playing Chopin in the cathedral. I am tempted, but then decide
to stay – to dream about our last visit to the same place.

I suddenly have that image of Janna, sitting in front of me. She
had an insatiable appetite for local food and loved hanging out
with the hippies. Once I found her at the Café de l'Union with
a group of them, happily smoking roll-ups, discussing Herbert
Marcuse's *One Dimensional Man* in broken French.

'Being a Bosnian in Britain is sometimes so weird. I'm sure that
Marcuse meant more than those hippies when he talked about
those on the perimeters of society. And I often feel not part of
society either. I quite understand their views, their way of life. I'd
even like to live in a farmhouse without electricity and running
water, growing carrots and hash in the garden. Can you imagine?'

'What – cold rooms for most of the year?' I asked.

'Yeah. No shower, no washing machine. No electricity to switch
a light on when you want to read or to watch the telly…'

'You wouldn't last a day,' I told her. 'That's life in Sarajevo
today.'

She looked with sad eyes into the distance and sighed, 'Yes, but in the case of the hippies here in St Girons it's their own choice. No one forces them to live the way they live. Most of them have the brains to earn a living. They could teach, be doctors, or buy and sell companies like you.' She thought for a moment, and then concluded, 'So I guess I could live like that if I were forced to. But I'd definitely miss my cappuccino in the sunshine.'

She looked around. 'This place will never change, these old houses...' she said.

We looked at the houses around the square, their shutters closed against the scorching sunlight, grey paint peeling off the wood. Normally, there are only a few tourists around, looking into the little shops around the corner. Otherwise it is quiet. This could be life in a small Bosnian town. Why can they not enjoy the same tranquillity? Why do they have to be filled with such hatred as to kill their neighbours, to shoot and maim innocent children?

Is there an answer? Yet France also had its ugly days, only some fifty years ago, with Jews being rounded up, children sent to die in German concentration camps, resistance fighters either tortured and killed or sent to concentration camps in Vichy France, which showed a similar degree of cruelty as those in Bosnia today. And now, people live in peace and tranquillity, the hatred seemingly gone. How many years will it take in Bosnia until Serbs, Croats and Muslims live together again just as the French resistance and collaborators do now?

As my parents set off to the concert, I walk back to my room and sit down at my desk. The air in the house is cool, as the thick walls keep out the heat, even in the summer. I open both windows to feel the draught as the wind passes through the house on its way from the mountains.

St Lizier main square, outside the Cathedral. Ext.

There is a fountain in the middle. The houses are grey, their shutters closed. The cathedral is relatively low-built. It is an old, simple, Romanesque cathedral, of smallish proportions,

with the upper windows in gothic style. The main door is wide open and organ music can be heard from inside. A grey Jeep Cherokee can be seen approaching. Rebecca parks the car and they get out. Rebecca, Janna and Dan are seen walking towards the cathedral whilst Seth goes off towards the café. Rebecca holds Janna's arm and explains the scene to her, pointing out details. They look at the houses, then at the cathedral, which they enter.
Cut.

St Lizier Cathedral. Ext.

They are visiting the cathedral, looking around. Morning light enters through the high windows, casting colourful shadows on the opposite walls. They are walking quietly on the stone floor, pointing at the organ, while organ music is playing. The church is quiet and empty; they are the only visitors. A door opens at the side and a priest enters, coming towards them. He stops to shake hands briefly, before he leaves through a side door that leads to the cloister garden. They follow him through the small, low door.

St Lizier Cathedral cloister. Ext.

It has a lawn in the middle, surrounded on four sides by a walkway. They tour the cloister, looking at the pillar carvings, walking around the garden. Janna and Dan are now arm in arm, Rebecca accompanying them. As they talk, the camera shows the carvings, geometrical shapes, heads carved in stone.

JANNA: This really is amazing. Can you imagine the life of the monks here? Chiselling away to create all these carvings?

REBECCA: I like Romanesque and Gothic cathedrals best.
They are simple, elegant, without the pomposity of
Austrian or Bavarian baroque.

DAN: Couldn't agree more. I hate all that kitsch over there.
Flying angels everywhere. It's all a bit much.

REBECCA: On top of that, the other day Seth and I were in
Bavaria, you know, at that conference in Starnberg,
and we visited an enormous, pretty impressive church.
But you won't believe it – the marble was fake. It was
all painted on cardboard. Seth tapped on the columns
and they made a hollow and cheap sound. We were
having a fit, giggling like schoolkids. How can you take
church seriously? The local priest almost threw us out.
Cut.

St Lizier main square. Ext.

*They are coming out of the cathedral again, and walk
across the main square towards a café, where they join Seth
at a table.*

REBECCA *addressing Janna*: In a way I feel quite ashamed.
Here we are strolling around a peaceful little town,
marvelling at churches, while your parents must be
struggling right now to find food to eat. I guess we
cannot imagine how awful it really is. I mean, TV and
all gives you a pretty grim picture right in your living
room. You can watch it from the comfort of your
couch, hiding behind a glass of wine when the
shrapnel is flying. But reality? I don't know. *She
pauses to reflect, looking over to the cathedral, from which
organ music can be heard.* I only have very faint
memories of the war. I was a child, and after it was
over I tried to block things out, though I can still
remember the hissing of shells and bombs and the

thud in the earth as they hit their targets. *Turning towards Janna*: I do remember the feeling of permanent hunger, the bitterness of empty stomach cramps, though.

JANNA: My father shoots rabbits and grows carrots in our garden, so they aren't that hungry for the moment. And he has a fantastic wine cellar. He inherited a collection from his father and grandfather, and bought and sold wine himself too. Bordeaux. Only the best Châteaux. And now he finally drinks it all.

SETH: Why doesn't he sell it to the UN?

JANNA: He can't. *She turns quiet.* This is what he inherited from his family. Under communism there was no wealth, except for a select few, but we certainly were not part of them. So this is what is left of his family's possessions, and I think this means a lot to him. This is for him now a reminder of the culture of Sarajevo, which was different from communist cultures in the other communist countries. *She looks at them and smiles.* So he drinks it to enjoy culture.

REBECCA: Gosh! *Faintly smiling.* You have to have a sense of humour. This is so horrid. *She stirs her cappuccino, observing the froth turning in her cup, getting lost in thoughts. Finally she looks up again into Janna's eyes.* How about the rest of your family? You've got a brother and a sister, haven't you?

JANNA: I…we haven't heard much from my brother for a long time. At the beginning of the war he joined the Bosnian army and disappeared. He simply didn't write any more, or…well, you know, I guess it's not easy. You can't simply call home on your mobile phone when you're in a trench in the mountains and Serbs are shooting at you. Besides, he wouldn't write to me anyway. We had a major row before he volunteered to fight.

REBECCA: Why?

JANNA: I told him I'd consider him a murderer, and would prefer…well, it got all very heated. *She looks in silence into the distance past Rebecca.* You can imagine, that though I meant it, I now regret having said what I said. I mean, he is still my brother. *Rebecca sighs and puts her hand on Janna's arm.* But my sister is there with my parents.

REBECCA: And what does she do?

JANNA *shrugging her shoulders*: She still tries to study with her friends or play with them. There's no school. The kids do get help from their former teachers though, from time to time.

REBECCA: And otherwise?

JANNA: Otherwise? *She looks at Dan.* Well, she plays at home, builds traps to catch rabbits, looks after our chicken, her cat, the usual stuff. Mum teaches her to play the piano. *She pauses to think.* You know, when you're in a situation like that, it's not like having a weekend off. You simply can't concentrate. You can read, but your mind wanders off. You constantly live in fear. Even if they're not shelling your neighbour-hood or your house, you never know when a stray shell is suddenly going to hit you.

REBECCA *looking puzzled, addressing Janna slowly, trying to find the right words*: But why are you even thinking of going back? Because of your family? Why don't you rather get them out of there? Fly them out to Britain or the States. *Janna smiles vaguely without answering.* Look, if it's just a question of money, I'm sure Dan can help. We can help. You can't leave them there.

JANNA: I guess my father would never leave his wine collection.

DAN *looking at her with serious eyes*: Janna, please!

JANNA: No, seriously. They would never leave. Sarajevo is their home. They don't want to be ethnically cleansed. I guess it's a matter of principle for them. *Janna looks pensively at the cathedral, then at the floor.* I mean, why did your son go to Israel? And stay during the war? He didn't leave. He could have gone back to Britain or the States. And as for me? I still haven't decided yet. But I sometimes think that if things are half-way safe, I'd consider going. I mean, I could work as a surgeon – there are simply not enough doctors left to help. *Rebecca looks at her, and puts her hand on Janna's arm again.*

REBECCA: I guess I know what you mean. But you're pregnant, and that means double responsibility.

JANNA: I'd fly back for the birth.

DAN *looking lost and not really part of the conversation*: I don't know what to say. I think it's pure madness to go there. And you're needed in London too. Think of all the children there. Think of Christina. Do you want to leave her?

JANNA *looking down again*: I know. Please give me some time. I need to think about it.
Fading.

Walking in the Pyrenees. Ext.

Dan and Janna are seen hiking in the mountains, hand in hand, filmed from a distance, so that they can be heard laughing but their words cannot be understood. It is a beautiful day; birds are singing; big, white, cumulus clouds are overhead. Janna is picking flowers while walking. Dan crouches down to pick up some blueberries.

DAN: Hey, come here. Look what I've got for you. *Janna walks up to him. He shows her a handful of blueberries and puts them one by one into her mouth.*

JANNA: God, they are delicious! So sweet! Let me get you some. *Both are bending down again to pick berries. They lie down next to each other, putting them into each other's mouths, then kiss. When they stop, Dan has blueberry juice all over his chin.* Hey, wait. *She bends over his face and kisses Dan's chin, licking off the juice.* We should make love over here. No one can see us.

The blueberry field was wonderful – the intense smell of the mountain air, the solitude, the warmth of the grass on our skin. Afterwards, we lay in the sunshine, dreaming, talking. Janna made sketches of the scenery, capturing the wildness of the valleys, the bulging cumulus clouds over the plain in the distance, the heat rising into the air, blurring the view. Other times, she took out her flute and sat down on a stone, improvising. Her tanned body was getting darker every day. Those were the days when she tried to push away the clouds that were growing around us. I loved to hold her in my arms, trying to feel whether her belly showed the first signs of pregnancy, but she remained as slim as ever.

Most mornings we drove to the market in St Girons, where we joined the hippies who were having cappuccino at the Café de l'Union. We walked slowly along the stands, set up next to the river, where farmers, traders and hippies gather in the mornings to sell anything: bread, cheese, shoes, vegetables and wonderful golden honey from the mountains. The local hippies discovered that by adding the word 'bio' they can sell all their rotten vegetables for triple the price.

'They always look at me with a certain degree of suspicion,' I said.

Janna looked at me curiously. 'Why?'

'Well, they rightly suspect the class enemy Marx had warned them about, hidden inside my dirty jeans and T-shirt.'

'I bet they haven't read Marx.'

'But you think they've read Marcuse…' She laughed, picking up a pot of honey.

'Oh, look!' Janna interjected as we passed a little girl who was trying to sell her kitten, which was totally black. We both had difficulty resisting the temptation of buying it.

Further towards the end of the market a crowd of people had gathered. As we approached, we saw a man holding a huge bear on a leash. It was dancing to some sad tunes the man's companion was playing on a battered harmonica. We watched the bear perform his sad movements to the sound of gypsy music, tame and distant.

Janna turned to me. 'Look at the kids in the first row.' They seemed awe-struck, completely motionless and quiet. 'Children instinctively feel the sadness in this show, a wild and strong animal, pathetically imitating tameness brought about by a ring through the nose and a whip.' She paused, and added a moment later, 'Look they don't even smile. Just look at the blank expression in their little eyes!'

I could not see their blank expressions, but knew that Janna felt exactly what they felt. Her intuition was always right.

Our last day was bitter and heavy. A dense layer of clouds was already hanging low over our valley early in the morning and the sun never broke through. Janna was unusually quiet. For breakfast she stayed in our room, drinking coffee, so I went alone to the market at St Girons. When I returned, I found her sitting at the end of the garden in a chair, with a book on her lap, writing a letter. I observed her from a distance. She wrote slowly at first, stopping to think, gazing into the distance as if searching for something. She picked up a glass of red wine that was standing by her side, and looked at the sun shining through the wine. Slowly, she put the glass to her lips and drank two sips, pausing to think. When she continued writing, it was as if she had found what she had been looking for – no, as if she was trying to hold on to what she had caught. She wrote fast, rushing the lines. I slowly and quietly approached her and stopped behind her to watch her write. She must have sensed my presence, and turned round and smiled.

'Don't try to read it. It's not in English anyway.'

'Who are you writing to?'

'My father.'

She turned round again and picked up the letter and looked at it.

'Let me read it to you… I'll translate it.'

Her face turned serious as she read it. From time to time she glanced up to see whether I was still listening, whether I was following the thoughts she had put down on paper.

Dear Dad,

I am in France, at the foot of the Pyrenees, sitting in the middle of a beautiful garden in one of the most peaceful places I have ever been to, listening to the bees humming above the flowers, to the river in the background. I'm sipping wonderful wine, which you would appreciate, looking at the silhouette of the mountains in the background. The air is hazy, and birds are flying high above us.

I remember the days when we were sitting in our garden, looking up at the hills, at the forest, with the summer's heat burning down on us, when you and Mum used to come out with fresh strawberries and ice-cold tea. When we were spraying our neighbour's cat, pretending to be watering our flowers. I wonder where they are now. In all this tranquillity I have to think about you, about Sarajevo, today.

Dad, why did you have to ask me that question? Why did you have to ask me to come back? Why now? This is not the time. I still do not know. On the one hand, of course, I am convinced that I have to come to help. Yes, I was a surgeon. On the other hand, Sarajevo is the part of my life I am trying to block out. I am trying to move on...forward. Going back there now would be moving backward. But then again, I somehow feel that I need to move through Sarajevo in order to advance further, to find my mission. (If only I knew what my mission was.)

What, Dad, is my mission in life? To sew together those whom brainless soldiers have tried to kill? To try to save the lives of individuals, when I would always be trying to catch up? If I wanted to save their lives, I think I should have become a UN politician who negotiates peace. I should be out there with David Owen and Cyrus Vance, negotiating. I can deal with our lot, because I understand their thinking. Owen and Vance are better off dealing with the Serbs, as they do not seem to be able to understand the Bosnian position.

Dad, peace is the only condition that will help all those children who are getting maimed now. Doctors are just running behind, clearing up the mess. I do not see it as the purpose of my life to be the janitor of the Serbian army that shells our city. Then again, I also see that if you are a child, hit by shrapnel, you do not care about the UN negotiating peace. What you need at that moment is someone to stop the bleeding, to take the shrapnel out, to put you on a drip. And Dad, that's me.

'Dan, that's as far as I've got. Please let me finish this so that I can express-mail it to Budapest, as Milas can pick it up from there in three days' time.'

She smiled at me, turned away and continued writing. I watched how she scribbled hastily line after line. Her smile was warm, so innocent and open. Such a perfect way to hide her torn emotions. Such a contrast to the letter! I retreated back to my room, realising that I could not help her bridge the two forces pulling her apart – sensing, however, that one force was stronger, and gradually seemed to be winning.

Lujeron salon. Int.

All four enter the salon, sitting down at the gently burning open fire. Seth adds some pieces of wood. He opens a bottle of Cognac and pours three glasses, as Janna indicates that she does not want any. Seth sits down too, with a big sigh.

SETH: Well, Janna, let me be very direct. If you go, when will you go? *Janna moves about in her chair, not having expected this direct question from Seth. She blushes.*

JANNA *muttering*: In a…I don't actually know. I've still got so much work to do. I have a contract, after all. And of course I have all these little patients, and I can't simply leave them. Not now, for sure. *She pauses and looks for a long time silently into the fire, the flames reflected on her face.* I know it sounds awful. But as a doctor you're normally quite detached. But sometimes there's one little patient who gets to you. *She pauses, reflecting.* There's one little girl, Christina, who I really love.

SETH: Hmm…

JANNA *pensive*: I don't think she will make it. I just fear she won't. She is so brave, despite her pain. You know, I somehow feel as if I cannot leave her alone. I have to be there for her. *She pauses again for a while.* I think we'll know in two weeks' time…I mean the results of the treatment.

REBECCA *after some moments of silence*: And then?

JANNA: Then I'll have to see. *The telephone is ringing, and Seth and Rebecca get up and leave the room.*

SETH: Please excuse us a minute. *Janna looks at Dan, moving to the edge of her chair to be closer to him.*

JANNA: I know I don't say it very often, but it's not easy for me. Harder than leaving my patients is leaving you, Dan. To be honest, this is the first time I've really been in love, that I've found total happiness. *She smiles, disarmingly.* I hope this doesn't sound too banal. *Dan stares into the fireplace, sipping his cognac, so that he does not need to meet her eye. Janna turns to him again.* To be honest, you're the only person I want to be with – I've ever wanted to be with. *She too stares into the fire.* Parting is not easy for me either. I know it sounds stupid. But I just don't know.
Both are quiet, looking into their glasses. Rebecca and Seth re-enter the room and sit down again. Janna pauses. There is silence, only the noise of the fire is audible.

JANNA *looking at Seth and Rebecca*: I guess I have to speak to my father. *She pauses and sighs.* Look, in the end I'm a coward too. I'd only go if the situation is relatively safe. I mean, if street fighting were about to start it would be stupid to go, but the situation at the moment is pretty clear: Sarajevo itself is free.

SETH: But surrounded by Serbian tanks and artillery.

JANNA: Yes, but they aren't getting into town.

DAN: And the snipers?

JANNA: They shoot from houses on the main road to the airport.

SETH: Oh, that's 'Sniper Alley'? *Janna nods. Seth looks at her, shaking his head.*

JANNA: That road is grim. A lot of people need to use it to get food or water, and snipers are actually sitting in buildings on the other side, shooting at anyone who takes that road. *She tries to smile at them.* But there's no fighting in the town itself. That's what I mean by 'relatively safe'. As long as the Serbs remain on the hills, life is normal. Besides, I only want to go to set things up, so that life will continue after I leave.
Seth gets up and walks over to the desk near the window, opens the humidor and takes out a cigar. He carefully cuts it with a silver cutter and lights it with a burning twig which he takes out of the fireplace.

SETH: Hmm.
He sits down again, looks into his glass, letting the cognac swirl around, and starts puffing. Silence again. Dan also gets up and goes over to the humidor, takes a cigar and lights it.

JANNA: I'll only go once. And then I'll never go back for the rest of my life, probably not even once there's peace.

REBECCA: But Sarajevo was so beautiful before the war – and I'm sure it will be the same again once this fighting is over.

JANNA: Yes, but I think that the people will have changed and that change will be permanent. Once you have killed your neighbour, you cannot simply continue living next to his family once the war is over. We won't live as we did before the war. Our tolerance is gone.

SETH: Hmm. *They sit in silence, Dan and Seth puffing their cigars, Rebecca looking into the fireplace.*

REBECCA *suddenly looking up*: Have you two thought about the religion of your baby at all?

DAN: Mum. Baby isn't born yet. But no. I'm not that obsessed with religion that I'd start arguing with Janna now. I don't want our child to be either an orthodox Jew or an Islamic fundamentalist...

REBECCA: Dan, you have to be serious. Religion is really important when it comes to the bringing up of children. It's the basis of our values.

JANNA *quietly*: I don't know how to say this without hurting any feelings, as I know how important this issue is for you, but I'm just not very religious. For me the most important thing is our humanistic values. Most Muslims in Sarajevo are tolerant. Far more tolerant than the Christians in Serbia or Croatia. We've been living together for years, respecting each other's religions, or simply ignoring religion as more and more people turned atheist. But being a Muslim in Bosnia isn't the same as in Afghanistan. *She gets up and walks over to the fireplace, picks up a log and puts it into the fire. The wood starts crackling. She turns to them, smiling disarmingly.* Knowing Dan, we'd probably argue more about whether baby should become a pacifist or read the children Clausewitz *On War* before the age of five. *She pauses and thinks and becomes serious once more.* I want our child to be brought up to be open towards religion. But I won't teach the Koran, the Old or the New Testament, and at school we'll make sure there's no bias towards any religion. *Rebecca is sitting in silence, slightly shaking her head.*

DAN: Mum. Don't look so glum. You know I don't share your rather orthodox views...

REBECCA *interrupting*: I have no orthodox views. But yes, I am religious and it hurts that you... *She sits back and remains silent, sighing.*

JANNA: I'm sorry I hurt your feelings. *She tries to smile at Rebecca.* But coming from Sarajevo, or rather, having left Sarajevo and seeing what is happening over there today, I just cannot be very religious, and I don't want to perpetuate religion. For me religion is the ultimate reason for all that killing.

SETH: And nationalism.

JANNA: Well, yes. But religion is more important. And besides, after Nazi Germany you really have to wonder whether God exists, what the heck he was doing whilst six million Jews were gassed. *She pauses, exhausted, and looks at them.* That's why I don't want religion for my children. Just humanistic principles. *She looks at Dan, who nods. Seth and Rebecca stay silent.*
Cut.

Lujeron garden. Ext.

Night. Dan is sitting alone, smoking and drinking cognac. It is completely dark, and quiet. A Chopin piano sonata can be heard from the open window. Seth comes out of the house towards him.

SETH *whispering*: Is Janna upstairs?

DAN: Yes. She's gone to bed. She has a 24-hour duty tomorrow, as soon as we arrive. *Rebecca also joins them.*

REBECCA *quietly*: I think there's nothing you can do – that is, if she really wants to go. You've got to let her do what her conscience dictates. *Silence.*

SETH *sitting down next to Dan, and putting his hand on Dan's arm*: I somehow feel that she's set to go. Not today, but tomorrow. And I think you should not try to stop her.

DAN: I know. Yes, I know. But still it's hard to grasp.

REBECCA: You have to support her. *They are quiet for some time.*

SETH: Do you have another cigar? *Dan gives him one. He lights it. Seth draws in the air so that the cigar is glowing in the night.*

REBECCA *sighing*: You should be happy that she's pregnant. At least she'll come back in a couple of months.

SETH: And then she'll be feeling better. *He pauses and puffs his cigar.* If she doesn't go now, she'll always be ashamed. Ashamed not to have helped. She would always have a bad conscience: to have lived in her peaceful and beautiful London, while around her her friends and their children were dying, dying because she didn't help where she could have helped, where she was one of the few people who could really help. *Both smoke in silence. Seth sighs. Both continue smoking in silence.* I don't know what to advise. Buy her a bodyguard. Make sure she never has to queue for bread or water. That's where the snipers shoot. Make sure her home is safe.

DAN: Me? How? I mean... I'll be sitting in London. Do you want me to go too? I'd be mad!

REBECCA: No. Of course not. Just pack her off with enough medicine.

SETH: And dollars or deutschmarks. Cash is what counts in war. She will need a lot to buy herself peace. That's the way to survive. You know, I've read that the enemy is not only on the hills surrounding town, but right inside it. Sarajevo is infested by Mafia who are profiteering from the suffering of others. Most aid shipments go to the Croats or the Serbs rather than the children in Sarajevo. *He looks at Dan, and Dan nods back.* And make sure you can always fly her out if needed.

DAN *a little annoyed*: Dad, I'm not Mossad!

SETH *comforting*: Just always make sure you do the utmost to protect her. All women are crazy. Janna is, in a positive sense. Let me be honest with you. Becks and I supported your brother when he wanted to go to Israel. And we also support her. I – maybe because of the shame I feel never to have fought against the Nazis in the Resistance myself when I could have.

DAN *annoyed*: But Dad, you were far too young.

SETH: I had a friend later on, who at the age of eleven laid mines with his brother. His brother was nine. Two little kids. His brother was shot. But my friend continued laying mines. I sometimes wonder whether I shouldn't go myself. To Sarajevo.

DAN *laughing*: That's absurd.

SETH: Yes, I know. And I guess that I won't. But I understand Janna.

DAN: Well, let me just say that despite all the self-doubts I occasionally have, despite my…well, what Janna calls bellicose notions…I would not go to live in Sarajevo. Forget it! It's all very noble to go and help, but to risk your life when you're surrounded by nutters who are trying to kill anything that moves? No way! *He becomes quiet.* But then again, I'm not a doctor, and I somehow do understand that if you can help you want to help.

SETH: Well, of course it's that. But also, don't forget, it may not be quite as ugly as everyone thinks – I mean, if you don't have to walk down Sniper Alley to fetch water. *Seth gets up, as do Dan and Rebecca.*

REBECCA: Daniel. Don't let her down. *They embrace. Seth and Rebecca walk back into the house. Dan stays behind and sits down again, smoking. The church bell strikes twelve.*
Fading.

Departure

We left the next morning. It was our only visit to Lujeron, a place I wanted her to love as much as I love it. The solitude, the people, the mountains. I had hoped that she would be able to think things over during our stay and decide not to go. But in the end I achieved the opposite – she thought things over, and I feel that deep inside, more subconsciously than consciously, she decided to go.

Rationally thinking, I did not want to understand her. If you are worried about children dying, you should be helping all the time. You could tour the world like Médecins Sans Frontières and go from one trouble spot to the next – operate in Vietnam, North Korea, Mongolia, Haiti, Africa. There are enough places in this world. I am becoming slightly cynical: why help only in your hometown?

Maybe I am cynical because my personal contribution to people in need is limited to making financial donations, from a safe distance, without getting involved. I save lives by sending money to trouble-spots with my American Express card – don't leave home without it. I don't even leave home...

But then again, I loved her, and her sincerity fascinated me and made me feel humble. I needed to help her so that she could achieve what she wanted to achieve. I decided to help her, still vaguely hoping that she would convince herself not to go.

Dan's bedroom. Int.

Dan is lying on his stomach diagonally across his bed, reading Anna Karenina. *It is evening. The bedside light is on. He is wearing a T-shirt and boxer shorts. The curtains are drawn. The doorbell rings. He gets up to answer the door and returns to bed. Janna is coming into the room. He gets up again and they embrace and kiss.*

DAN *happy to see her*: How are you? How was work?

JANNA *looking very tired, yawning*: I'm exhausted. Twenty-four hours non-stop. Even in the night I got called a couple of times, so I didn't sleep at all last night.

DAN: How is Christina?

JANNA *smiling pensively*: OK. Not much better, not much worse. Just always smiling. Yet pretty weak. I told her about you, and she wants to see you.

DAN: Maybe I should go one day.

JANNA: I think she'll insist. How is your deal going? *While talking Janna undresses and puts on a long nightgown.* I stole this one from the hospital. *He smiles and indicates that she should join him in bed. She lies down on her back, putting her head on his stomach. He is lying on his back, his head on cushions.* Your deal?

DAN: It's becoming a boring story now. It's up to the lawyers to sort out the details. *He sits up with a jolt.* By the way, I phoned my mother today. She's absolutely nuts. I'm sitting here trying to persuade you not to go to Sarajevo, and she tells me to tell you she'll be fundraising for you in New York.

JANNA: I know.

DAN *perplexed*: How do you know?

JANNA *smiling with a knowing face*: She rang me at work to discuss details – basically, whether I needed money or medicine.

DAN *annoyed*: I can't believe it! Behind my back! *He laughs.* Women! No: mothers.

JANNA: How will she get the money?

DAN: No idea. Years ago, when they lived in the States, she used to do this all the time. For orphans, for artists, but mostly to support their institute and research. Once she got Menuhin to play in aid of a Polish orphanage. I bet for you she'll get Lichtenstein to make special lithos, or Schwarzenegger to do a charity run.

JANNA: Really?

DAN: Sorry, just joking. But she'll get you the cash. She still has lots of wealthy friends.

JANNA: You said she could get Lichtenstein to make special lithos? *Her face becomes pensive.*

DAN: What are you thinking about?

JANNA: Nothing. No, nothing, really. *Shaking her head.* Anyway. So you really think she can raise some money?

DAN: Sure. But tell me, what was your answer? Money or medicine?

JANNA: How do I know? I haven't seen what's missing. Maybe we don't need medicine but an x-ray machine instead. Maybe…God, how am I supposed to know? Maybe it would be better just to buy bullet-proof vests for everyone in town. *She turns around and rolls on top of him.* Anyway (*she looks into his eyes and puts her finger across his lips*) let's stop talking about it now. I'm just too tired. *They kiss.* But do keep a Lichtenstein for me for when I'm back.
Fading.

Jann's hospital. Int.

Inside the hospital, Janna is standing in an open telephone booth at the end of a long hospital corridor. The walls are covered on both sides with Janna's paintings. Each painting has a little tag. Janna is wearing her green uniform. Her face is concentrated and she is shouting into the phone.

JANNA: No, Milas. You have to tell them I'm definitely coming. You've got to pick me up. Yes. But when will you know? OK, I'll ring you again tonight. OK. Speak to you later.

Dan's office. Int.

A meeting room. Dan is sitting with his six colleagues around a large table. They are in the middle of discussing a transaction; documents are on the table, as well as coffee pots and cups. A secretary knocks and enters.

SECRETARY *nodding at Dan*: There's a call for you. *Dan looks up.*

DAN: Can it wait? Who is it?

SECRETARY: It's your mother.

DAN: I'll take it right outside. *Addressing Tom*: Tom, can you take the document out of my briefcase and start with page 24, the taxation stuff?

Tom opens Dan's briefcase and takes out a book. It is a baby book for fathers. He smiles and puts it back. Dan goes out to the phone on the desk outside the room and waits. A moment later the phone rings.

DAN: Thanks … Hi Mum.

REBECCA: Hi Daniel. Just to let you know: I have two charity events lined up in New York. And Mark, you know, this Yugoslavian guy who runs that hedge fund, or whatever you call it, is going to give Janna one hundred thousand bucks in cash. *He listens for some time.*

DAN: Mum, you're nuts! The more dosh she gets the longer she's going to stay in Sarajevo!

REBECCA: Oh, come on, Daniel. You've got to accept that she's going. Be more supportive. Please Daniel.

DAN: Mum, I wish you would be a bit more constructive. It's crazy, in her state. *Silence. Then, hesitatingly, sitting down and staring out of the window*: Yes I know she's set on doing it. And I realise we can't change her mind. Thanks for helping her.

REBECCA: Well, this is the least I could do for her right now. Later, when she knows what she needs, I'll get her the stuff and ship it over to Sarajevo.

DAN: Mum, she really appreciates it. Me too!

REBECCA: Ciao. I need to dash.

DAN: Ciao, Mum. Take care. *He hangs up. He is about to go back into the meeting room to sit down when the phone rings again. The secretary appears at the door.*

SECRETARY: It's Janna. *Dan picks up the phone.*

DAN: Hi!

JANNA: Am I disturbing you?

DAN *laughing*: Of course not. *He pauses and listens.*

JANNA: Daniel. I was wondering. Could you come over to see Christina straight away? She's having her operation either tonight or tomorrow morning.

DAN: Yes. Yes of course, I'll be right there.

JANNA: That's sweet of you. She's so much looking forward to seeing you. Well then. See you in a minute!

DAN: OK. Take care. I'll be right there. *Dan hangs up. He walks thoughtfully back to his colleagues.*

DAN: I'm sorry, I've got to go. Tom, sorry, can you just finalise the last points?
Cut.

I parked my Land Rover right in front of the entrance and ran up the stairs to her ward. She was standing at the other end of the long corridor, smiling. As I was rushing up to her I realised something was weird, and then it hit me: the walls were covered with Janna's paintings, probably more than fifty of them, each neatly labelled with a price tag. 'What's this all about?'

Janna smiled innocently. 'I'll tell you later.' She turned serious. 'Professor Douglas decided to operate on Christina tomorrow morning.' She paused, reflecting, looking to the ground and heading for the ward, taking me by the arm.

'There's only a slim chance she'll pull through. You had to come to see her today. I had promised her.'

We entered her room and walked up to her bed. Christina was smiling, stretching her little hands out to us.

'Hi, sweetie,' said Janna. 'This is my prince. I promised you he'd come to visit you…here he is!'

I took her little hand and kissed her cheek. She was amazingly sweet. We chatted for a while until Janna pulled me away.

'What a smile she has!' I said, turning to Janna, when we were walking back to their common room. 'She's so full of hope.'

I understood why Janna loved this little creature so much, why she felt emotionally so drained when Christina was unwell, why she was so happy when Christina was so much better.

You always hear that doctors are emotionally detached. I think that Janna could be quite detached, even cold, but there are always exceptions. Christina certainly was one such exception.

I had been looking forward to meeting her colleagues, to meeting the people she shared her life with. I had already met the head of the ward, Professor Douglas, but not the rest. In a way I felt slightly self-conscious, and maybe even jealous of doctors, who changed other peoples' lives and who could live and work with Janna every day.

When we entered the meeting room, three of her colleagues were already sitting around the table, feet up, relaxed, drinking tea, chatting. They looked exhausted. Janna smiled at them as they looked me over inquisitively.

'This is Daniel, I told you about.'

Dr Walker, who was still wearing his green surgeon's outfit, got up and shook my hand rather formally. Two younger female colleagues, Dr Annan and Dr Khan, smiled and remained seated. I walked over and shook their hands too. Neither could have been more than twenty-five years old. At least, despite their tired faces, they looked that young. Two nurses, Angela and Funmi entered the room and greeted us too.

Janna looked around, and everyone fell silent, expecting her to say something. She waited a moment, searching for words. Finally she sighed. 'Well, I have to tell you something.' She paused again. I watched her. It was evidently difficult for her to break the news. 'I'm going to leave London. At least temporarily.' She surveyed their reactions as they silently greeted the news.

Eventually Dr Annan asked, 'Why? What are you going to do?'

'Well,' Janna replied, 'I want to – I need to – go home. To work at home. In a hospital over there.'

Angela stared at her, astonished. 'Where?'

'Sarajevo.'

There was silence, and I tried to see their reactions. They seemed dismayed. Angela, Dr Annan and Funmi gazed down. Dr Khan broke the silence.

'Have you spoken with Douglas?' she asked.

'Yes. He has given me a year's leave.'

They looked at the table in silence, avoiding each others' eyes, as neither wished to raise the topic that was obvious to each one of them. It took Dr Walker to spell out what everyone thought. 'But that's crazy. There's war. I mean, it's a pretty dangerous place, Sarajevo.'

'No. It's not that bad. I'll take care. My whole family is there.'

'But you're pregnant,' said Funmi.

'I'll be back for the birth.'

Dr Annan looked at Janna, touched her shoulder and sighed, shaking her head.

'Christ! What a decision!'

'You're a Muslim, aren't you?' asked Dr Walker.

Janna nodded, and Dr Walker shook his head in disbelief. 'Janna, they're the ones who get shot.'

'Please. I know all of that,' Janna retorted. 'Do you think I'm naïve?'

'So when do you want to go?' asked Dr Khan. Janna looked around in silence, not knowing what to say. She had not even told me yet.

At that moment Professor Douglas entered, smiling warmly at Janna. He came over to me and shook my hand.

'Good evening, Dan. Good to see you again. Sorry to be inter-rupting.' He laughed.

'I'd just asked Janna when she was planning to go,' Dr Khan said.

'Well, pretty soon, I think.' Professor Douglas answered for her.

'But you know, I'm not resigning,' said Janna. 'I'm just asking for some sort of sabbatical. A break for some time.' She looked around at their faces, searching their expressions, but nobody seemed to return her gaze. So she added, glancing down at her tea mug, sighing, 'I'll be back, you know. I won't stay there for ever.'

'That's no problem,' Professor Douglas replied. 'As I told you. I think it's remarkably brave what you want to do. I certainly have a lot of respect.'

Janna smiled at him, and then at everyone.

We stayed for more than three hours, in the end ordering pizzas to have supper together. After the initial shock and silence, they showed their interest in her plans, her life in Sarajevo, her views about the war, the Serbs and her own people. Janna was excited by this support.

The shift was quiet, and only Dr Khan was called out during our meal.

I felt sad when we finally left them and I drove Janna back to her place.

In the car I couldn't wait any longer.

'What the heck is happening? What are you doing with your paintings?' I asked.

'I decided to sell them to raise cash. If your mother gets Lichtenstein to do lithos for me, then I can sell my paintings too.'

'But that was a joke. And you told me that you'd never…'

'I decided not to be too precious,' she said. 'After all, they're just paintings.' She looked at me, trying to smile, but her smile seemed sad and forced.

'I've kept three paintings for you and one for your parents, though.'

'Can I not buy the others?'

'No, I've actually sold them all.'

I was speechless.

'It turned out that Christina's father is an art dealer, and he bought the lot when Douglas told him why I was selling.' She tried to sound happy, but her voice had a strange and unnatural tone. 'I've already spent all the money on paracetamol, syringes, disinfectants, latex gloves and more specialised medicine, which I managed to buy here from the hospital.'

I touched her hand and realised it was cold and tense.

'I guess I got a good price considering it was my first exhibition ever. I did better than Van Gogh!' She laughed. 'And I'll paint new ones when I'm in Sarajevo.'

She turned quiet again and, when we got out of the car, held me tight so that I could not see her face. When she turned round, there were no tears, even though her eyes were covered with deep shadows.

Janna's room. Int.

Janna is alone, on the phone, sitting on the floor. She is barefoot, wearing jeans and a T-shirt. Slowly she gets up, and her silhouette can be seen against the light. The floor is littered with suitcases, bags and plastic bags.

JANNA: Dad, no. *Silence.*

DJEMAL: Well. It's just that Milas and your Mum and I have been talking this over ever since I first asked you to come back. You know, Mum and I had quite a row. And we are just not sure any more.

JANNA: But I'm sure.

DJEMAL: Please, Janna, think about it again. Really. Well, I mean…*Silence.* I mean – I, er, we really think you shouldn't come. Particularly Mum.

JANNA: What do you mean, I shouldn't come? *Silence. And then insisting*: Dad, I'm determined. I've made up my mind. I'm coming. *Silence again, and Janna looks out of the window.* You have to arrange for Milas to pick me up.

DJEMAL: Milas could meet you in Budapest. But think about it again.

JANNA: Please, Dad. You've asked me to come. Don't say now that I should stay in London. Oh God, please!

DJEMAL: Well, I don't know what to say. We had not really expected you to be so determined. Mum was a bit – no

– she was very doubtful. But look, Janna, we'll take
care of you, starting from the moment when you arrive
in Budapest in the evening. Milas will meet you at the
Forum Hotel in the morning. Wednesday morning.

JANNA: OK! Can I rely on that?

DJEMAL: Yes, Janna.

JANNA: Thanks so much, Dad. Really. But now I need to
dash. See you soon. Take care.

*She hangs up and wanders around, taking a book from her
shelves, putting it into a bag on the floor. She goes over to
her medical books and selects four tomes, placing them into
the bag. She opens a drawer and empties the contents – a
stethoscope and other medical equipment – into the bag.
She picks up a plastic bag from the floor and pours
bandages, syringes and boxes of medicine into a suitcase.
She opens the wardrobe and pulls out a sleeping-bag and
winter clothes. She puts a CD into her CD player and
switches it on, crouching down in front of it for a minute.
Cello music, the second movement of Haydn's concerto in C
major, sets in. She looks at a picture of Dan, and places it,
together with a photo showing the two of them in Lujeron,
in the bag with the books. Then she sits down and looks at
another picture of Dan, dreaming.*

JANNA: Oh damn it. Oh God damn it!

*She sighs and gets up again, slipping the picture into the
bag. The doorbell rings. She presses the buzzer. Dan comes
up. They embrace in silence. She sits down and he walks
silently through the room, pausing over her recent painting.
He takes her flute and packs it into its case, placing it in
her bag. He smiles at her, caressing her hair, and looks
down, touching her belly:*

DAN: You have to take care of him.

JANNA: Him?

DAN *smiles vaguely*: I somehow think it's going to be a boy.
I've always dreamed of having a son. *He sits down next
to her, caressing her hair.* I've always dreamed of having

a little son to play with, who explores the world with me, travels with me. *Looking into the distance, dreaming*: Someone for whom I'm the same as my brother was for me. For some reason I've never dreamed of having a family…just a son. *Janna has tears in her eyes.* Don't cry. Please. Crying makes your leaving so finite. *He wipes her tears away. He looks at her, caressing her head.* I've promised myself that you'll never have to cry because of me. You'll probably have to cry often – too often – because of other people. So please.

JANNA: Please don't be so poetic. We really are a strange couple. Poetic and pathetic. *She gets up, and so does he. They embrace in silence for a long time. Only cello music can be heard. They look into each other's eyes. Janna turns away, freeing herself from the embrace, and goes into the bathroom. There is the sound of water running. She comes out smiling, with a wet face.*

JANNA: I had great news today. Christina will make it. The operation was a success. She's much better. She knew that I'm off to help other children, and that I won't see her again, as she'll be out when I'm back. She didn't even cry. She smiled and held back her tears. She just said, 'You can go, I don't need you any more. I'm all right now.' She smiled a wonderful smile, and then said: 'When I'm able to write, I'll write to you. And every birthday I'll send you a present, because I love you so much.' I was so happy to see her face, so relieved that Douglas succeeded where I, honestly, had already given up hope. *She sighs and smiles at Dan.*

DAN: I've got some good news for you too. My mother has raised two hundred and fifty thousand dollars for you. *Janna looks at him in amazement.* You'll need the money.

JANNA: That's terrific! Her friends don't even know me! I hope I can live up to their expectations.

DAN: And look what I've got for you. *He picks up his bag.*

JANNA: What is it?

DAN: A bulletproof vest for you. And for him. You should both be able to fit into it.

JANNA: That's really sweet and thoughtful. I'll need it. And I'll wear it. Let me try it on. *She puts it on, and reads the attached leaflet.* Wow! This will protect me against everything – bullets, shrapnel, back-stabbers, shark bites. But where's the Gucci label? *They laugh.*
Fading.

We went shopping that afternoon. Since I normally do my charity work with my American Express card, I realised that it would be incredibly mean and cynical not to help Janna in her endeavour. Why had it taken me so long to start supporting her? We bought equipment, and with Douglas's help medicine.

'I don't really know yet what we'll need.'

'If in doubt, just buy tons of aspirin.'

'No, I'll buy bandages, sterilised stuff. Needles. Anti this and anti that. You won't know what it's for or against in any event.' She smiled at me. I paid. And felt mean.

I also felt mean for not throwing a farewell party for her, but she insisted on leaving without much fuss.

'You know, if it's a big party, people will think that I won't be coming back. And for me it's just like a longish holiday. Besides, outside work, I don't really have any friends, and my friends at hospital have all said good-bye to me so many times.'

Heathrow Airport. Int.

Janna and Dan are walking inside the airport terminal. He is carrying her bag. They are dressed the same way as on their first day. Airport noise in the background. They reach passport control, and hold each others' hands, kissing a long farewell, Dan caressing her head.

DAN *in a very quiet, sad voice*: Look after yourself. *He pauses*. Take care.

JANNA: Don't be so sad. I'll be back soon. Really. *She caresses his head*. Take good care of yourself.

DAN: You too.

Janna frees herself from his embrace and slowly looks into his eyes. Suddenly, she turns round and walks away. Dan watches her. Janna is filmed from above. She walks through the gate. He looks at her and waves at her. She returns the wave and smiles. Then she walks off. Filmed from above, she can be seen walking slowly through the metal detectors. She picks up her bags again. Next she is seen walking along the long airport corridor towards the departure gate.
Cut.

The moment Janna disappeared out of sight, I went to work, from early morning to late in the evening. Every day. I cared for little else. In the evenings I could not play the cello, so I met up with Tom instead. We sometimes went to the cinema or played chess together. I also travelled a lot, saw new companies, met with investors. I wanted to like my job again, the way I had before I met Janna, but I was not sure I could regain that hunger to produce and achieve.

I am writing this in reflection, sitting at my desk in the same room where Janna and I dreamt in bed together. I turn around and seek her out as a silhouette in the darkness. But she's gone. She forgot a bottle of her perfume on the chest of drawers, or maybe she left it there on purpose, and I smell it now and then. But then again I do not need the scent to bring back memories; they are still fresh, and every second comes back without the need of sensory help. Nevertheless I love her perfume as its particular fragrance intensifies my feelings. It is like feeling her on a warm summer day.

I called her a week later. A week is longer than you think when time is slowing down. Six hundred and four thousand, eight hundred seconds slowly ticking past.

Sarajevo

Sarajevo hospital. Int.

A big ward with lots of children, all ages, up to about fifteen. The conditions are squalid and primitive. The sheets are not the cleanest, the equipment is old and shabby, the windows are broken and repaired with plastic panes.

Janna is in the middle, moving around in her green operating outfit. Her clothing is dirty and covered with old blood stains. She has cut her hair extremely short. Agile, she is moving from bed to bed, examining patients, giving orders to other doctors and nurses, examining bandages. Her face appears tired, looking worried, with slight lines under her eyes. She sits down on a chair, having finished with the last bed. A voice is heard in the background. Dr Halim, one of her colleagues, is a female doctor aged thirty-two.

DR HALIM: Janna, it's Milas outside for you.

JANNA: Please ask him to come in. I'm too tired to go outside. *She puts her feet up on another chair and examines her stethoscope absentmindedly. Dr Halim comes through the door.*

DR HALIM *shouting*: It's Milas with his phone. He says he's got Dan on the line. *Janna's face shows that she is overjoyed. She jumps up as Milas enters with the telephone. Impatiently she grabs the receiver, walking off towards the window. Milas sits down.*

DAN: Janna?

JANNA: Yes! Dan, hi! How are you? It's so great to hear you!

DAN: Finally, Janna. Why didn't you call? I was getting worried!

JANNA: Oh, please, Dan, I've been incredibly busy! You know there are no lines. And it's impossible to get Milas.

DAN: So how are you? How is it going?

JANNA: It's pretty incredible. The people are so nice. I'm working day and night…I don't know where to start. It's been utterly amazing. Operating. I thought I had forgotten. But it all came back. Can you believe it? I've taken shrapnel out. Stitched wounds. It's been…I don't know what to say. Overwhelming!

DAN: Are you safe?

JANNA: Absolutely. The hospital is great.

DAN: But I read every day that they are shelling the hospitals too. How can you say it's safe?

JANNA: Ours is completely safe, as you can't see it directly from the hills. And it's relatively small, not a high-rise, so we haven't been hit by shells the same way. I'm actually staying here rather than at my parents' place. It's far more convenient. And then it's safer, as I don't need to commute. *She pauses, looking around.* 'Commute' – what a word! But, really, don't worry!

DAN: OK. OK. But do you have enough medicine?

JANNA: No. Not yet. It's a pretty grim story. We are missing everything. You can't imagine how fast we're getting through all the things we bought together. We'll soon be out of even basic stuff like aspirin, narcotics, iodine…But the first shipment of things bought with the money your mother raised should be arriving soon.

DAN: Who put that together?

JANNA: Douglas and my colleagues. Your mother sent the money straight to them. And Milas is picking it up.

DAN: You're amazing. You didn't even tell me about it.

JANNA: Oh, by the way: mega thanks for the plastic bag full of cash. I almost threw it in the bin without realising what was in it. *She pauses smiling, but then her face becomes serious again.* But I guess we need a lot more. More money, more medicine.

DAN: But you get stuff from the WHO.

JANNA: Stop dreaming. It's next to nothing. But we've got plenty of candles. With no electricity we operate in semi-darkness, using candles. Can you imagine? Trying to find shrapnel without proper light? Metal is OK, but plastic? Try reconnecting an artery when you only have candlelight and a torch-lamp attached to your head like a miner. Dan. Damn it. It's more primitive than bloody Timbuktu. And we're supposed to be in the middle of Europe. The centre of civilisation! *Silence. Janna walks over to a chair and sits down, getting up again to take another chair, so that she can put her feet up.* Anyway, it doesn't matter. We're OK, in general. *She is silent, looking at Milas, who is sitting on a chair, watching her. He smiles back at her.* Oh, by the way, do you know what I've been thinking about? I'll be working like this for a month or two...*She hesitates, staring into the room*...or maybe three, and then I'll take two days off. I can meet you in Vienna or Budapest. What do you think?

DAN: I'd love to see you. Really. But how are you going to get out of Sarajevo?

JANNA: Same plane we took the other day. Or I'll crawl in the night over the runway and then drive over the mountains, or bribe myself on to the Vance–Owen plane. I need their plane on my way back, as I want to buy a better x-ray machine and bring it back. In hand luggage. *She chuckles.*

DAN: But how safe is it to travel out of Sarajevo?

JANNA: Oh, come on, Dan. Milas does it all the time. You did it!

DAN: But they close the airport all the time because planes get shot at.

JANNA: See how safe it is? When there's shooting they stop flying. Please don't worry. You get used to things. It's really not that bad. And I'd love to see you. I really, really miss you. Every day. All the time.

DR HALIM *coming in, pulling at her sleeve*: Janna, they've brought in some idiot who fell off a ladder. Can you have a look at him? He's in shock...

JANNA: Dan, I need to run. They brought someone in. What a joke! We are in the middle of a war and that guy falls off a bloody ladder. See how meaningful my life is over here? *She laughs.* Must have been a Serbian ladder. *She pauses and looks around.* I'll call you some time next week when Milas is back at the hospital. Please don't worry about me. I am fine and it's fantastic. I really love you! Big kiss and big, big hug!

DAN: You too!

Janna runs off.

Cut.

I slowly hung up, elated by her words. I thought I smelled her skin and saw the depth of her eyes in the darkness in front of me. I heard the crystal clarity of her voice, her determination, her joy of helping others. It was a relief to know that there was a strange normality to her life – operating, seeing patients, checking wounds. I had a vague idea from my own visit to Sarajevo – and the hospital I saw – of how her hospital might look inside, how the patients were, who they were.

I later discovered the diary she kept, writing almost every day about her work, her operations, the progress of the patients. It was not only a medical journal, but also personal reflections, about hope and hopelessness, about the warmth of her family and friends against the coldness of the snipers.

I am sitting in the garden under the old willow tree, listening to the river and the wind blowing through the leaves. The air smells of open fire as farmers burn bushes and branches from fir trees they have just felled, an immensely intensive smell, reminding me of Christmas, the holiday neither of us would celebrate, when both Jews and Muslims are like outcasts in the Christian world.

I am reading the fine black lines of her handwriting, which must have been composed in the darkness of night, shells falling onto Sarajevo around her. I imagine her bare room, the bed, a candle, a desk, a chair, and Janna, dressed in pullovers against the cold, writing page after page to deal with all the misery – and sometimes joy – she experienced.

'You have to quote from Janna's diary,' my mother remarks as she joins me in the garden.

'Mum, it's a log book, of every single bullet she removed, every artery she repaired.'

'I guess there were many.' She sits down next to me, looking at the pages.

'And then it was also her normal diary and thought book, containing reflections, thoughts, hopes, crystallising her dreams, black on white paper. There are some passages I can't read.' My mother looks at me sideways. 'Others I can't understand,' I continue, 'though I can feel the pain Janna must have felt when cutting through the flesh, when sewing together meat and skin. And I'm puzzled by her black sense of humour, which she didn't lose even in those dire hours of war. Listen to what she wrote on her second day.

2 October 1992

Today I had five operations. Five times I took shrapnel and bullets out of various legs, shoulders and one guy's fat bum that was a 'too easy to miss' target for any amateur sniper. When I finished stitching them up I always marvelled at the wonderfully symmetrical stitching. A Singer sewing machine could not have done a better job than me. I felt like putting my signature underneath the stitching. That reminds me, I have a friend who is a surgeon and who once told me that he can always recognise his work from the stitches. When he looks at someone, he can say, 'This is mine' or 'This was done by someone else.' I wonder whether I will leave my signature on Sarajevo's kids, whether one day when the war is over we'll be sitting back there at the town's swimming-pool and observe, 'Yes, this was me, I remember it from the way it's stitched. Yes, this was shrapnel and this was a bullet.' Most of my patients will probably … hopefully … be alive once this war is over.

My mother sits down, putting her feet up, looking at me.

'The snipers are most probably still alive too, able to sleep well, having forgotten the images of the children they shot.'

I light a cigar and follow the smoke as the wind blows it away over my head. The smell of burning Cuban tobacco leaves mixes with the smell of burning fir trees.

'But at some stage there will be justice,' she adds, after thinking silently for a long time. 'Remember the Nuremberg trials after the war.'

I close the diary and look at her.

'They will catch a couple of big fish and do some show trials in order to satisfy their own consciences, but all those who were responsible for the wounds Janna repaired will go free. That's so disgusting. Disgusting about us here in the West, most of all. We don't have the guts to intervene. And we won't have the guts to make justice happen, or to help those who could make it happen.'

I stop, as I try to search Janna's voice echoed in mine. I feel the bitterness in my stomach affecting the tastebuds in my mouth. My mother must be sensing how I feel, as she gets up and touches my shoulder, without saying anything. She goes into the house, leaving me alone with my thoughts, surrounded by blue smoke which the wind disperses only slowly. But she returns minutes later, with a large glass of Armagnac.

'The best antidote against bitterness: only be angry if you can change things. Only be bitter if you can improve things the next time round.'

I wonder whether Janna would have felt the same way. Probably when we got to know each other. When she was working in the cancer ward. But later? I tried to understand her also through her letters, which arrived occasionally after days of travel. The first one reached me three weeks after her arrival in Sarajevo.

8 October 1992

Dear Dan,

This is my first letter to you, and I am writing these lines in the early hours of the morning, sitting in my bed, which is wonderfully warm now, though I dread to think of what the temperature is going to be once winter starts and the heating fails. My bed is cosy, so that anyone in this room who can crawl, abseil or jump into it has already done so during the last few days. I am sharing this bed with probably fifty other inhabitants, who, as a sign of gratitude, bite me during the night. No need for pity, sympathy or jealousy.

Dan, I have arrived. And I arrived with a bang. I started operating the moment I had dumped my bag in my room and washed my hands.

This place is pretty amazing. The people are great. The doctors are wonderful. What a team! A number of patients who arrived once I got here have already gone home. This is extremely satisfying.

I have not seen my family a lot. I work most of the day, and in the evenings you cannot simply go out. At least I don't feel too safe at night, it's different during the day. And people do go out, as you know, as they need to buy bread and fetch water. Yes, fetch water. Most of the time the town has no running water, or electricity for that matter.

From time to time, I go and watch from the corner, at the end of the block, where there is the big road junction, and I can see the hills and the sky. We are in a big prison, being shot at and shelled. And then I look at the sky and the lonely birds, that circle from time to time high in the air. They are free. How long will this last? It is all so absurd that I want to leave and just return to the world of sanity I know. The truth is: we are prisoners and the world is keeping us prisoners.

As you know, Dan, our only way out of town is crawling across the runway of the airport at night and then taking the road across the mountains. And what do the Unprofor troops, who are guarding the airport, do at night? They illuminate it, shining their powerful lights on the runway so that all the snipers can have a round of night-time shooting. I recently operated on three guys who were shot on the runway. Two of them died on the spot and the third one is still in intensive care, and I fear that he won't make it either, as a dum-dum bullet ripped through his side and hit his intestines. I am so angry about these atrocities. And furious about the UN. Daniel, you can't imagine what a dum-dum bullet does to you when it enters your body. It rips everything apart leaving an unimaginably grotesque hole. Who are those swine that kill with such bestial calculation and precision? How do you punish them if you ever find them? And how do you punish the guys who shine their lights for the snipers? I know what you would do, and ... I just hope that the images of people dying in spasms on their runway will haunt them forever.

But there is hope, as they are building a tunnel. One tunnel as the only exit out of town. Dug by hand. You'll have to crawl. Two people with rucksacks would have difficulty passing each other. Dan, this will be our contact with civilisation. Or rather, this is how the world's wonderful civilisation will be forced to keep in touch with us.

Dear Dan, I wish I could be with you. I am thinking a lot about you, even if you do not hear a lot from me. I wish you could be here with me in my bed, but then again, my fifty friends might not appreciate your presence as much as I.

Big kiss and big hug and lots of love Janna

The evening I received that letter, I watched the news with disgust: Belgrade. The sickening faces of Milosevic and his sycophantic cabinet. And conferences, meetings, but no action. Cowardice of the EU. And Sarajevo was nearing its first winter with no electricity, no heating, not enough food.

10 November 92

Dear Dan,

My second letter! Today was a day of respite. No shelling. No sniper fire. As a result, we are sitting around, sipping peppermint tea, chatting. War breeds a very special sense of humour. Our sarcasm is better than any you can find in Britain.

At lunchtime I sometimes go to my Dad's favourite café, the one you know. On my way, I see dogs and cats, left to their own devices, going through the rubbish. Rubbish! It is piled up every-where and it stinks. People who have no running water shit into anything they can put in a rubbish bin. And bins and bags are dumped outside the houses. So some high-rises have weeks of shit in front of them. You cannot imagine the stench. Thank God it's getting cold. The shit stops smelling once the temperature starts dropping. It's awful.

Yet people try to keep up appearances. Right outside the café was a woman with a spotlessly clean blouse and red lipstick, which emphasized her broad and gentle smile. I think it was the same woman we saw during our visit to Sarajevo, right outside the hospital. We noticed we were staring at each other.

'We have to keep up appearances, dear. They should not take our dignity, even if they take our electricity,' she said, looking at me, and I became aware of my dirty jeans, my boots and my punky hair. I smiled, and then had to laugh and replied, 'Even when you're bombed, you have to cultivate a punky subculture, Madame!'

The woman laughed too, somehow not too convinced of my punk convictions.

My father was not in the café, but I saw a group of men who were sitting around a table, discussing politics. I sat down in the corner and tried to hide behind a newspaper. It is amazing that despite the fact that nothing works, they still publish the *Oslobodjenje*. It's not the *FT* or *The Times*, but an excellent paper here in Sarajevo. When the door opened I saw three well-dressed men enter. Armani suits, big golden Rolex watches, flashy sunglasses, but tacky shoes. (The shoes always give men away – I learned that from you. You're such a snob, Dan, but of course you were right.) The group of men in the café all got up at the same time and blocked the entrance. I thought I'd witness the beginning of a fight, but the three characters left without a word. Turning towards me, one of the men in the café introduced himself as Braco Bobar. I remembered him as a former colleague of my father. He explained that those were Bosnians who were dealing with the UN and with the Serbian army, trading anything that moved, and obviously taking a major cut.

'Bloody Mafia. Bojan and Ardo. Worse than in Italy or New York!' He said angrily, but then smiled and turned to his friends.

'Hey, come and meet Djemal's little daughter Janna who is here on holiday from London. The last time I saw her was when she was a little teenager, and now she's here sewing people together.'

But now to the greatest news: outside the café I met a dog, who has started following me around. He used to be a strong animal, muscular, with a fine coat. Now he is haggard, looking not only for food but also for an owner. He followed me back to the hospital. I shouldn't have touched him. I patted his back as he approached me, and I guess that he took this as a sign. I called him Sirius.

So, that's life. I need to finish…Lots of Love. Speak to you soon.

Janna

Tania called. She sounded desperate. The *Journal* refused to accredit me again for the month of November or December. I had offered to stay in Sarajevo for them over Christmas. They refused. I offered a big advertisement as a bribe, but it did not work. Tom helped me with *The Times*, and then I tried a number of other papers. None was willing to send me to Bosnia. When I could not reach Janna, I called Milas in the end, asking him to let Janna know. She did not call back, but I found her sadness reflected in her diary.

November/December 1992

Another evening. I've lost count of the day, the week. This is my longest evening. I am sitting in my room, and I am crying, and am ashamed of crying. Why do people cry? God, what a question to ask in war, where the answer is so obvious every day in front of my eyes, under my hands, in the morgue! And yet I am crying not because of hurt or tangible loss, but because of the loss of my little ray of light, which you just extinguished, Dan. Why, why can't the *Journal* give you another accreditation? Why does *The Times* object? Why this bureaucracy? I had been so much looking forward to seeing you again in your journalistic parka. When will I see you again? How many pages in this diary will have to be filled before I can be with you again?

Why can't I get a flight out of this place on a UN plane? I thought that as a foreigner I could get out anytime, but now they're treating me like a local. Well, in a way, they're right of course: I am a local Bosniak. But, still, everything and everyone seem to be conspiring against us.

To stop the pain I paint. There are a lot of things to paint over here, though I do not need many colours. As long as there is war, I decided, I paint only in black and white. And red. I have made paintings of the hospital, of town, of my parents. I paint some of my patients. And I paint abstracts, similar to the Srebrenica painting.

It is six in the morning. I have had two hours of sleep. Nobody died. Just shrapnel wounds. No amputations. What a relief.

Hospital. Staff room. Int.

A shabby room. Dirty, white-painted walls. A calendar hangs on the wall with the months November and December circled in red. Two of Janna's black, white and red abstract paintings are on another wall. A table is in the middle of the room; around it there are eight chairs. On the table a white teapot and a few mugs are left standing. Janna and her colleague Dr Halim are sitting with their feet up, drinking tea. Dr Halim picks up a folder and starts studying the pages.

DR HALIM: We are seriously running out of some supplies again. If we don't get the next WHO shipment soon…I don't know…

JANNA: Actually, wasn't that due to arrive last week?

DR HALIM: Yes, but it hasn't! *The door opens and Janna's father appears. He goes straight up to her.*

DJEMAL *smiling broadly*: Hello my little one! Don't get up. *They embrace before she can get up from her chair. He turns to Dr Halim, greeting her, shaking her hand.* I hope I'm not disturbing you.

DR HALIM: No, of course not. How are you?

DJEMAL: Excellent, thank you. Look what I've got for you. *He gives Dr Halim a package of Marlboros.*

DR HALIM: That's really sweet of you. Thank you so much. I haven't had a decent cigarette for days. *She walks around the table and kisses him on the cheek.*

DJEMAL *turning to Janna*: Now, Janna, have you finished work for today? I've come to pick you up. It's about time you came home to us again. You've been here for ages, and only visited us twice. *Laughing*: Not quite enough! Come home and have dinner with us. *He turns to Dr Halim.* Can she leave you here?

DR HALIM *smiling*: Well, sure! I'm supposed to be on duty anyway.

JANNA: Are you sure?

DR HALIM: Positive. It's not that I'm in a big rush to go anywhere because the war might be over tomorrow morning...

JANNA *with an apologising smile*: I'm sorry, Dad. You know how it's been. Let me just go to my room and change. I'll be right with you.

She goes out. Her father accompanies her out into the corridor. She disappears through a door and he looks into a ward, glancing over the beds. The children are staring at him in silence. Janna returns, now changed, wearing army boots and a big army parka, beneath which her belly is barely noticeable. She looks through the door and smiles at the children, waving her hand. They smile back at her. Dr Halim joins them in the corridor.

JANNA *turning to Djemal*: Look, I really am sorry. I really should have come home more often. But I'm always on call.

DJEMAL: I know. Don't worry. I know you didn't come here simply for family reunions. But it's still nice to see you from time to time at home. Let's go. *They leave through the door, Janna waving good-bye to Dr Halim. Cut.*

I pause as I read what she wrote that evening in her diary.

3 December 92

I'm walking the streets – no, walking is the wrong word. We are rushing, ducking for cover, hiding. Hiding in my own town. Why? This is my town, the streets I used to go along every day to school, with my friends, to flute lessons and to ballet. Dad was pushing me, as if the snipers were running behind us, but it was like a graveyard, quiet, the wind hissing through the open windows of the bombed-out houses. Spooky, but no one to shoot at us.

Where are my friends? I suddenly remember all my friends. Where are they now? Many live abroad, escaping, driven by a premonition, living in Germany or the States. Some others have remained. I remember the days when we were hanging out around our school, bunking off lessons in order to meet the local boys, smoke a secret cigarette in a café and kiss when others were not watching. Where are the boys? At the front? In the mountains?

I'm looking through a window, where a candle is shining. Its flame is moving in the draught, as the windows are destroyed. This is the flat where Biljana lived. I remember her living room, where we played Monopoly when the world was normal, while her father swore at Marshall Tito when he appeared on television – which he seemed to do all the time. Biljana is gone. I cannot find her, though I tried. I keep quiet and we rush on, home, my way from school, the leisurely stroll, now hunted, haunted.

And then I am at home. My home. Is this my home? I hug my mother and touch the wood of our table, the ivory of the piano. These are our rooms, where I lived in my childhood. But now I am detached, although I cannot show my detachment, lest I hurt my parents. Before dinner I go to my room. My bed is there, my desk, my books from school. I close the door, as memories flood my brain and bring pain, long-forgotten feelings.

Last, I go into my brother's room. There it is: his Märklin train set still hanging on the wall, and many photos. Where are you Milutin? In Srebrenica? Or are you in the mountains surrounding Sarajevo, shooting at the Serbs who shoot at us? You should not kill, Milutin. And yet I forgive you for your killing, since I finally seem to understand how you came to think the way you do. You are wrong, but still I understand you, and I torture myself for having quarrelled with you so that now you do not want to hear from me or write to me. I think of you, Milutin, all the time.

I feel the pain inside my stomach, bitterness defying gravity, reaching my throat. I close the door, stumble down the stairs and gulp down the rest of the single malt my father had left in his glass, the smoky peat of Lagavulin smothering the bitterness of my reflections. Oh, Milutin! I pray for you. Do you remember what Mum had told us about our Guardian Angels? I just hope that yours is powerful, stronger than the hatred in the trenches.

Janna's parents' house. Int.

The living and dining rooms are simply but tastefully furnished with old, quasi-antique tables, chests, a mantelpiece and bookshelves full of books all round the walls. The walls are also decorated with two of Janna's colourful oil paintings and a number of black and white photographs. In the dining room, the table is prepared for dinner; simple porcelain and unpolished silver cutlery, candlelight. Two bottles of wine are on the table.

Janna embraces Jasminka, her little sister. Jasminka is twelve years old and a typical teenager, in jeans, sneakers and a big sweatshirt. She is pale despite her dark skin, quiet, but smiling happily. Janna's mother Leila brings in the dishes from the kitchen. Leila is a tall and attractive woman of about fifty with dark hair, a very fine face, tanned skin and deep shadows under her eyes. Djemal puts a cassette into the stereo. Rachmaninoff's piano concerto no 3 can be heard.

JANNA: So how are you?

JASMINKA *smile vanishing*: Bored. No school, only two friends. All day at home, with Mum giving me homework to do. And I can't even go and see you. I hate life. Why do you have to sleep at the hospital?

JANNA *smiling a bit*: If I only had time to sleep! Most of the nights I don't.

LEILA *bossy, but sweet*: Come, let's sit down and eat. Dad shot a rabbit today. A real one for once. Let's celebrate.

JASMINKA *quietly*: There isn't much to celebrate. *They all sit around the table.*

DJEMAL: Well, then. Bon appétit. *He is about to serve the wine when Janna takes the bottle from his hand.*

JANNA: At least you keep culture up over here. Let's see what year we are having today. *She reads the label with an expression of disgust. Mocking*: Oh, how plebeian! Only 1964. *She reads*: Château Chasse Spleen. Well, that's not too bad. *She smiles at her parents.* It's so nice to be at home! *They all eat in silence.* On the other hand, it's incredibly depressing operating on all those kids and adults. Particularly the kids. *She looks at them.* I've had to amputate legs and little arms. These children are crippled for life. *She looks angrily at her parents.* Why can't this end? Why the hell can't this end?

DJEMAL *putting his hand on her arm to calm her*: Janna, please.

JANNA: What do you mean: 'please'? Why? Just tell me why. Just one reason, please. S*he eats and calms down again, slowly drinking her glass of wine. She looks through the wine into the light.* This is wonderful – what wine! What culture!

LEILA *changing the subject and smiling warmly at her daughter*: Janna, you haven't told us much about Dan. And all we see is that your belly's getting rounder. *Janna sips the wine. She pauses, reflecting, looking into the glass as if to find the words.*

JANNA: Well, he is … well, you have seen pictures of him. He is … I don't know how to say it. *She sips from the wine again.* I've never been in love before like this before …

DJEMAL *interrupting*: But what does he do? He isn't a doctor, is he?

JANNA: No, not at all. He buys and sells companies. Does M&A and stuff. *They look puzzled.* He's a banker. He does mergers and acquisitions of companies, private equity, venture capital and things. *They still look slightly puzzled.*

DJEMAL: What does that mean?

JANNA: Well, he buys companies that are undervalued, restructures them, sells off unnecessary subsidiaries, changes the management, improves productivity and then sells them on, either to another buyer or through a…what do you call it?…a floatation on the stock market. And that's how he makes money.

DJEMAL: Sounds complicated. Communism was a lot simpler.

JANNA: But then, he has a completely different side. A melancholy side…and he plays the cello, like you, Dad. In fact, I met him as he was playing the cello. *She pauses.* In a cemetery. *She pauses again, looking into her glass.* He told me that he plays in cemeteries because his brother died when he was very young and I think he never got over this loss. *Djemal looks into his glass, examining the wine against the light of the candle. She smells the wine, takes another sip and looks through the wine at the candles.* This really is an amazingly beautiful colour, such an intense crimson red, almost like a Rothko painting. *She drinks again and smiles disarmingly at her parents.* I've never met anyone like him. Never loved anyone like this. *Everyone drinks in silence.*

LEILA: Where did his brother die?

JANNA: In Israel.

JASMINKA: So, is Dan Jewish?

JANNA: Yes.

DJEMAL *looking at her inquisitively*: Doesn't he mind that you're not?

JANNA: His mother did, initially. But when we met, she turned out to be incredibly sweet. That is, after a first argument. *She looks at Djemal.* I hope you don't mind.

DJEMAL: God, Janna, what a question. You know we have all sorts of religions in our blood…But why did you need to get pregnant?

JANNA *laughing disarmingly*: It just happened.

LEILA *also laughing*: But, Janna, you're a doctor.

JANNA *serious*: To be honest, it's fate. Well, we did take
　　care, of course, but, you know, then...*She pauses*. And,
　　anyway, I just knew he's the one and that I want to
　　have his child.
LEILA *doubting*: And does he share this feeling?
JANNA: Yes. Absolutely. *She pauses, looking into her glass again.*
LEILA: But then why did he let you go to Sarajevo?
JANNA *looking seriously at her mother*: He didn't. He was
　　dead set against it. But I had to come here. I couldn't
　　stay in London, go to great restaurants, stay at five-star
　　hotels and have great holidays all the time when I
　　know what shit is happening over here. *She pauses.*
　　How could I? How could I look myself in the eye in
　　the mirror each morning, staying at a Four Seasons,
　　being pampered. *She looks around, searching their eyes.*
　　In the end, I think, he understood.
　　Fading.

3 December 92 cont.
It is night. I've got used to eating nothing, or just sticky rice and
old potatoes. So even tiny portions of meat are wonderful and
luxurious for me nowadays. And we had electricity for once and
gas to cook on, and water to do the washing up. And water to flush
the loo, rather than having to shit into bags. This has been the
most civilised evening for weeks – like pre-war times.

　　Sirius follows me around, and yet has the decency not to enter
the hospital. He is immensely loyal, but I fear that I am a bad owner.
I have no food for him, as we have so little food for ourselves and
for the patients. Most patients get food that families and friends
bring in during the day or the occasional UN ration. We have to
save the crumbs for ourselves and for the orphans, or for those who
don't have any relatives left in town. Sirius, I suspect, goes out
hunting at night, killing rats, eating shit. He is still amazingly fast.
I should know what race he is. Race seems nowadays to be of
paramount importance in this godforsaken town. Race and religion.
I guess Sirius is like all of us in Sarajevo – a mixture with no trace of
original race, or of religion for that matter.

I try to put together the puzzle of what really had been going on in her mind, in her thoughts, which in one sense I knew so well and which had developed so fast while I was absent, stagnating back in London. But nobody can remain the same when coming face to face with atrocities every day. And the atrocities were there in every dimension, robbing people of their values, their beliefs and strength.

'You know,' Janna said on the phone, 'I've toughened up already. I operate on shrapnel wounds nowadays without the slightest emotion. I take out the splinters, patch up the bodies, do my stitches, marvel at my "signature" and move on to the next job.' She sighed in silence and continued. 'I don't feel that hatred any more. I rationalise my job, and it is almost as if I rationalise the "job" the soldiers on the other side have to do. Reflecting back, in the evenings, I am of course disgusted at them and at myself. But the next morning I begin to operate again without any emotion. Is that my survival mechanism kicking in? A stupid question from a doctor, don't you think?'

She waited in silence for my answer, which did not come. So she continued, 'But then again I get so furious and so upset when I hear that our own guys are swine. Our own Mafia has kept the WHO shipment. Full of vital medicine and equipment.'

'What did they do with the shipment?' I asked. 'Can't you simply buy it back from them?'

'No. They'd already sold it on to the Croats.'

'That's awful. But my mother is in New York again. And she is raising funds for you again.'

'Dan, please tell her how grateful we all are. I should write to her, but I hardly get round to writing to you. Please let her know how well we use every dollar.' She paused. 'Before I forget, guess, what: Biljana, my kindergarten friend, turned up at the hospital! It's so amazing. We had somehow lost touch when I moved to London, and she had also moved on in life, studying biology in Zagreb. But then she got trapped in Sarajevo when the war started, while visiting her parents. That's Sarajevo. Surreal! One day you move about freely, the next the war starts and you can't get out of town any more!'

'At the beginning, surely nobody imagined that there would be a siege, so people made no effort to get out,' I said.

'I guess so…But once they realised this was for real it was too late. So Biljana stayed to work as a nurse, initially at another hospital. When she heard about me, she decided to come and join me here.'

On 24 December, Janna called me late in the evening, to my surprise, to wish me a Merry Christmas.

'We had a wonderful time, Dan. Milas, Biljana and I took five children to see the UN's Christmas show. It was marvellous. There were presents and sweets for everyone, and the French soldiers were singing after the show. Biljana was crying most of the time. Even the savages on the hills kept quiet, although Orthodox Christmas is on 6 January.'

'It's weird to think that the people who are lobbing shells at you to kill you are celebrating the birth of Christ, praying for peace and happiness to the same God you are praying to,' I said, trying to stay calm. I felt furious, but did not want to show her my emotions.

'Dan, I know. But today was wonderful, even for us Muslims. And it was just as if the war was over. After the singing, people hugged the French soldiers as if they were saviours who had succeeded in liberating town. But then we were driven back in armoured personnel carriers, which reminded us of reality.' She was silent for a while, and I heard doors banging in the background and Milas's voice.

'I gave Biljana, Milas and my parents each a painting I had painted in the evenings, and I've kept one for you.' She sighed.

'And then we had to go back to the hospital, and we saw the children lying in their cold beds, forgotten by everyone in Europe, while everyone in Europe was celebrating Christmas, stuffing themselves with good food and chocolates, wishing each other peace and happiness. Oh, Dan, I have to go. Christmas was so beautiful, and yet so fucking hypocritical!'

Thus Christmas came and went. And the war continued. And the year ended.

1993

1 January 1993

Last night we celebrated New Year. Today it's the first of a new year. 1993. Biljana and my other colleagues were there, and Milas came by, and we opened two bottles of champagne at midnight.

'I had wanted to keep them for the end of the war,' Milas said, popping the cork. 'But who knows when that will be? And anyway, I'm sure I can get another bottle from the French UN soldiers.'

We all sat around in our common room, listening to the local radio station, transmitting a show called *Nadrealisti*.

How can you have a comedy group on the radio in the middle of a war? But we were all cracking up, roaring with laughter at their stupid jokes.

As it was getting close to midnight, we all became quiet and thoughtful, watching the clock ticking towards twelve. In a way, I had been afraid that the soldiers on the hills would unleash spectacular fireworks for us that evening, lighting fires in town, filling the skies with red tracers. But things remained calm. We hugged and kissed, wishing each other what in a way none of us realistically believed would come to Sarajevo soon.

At six in the morning my parents came – yes, even my mother – and brought us fresh coffee, bread and jam. It was such a treat. Unbelievable. They stayed only half an hour, as my mother was anxious to get back before the shelling started. It was so good to see them! And the espresso we made over the fire was divine.

Janna's hospital. Staff room. Int.

Milas and Biljana are sitting in the staff room, smoking, drinking tea. Biljana looks very nervous and tired. A new painting by Janna is on the wall. It shows their hospital, the black holes where the windows once were, smoke coming out of a top-floor window. Sirius is sitting in front of the entrance.

MILAS: Daniel's been trying to reach her for the last couple of days, but she's never around. And Janna has been trying to reach him too…

BILJANA: Maybe it works now.

MILAS: Let me see. *He dials and waits.* Oh, I think it does. Dan? Can you hear me?

DAN: Sure, Milas. Let me just go to another room. Have you got Janna?

MILAS: Dan, just one second. I'm handing you over.

BILJANA: Janna! Telephone!

JANNA *shouting back from the distance*: Coming!

Janna *comes rushing in. She is wearing the same green operating dress. She picks up the receiver. Her face overjoyed.*

JANNA: Dan! Dan! I'm so glad to speak to you. Happy New Year! *To Milas and Biljana*: God, you guys are chimneys… *She sits down on a chair at the table, blowing away the smoke.*

DAN: Happy New Year, Sweetie! I've tried so many times to reach you, but Milas says you're always busy. We've got to talk more often than once every other week! I'm worried about you. Are you OK?

JANNA: Why? Yes! Everything is fine. Baby is fine. She… or rather he is moving about. Quite active. *She is smiling.* You'd be amazed to see how round I am. In fact, I wanted to tell you that I can be in Vienna next Saturday. I'm sorry about the short notice, and that it's taken me more than two months. Milas can get me there in the back of some UN bigwig's plane straight to Vienna. Finally. Can you imagine? I can stay for Saturday night, but have to leave again Sunday morning. Can you make it?

DAN: Great news. Of course I'll be there. I bought you the ultrasound scanner you wanted, and a lot of medicines you had on your list. I can probably take the stuff with me.

JANNA: Wow! That would be great. Despite all of Milas's connections, he often has to pay taxes on the way so that we only get a fraction of the stuff that's sent. But then again, we can pick up the rest later on the black market.

DAN: That's revolting.

JANNA: I know. I've never bought anything on the black market, but I know my colleagues do.

DAN: Where shall we meet? At the Sacher?

JANNA: That would be absolutely deliciously decadent and wonderful. Saturday late afternoon. I'll be there. Milas is absolutely reliable.

NURSE *shouting from the background*: Janna?

JANNA: Dan. I'm sorry, but I've to go now. See you then. Big big hug.

DAN: Big kiss. I cannot wait. *She hangs up and turns to Milas and Biljana.*

JANNA: I can't tell you how much I'm looking forward to getting out of here for a day.

BILJANA: You're so lucky. I wish I could get out of here. And I tell you, I wouldn't come back.

MILAS: But you don't even leave the hospital any more. Why do you want to leave this wonderful town?

BILJANA *looking at them*. I haven't told you, but I've received threats lately. Death threats.

JANNA *angry*: Why? Who from?

BILJANA: No idea. People accusing me of being a Serb...

JANNA: God, That's sick!

BILJANA: If it gets too much, I'll try to escape. Probably over the mountains.

MILAS: But you won't be able to get out like that.

JANNA *turning to Milas*: Can't you get her out?

MILAS: Probably only with the help of some unsavoury characters.

JANNA: Hmm. Let me know if you need money to bribe your way out.

BILJANA: Don't worry. I'm not going yet.

Cut.

That evening she wrote a letter. Her writing was difficult to read, scribbled in haste, and bitterness and anger.

Dear Dan,

I'm back in my room. I need to write to you. This place is getting more and more insane. Biljana is getting death threats. And tonight I was crying, just crying. I think I've seen a lot in this war, but a few hours ago they brought in a child, a six-year-old – a little girl. Her side was open. I could see her organs inside. She was awake, her eyes wide open, full of fear and hope and pain. Yet she was speechless, silent, not even crying. And she had lost a lot of blood, and was all white: white skin, pale lips. And big big pale blue eyes. She grabbed my arm, then my hand, with her little hand, and held it tight until her strength was fading. Her grip was loosening. It was too late, she had lost too much blood, her eyes were fighting, crying, 'Help me, save me!' But it was too late. Her light faded and the eyes became grey and empty. Empty. Dead.

Why, Dan? Why? What had she done to be killed?

I am thinking about my recent quarrel with my father. I challenged him the other day – I suspected him of taking out snipers, and his answers were evasive. So I argued with him. 'Thou shalt not kill holds also true for you!' I said. He only looked down. 'Dad. You must not kill. Please. You're becoming like them. You're the same, aren't you?' He just looked at me and shook his head and said: 'Janna, please don't judge.'

'But I do judge. Because I'm right. This commandment is a matter of principle! You cannot simply bend it whichever way you need to justify and cover your actions. Otherwise you become like the Serbs on the hills.' He looked at me and did not answer.

What gave me the right to judge him? Maybe he would have destroyed those perverted bastards who shot and killed this girl tonight? Maybe he did not do so because of our argument? If that is the case, am I not the one responsible for her death? Am I a murderer if I stop people stopping the killing? Dan – did I kill this child?

I feel lost. Nothing to hold on to any more. The ground is gone, the ground I had relied on when walking the path of life. When walking to the café. This sounds pathetic. I could just as well write in plainer English that my mind is fucked. I'm mind-fucked by the fucking war. I killed her. And I had preached to you the commandment 'Thou shalt not kill'. But the Bible is Bullshit in War!

Dan, I feel that I cannot go on preaching pacifism when they shoot little girls and rip them apart with fucking dum dum bullets.

Got to work. Love you. Janna

I will not melt

I cannot wait! I cannot wait! Warm rooms. Windows not broken or boarded up, but with clean windowpanes. A plane, a United Nations plane. What bribery and connections can do for you! I love the UN, it's such a useful organisation, providing the town with Humvees, barter trade, an endless supply of muscular males for the hookers and the occasional plane to fly to the decadence that awaits you only a few miles north. The Sacher: clean sheets, white, cool and ironed. A bath with essential oils to spoil yourself. Food that you can be sure will not be rat meat or cockroach salad. Baby will love it. Baby will have its first hot chocolate, its first Sacher torte. Only the wine will be less good than we have at home.

I am scared that my resolve will melt, that once I am in Dan's arms I will decide to leave it all, to stay. I am afraid of weakness taking hold of me. I am afraid of myself, which will tell me to stay in Vienna, fly back to London, sleep for hours without interruption, without the sound of shells, without the wind coming through broken windows, just melting in the warmth of Dan's embrace.

I read these lines and think, 'What kitsch, what crap!' Straight out of a trashy Barbara Cartland novel. But then, trashy novels reveal what we are all dreaming about, what we really would love to do if our super-ego did not control us better. How cheap I am, thinking of aromatic oils in warm bathtubs when children are still brought daily to the hospital? When Biljana is receiving death threats! When Milu is in the trenches.

I will not melt.

Sacher

The plane touched down in the late morning, and the Sacher was charming, warm, welcoming. I decided to go for a long jog through the parks and then read the papers in the Konditorei Demel, sipping hot chocolate, imagining Janna's face in the nothingness opposite me. In the end I even met with the CEO of a company and we talked about their planned leveraged buy-out and analysed the amount of capital they needed. All the while I was staring at the front door of the hotel, waiting for Janna to arrive, whilst the minutes ticked. I sent the CEO off, as I did not want him around when Janna finally came through the doors.

Vienna. Hotel Sacher. Int.

Dan is pacing up and down the elegant wood-panelled sitting room next to reception. He is restless, looking all the time at the door and at his watch. He is wearing a business suit and tie. The room is full of elegantly dressed people, sipping tea, carrying conspicuous shopping bags, chatting. A butler approaches Dan. They speak, but cannot be heard because of the distance. Dan shakes his head and looks at his watch. He sits down, trying to read, burying his head in the Financial Times. *The revolving door turns, and Janna enters, dressed in big army boots, old, dirty jeans, a polo shirt. She carries a green pullover, her flak jacket, and a thick army anorak over her shoulders. Her face is pale and her hair is cut extremely short. She looks around and hesitates, as she cannot see Dan. Then she sees the* Financial Times *and walks straight towards him, half hiding behind it.*

JANNA: Good evening, Sir.

DAN: Janna! *He jumps up, and holds her in his arms for a long time.* God! It's so good to see you! *They kiss.* I can't tell you how much I missed you. *He looks at her.* But God! What happened to you? Did you crawl through a coalmine?

What a contrast with her surroundings! Here she was, standing in old scruffy jeans, dried mud on her knees and on her anorak, and yet her smile, her face, the utmost beauty, her Henry Moorish belly a perfect curve. All the other women in the room, old or young, needed jewellery, gold, Cartier, pearls, Gucci and pashmina shawls to enhance their beauty. Janna stood out above them all.

JANNA: Hey, cheeky! *She flings her arms around his neck and kisses him again.*

DAN *looks at her belly*: Gosh, it's grown. It's really round. He touches her belly. I'm absolutely amazed and thrilled. *She smiles at him proudly. They embrace again. He touches her head.* What happened to your hair? You look like a punk.

JANNA: Please, stop it. Let's go to your room. I hope you've got one.
Cut.

Hotel Sacher. Bedroom. Int.

Janna and Dan are inside the large and lavishly decorated room. Antique furniture, elegant prints on the walls, two sofas, a low table and various Louis XVI-style chairs. Dan is sitting on the bed, changed into his usual black slacks and black pullover. Janna is taking a bath.

DAN: So what happened? How did you finally get here?

JANNA *from the bath*: Swissair first class, of course. What else?

DAN: No seriously.

JANNA: Well, Milas bribed us a ride on a UN plane. But we also had a bit on foot getting to the airport today. Quite a bit in fact, as we missed the UN guy's armoured personnel carrier.

DAN: What? You walked down Sniper Alley?

JANNA *laughing*: No, of course not. But we were late, so the first – er – the UN 'taxi' was gone. So we had to get a lift from someone else, and we needed to rush across town to the Holiday Inn and, as it had been snowing and raining a lot, the streets were muddy and I slipped and fell twice. Come here. See how bruised my bum is. In the end, we got the other carrier at the Holiday Inn. *She can be heard getting out of the bathtub. Dan walks over and waits at the open door. She comes out in a white hotel bathrobe. They kiss for a long time.*

JANNA: Hmm. That reminds me, I've not made love for ages.

DAN: I'm not sure whether it's such a good idea now...

JANNA: Rubbish! *She kisses him again. She frees herself and looks at him.* Maybe we should wait until after dinner. I'm actually starving. Let me just get dressed. *She goes back into the bathroom. Shouting from the bathroom*: I don't want to be arguing with you tonight. So may I say something now so we get it out of the way, since I can sense what you've been trying to say? Tomorrow morning I am going back. Milas will pick me up at nine o'clock here at the hotel. And I'm going back for another... well, until just before B-day. *She comes out again, still wearing a bathrobe.*

DAN *looking serious, getting up and taking her into his arms*: I had no intention of arguing with you. I know what this means to you. I know what you're doing, what you're achieving. I wouldn't ask you to stay here. I fully support your decision to go back and work at the hospital. Full stop. Besides, I've tons of equipment and stuff for you.

JANNA: Thank you. *She caresses his head with a sad face, closing her eyes.*
Fading.

Hotel Sacher. Restaurant. Int.

Janna and Dan are sitting at a table in the very formal restaurant, dining. The other people are very elegantly dressed, wearing jewellery and gold watches. There is a display of wealth. Janna is wearing a pair of grey corduroy trousers and a pale blue shirt. The atmosphere is hushed. Candlelight. Chopin piano music in the background. Janna smiles at him, reaching over the table to caress his hand.

JANNA *whispering, hushed*: I love this decadence, although I used to despise it. It's wonderful, so beautiful, quiet. *She pauses, reflecting.* But then, on the other hand, I can't bear this decadence when I see it in contrast to the life around me less than twelve hours ago, and which I'll be back to in twenty-four hours. The contrast is ghastly. It's so surreal. *She pauses again, looking into her glass of mineral water.* But then again, I'll only return once more, and then never again. Probably never again. Even once the war is over, I don't feel like going back.

DAN: I might wish to see it again one day, where you live, where you work, your parents, Jasminka, your brother and all.

JANNA: That's true. Maybe you're right. But that seems so far away. I can't imagine a day when this war will be over. *She pauses.* How can it be over? The sides are so deeply entrenched. *She looks into the distance and then into his eyes.* The people sitting in the hills are shelling their former neighbours. Everything is upside down. Worse than Kafka.

DAN: To be frank, I don't – I can't – understand it. What is going on in their minds?

JANNA: It's awful. *She becomes more silent and reflective*: So depressing. All those wounded adults and children. *She hesitates for a moment, reflecting on what to say, looking around at the people sitting at the other tables*. I operate most days. Take out bullets. Splinters. Amputate. Little legs. Stitch little arms together again. *Dan is silent. Tears fill her eyes.* And the kids are so hopeful. *She starts sobbing, shaking her head.* Dan, I can't handle it any more. I just don't know what to do. I can't simply fly to London and turn my back on everyone. I want to. I want to flee it all. Flee the hell, but I can't. I just can't. *She is crying silently. Suddenly she looks at Dan and hisses*: Why can't fucking NATO do something? *Raising her voice*: Why can't they bomb the shit out of those bastards on the hills? *The other guests turn their heads to look at her.* Who are those fucking bureaucrats who were in the Gulf to free Kuwait five minutes after the Iraqi invasion and who don't want to do anything here? *She bangs her fist on the table.* A couple of cruise missiles and the artillery on the hills would be gone. I can see them from the corner near our hospital. Everyone can see them. Give us the missiles and we'll knock them out. We'll bomb them back into the fucking Stone Age where they came from! *People are muttering, looking at them. The waiters are nervous, not sure what to do.* Oh, fuck them all! *She quietens down and stares with incredible determination and anger into Dan's eyes, hissing between clenched teeth*: Why is the West so gutless, Daniel? It's they who are the real murderers. They! Those gutless arseholes who do nothing. All those fucking spineless Western politicians. *She looks at him suddenly.* Or is this the West's strategy? Kill the Muslims? That's what it fucking feels like. That's what some people are saying.

She pauses and looks down again and adds in a quiet and resigned voice, shaking her head: The only guys who've come to defend us are some fucking nutters from Afghanistan. *Whispering*: Oh God damn them all!
Dan takes her hands and holds them for a long time, not saying anything. The business in the restaurant continues, the waiters continue serving, people continue eating. Janna closes her eyes and shakes her head silently.

We needed something sweet and bitter. Bitterness to numb our mouths, which had filled with stomach acids. Sweetness to block the memories of pain and disappointment. The waiter returned before we finished our thoughts in silence, unable to understand Janna's outburst. He took two beautiful plates of blue porcelain and ceremoniously dipped the large silver spoon into the mousse au chocolat, letting it slowly drip onto the plates. We watched the spectacle in fascination, like a film in slow motion. Our gaze followed the mousse as it dropped, trying to defy gravity. Janna's eyes were wide and empty, dreaming, distant. She ate automatically, licking her lips. I remember the day when we were eating mousse at a small restaurant in Toulouse, the sun burning down on us, melting the chocolate before we could indulge in its dark flavours. What was she dreaming of now? I felt I could not ask...

We left, having finished our dinner in silence. We did not need to speak. We felt each other's presence, looking into each other's eyes, searching and finding love and immensely deep feelings. Later, as we lay in bed, I felt the roundness of her belly and watched her face, her faint smile as she lay deep asleep.

Hotel Sacher. Bedroom. Int.

It is early morning. Dan and Janna are in bed together. The room is light, as the curtains are open.

JANNA: I'm sorry about the scene in the restaurant last night. I just couldn't handle it any more. *She smiles.* To be honest, I now have to laugh about all those fat self-satisfied people indulging in conspicuous consumption. In a weird way, I feel even sorry for them and their banal lives. *The phone rings. Dan answers it.*

DAN: Hello? OK. We're coming down in a minute. Can you please ask him to wait in the breakfast room. We'll be joining him there. *He hangs up. Turning to Janna.* I guess Milas is a bit early.

JANNA: Shit! It's him already. We'd better rush. You'll love him. He's really great.
Cut.

Hotel Sacher. Breakfast room. Int.

Milas is sitting at a table reading an International Herald Tribune. *He is unshaven, and looks rough and dirty, wearing old brown corduroys and a brown pullover, an army parka on the chair. Dan and Janna enter and walk to his table.*

JANNA: Hi Milas. Let me finally introduce Dan to you. Milas – this is Dan. Dan – Milas. *They shake hands.* You guys have spoken a lot over the phone. *She looks at Milas.* You look as if you've spent the night under a bridge.

MILAS: Don't worry. I visited some friends, and we were quarrelling until the early hours.

JANNA: Have you had breakfast yet? *Milas shakes his head.*

DAN: Well, let's dig in. *She puts her arm around Dan, and all three go off towards the buffet.*
Cut.

Hotel Sacher. Lobby. Int.

Dan and Janna are standing in the lobby, in the place where they met the day before. She is wearing her dirty clothes again.

DAN: So farewell. I hope to see you soon. *She remains silent.* Please take good care of baby and yourself. *She holds him, putting her face closer to his.* I really love you.
JANNA *whispering*: I'll be back soon. And will forever be with you. Be good.
They walk slowly towards the door. Milas enters and Janna kisses Dan one last time before they walk over to Milas, who shakes Dan's hand. Janna and Milas walk through the doors of the hotel, leaving Dan in the lobby looking at them through the glass doors. Janna and Milas get into a black S-class Mercedes with a Viennese CD number plate, into which the bellboy loads Janna's luggage and the packages Dan has given her. The car drives off fast. The street remains empty after the car has turned out of sight.
Cut.

It is once again night in Lujeron. My parents have gone to bed hours ago. I am drinking whisky and writing furiously, to capture those days that are now passing like an ever-faster-moving film in front of my eyes. I can still sense the loneliness of the hotel lobby, once she was swallowed by the revolving doors, which sucked her out of my arms and spat her out on the other side, on to the pavement, where the black Mercedes was waiting. Whose car was that? Whose plane was she using to get in and out of Sarajevo, when no citizen of Sarajevo could officially get in or out of town?

But then again, she had a foreign passport and I learned not to ask questions that would force people to lie. Two worlds. I looked for a long time at those doors, as they continued turning, hoping that they would swirl her back, back into my arms. But I waited in vain. I checked out and headed straight for the airport, straight back to the office. The next evening I found a letter, written on the hotel's letterhead, on my desk at work.

Der Verlust des Menschlichen
im Menschen

Dear Dan,

You are sleeping, and I can see you lying still and in complete peace of mind at my side. I caress your face and you smile in your sleep. I never told you how sweet you are when you are asleep.

You look almost pacifist.

I cannot sleep. I am sitting at the desk, thinking of my work, my patients, the dismal future of our hospital. The loss of hope. My parents, who are continuing the fight. I sometimes do not recognise my father any more. He tries to keep up a life of culture, but then I suspect him to be active in the defence of our town. He does not say so, but I am sure he is. It is disturbing to think that the father who rocked me in his arms, who scolded me when I whipped a horse too hard when we were riding through the forests – that this same gentle person is out there defending Sarajevo. Killing. Dad is a loner, and I think he climbs up into the high-rises and waits for snipers to appear on the other side. And then he takes them out. He is patient and precise.

I remember the dinner we had some time ago in London, when you invited this German priest who said that the biggest threat to mankind was the loss of the human dimension in human beings. Der Verlust des Menschlichen im Menschen. Dan, are we getting there? In Nazi Germany we got there. In Cambodia we got there. And now in Bosnia we have got there. I sometimes wonder whether you can ever regain it once it is lost. Das Menschliche.

From the way you held me in your arms, I know you will be sad as you read this letter. Please don't be sad. I am living life to the fullest, and I am so glad I am doing this.

Descartes said, cogito ergo sum. In my case it is one step further: I'm working so I am. I am so I am. Sum ergo sum.

This is fulfilment. Full Fulfilment.

Big hug and lots of love Janna

PS I had a peek into the boxes you gave me. Wow! I'm so grateful!

When I received the letter, I read it four times, studying every word; and now, in the garden of Lujeron, I'm reading it again. I walk away from the house to the willow and sit down at my favourite place, listening to the wind coming from the mountains. I am thinking back to the day when I was walking away from the Sacher in the coldness of the Sunday morning in Vienna, when the sky was grey, and black crows were flying low, landing only feet away from me, staring at me with curious but cruel eyes. Where were these birds the week before? Did they come from Sarajevo, from Bosnia, from the war? Were they picking at the dead soldiers rotting in the trenches? At children lying in Sniper Alley? Crows are cruel, and eat flesh. My mother told us – when we were kids – of crows which flew to Dachau, landing inside the fences, staring at the prisoners with cruel eyes, and then flying away, when there was nothing to pick at, like cynical black humour sent by the SS.

Forty-eight hours after Vienna I flew straight to Hong Kong, to dive into the world of South East Asia, forcing me to forget the past weekend whilst trying to find a buyer for one of our companies. I could not enjoy the luxury of the Mandarin Oriental, as I thought of the bitter coldness Janna was facing right now. After four hectic days I finished my work and had done enough forgetting, and flew back to London.

Janna's hospital. Corridor. Int.

Janna is on the phone to Dan. She is sitting on the floor in the corridor. Milas can be seen leaving through one door and entering the doctors' room. Janna is wearing baggy, very old tracksuit trousers and a black pullover.

JANNA: God, I'm really exhausted. But it's not so much the operating. It's the emotional stress. And I don't wish to toughen up. *Quietly*: Although I probably already have. *She wipes away her tears. Deliberately calm*: I'm sorry, I'm just emotional at the moment. It's probably hormonal. And I haven't seen Biljana since coming back from Vienna.

DAN *pleading*: Why don't you come back now? I mean, you have achieved all you can achieve. And you need to come back pretty soon in any event.

JANNA: No. *Pausing, reflecting.* Sorry Dan. You know I'll be back in a month or so. Please wait … And, once again, Dan, a big big thanks for sending all the medicine and stuff. It should arrive soon. How much did it all cost?

DAN: All the money Mum recently raised.

JANNA: What, four hundred thousand bucks? Phew!

DAN: I think she's doing some more fundraising. Next week she'll be speaking to some pacifist organisation…

JANNA: That's funny: pacifists. Gone are those days. You lose your naïveté in Sarajevo. Oh Dan, I've become so cynical … *She pauses.*

DAN: No, Janna. You've just grown up.

JANNA: Whatever. I don't mind where the money comes from, Daniel. Please thank your mother. And thank you, Dan, for all the cash you stuffed into my bag and anorak in Vienna. I only discovered it when I was back in my room. It's a huge amount. I could buy two Humvees with the dosh in the grey market. Dan. *There is silence.* I've got to go. *Janna slowly gets up and grabs a pile of clothes, getting ready to go back into the operating theatre.* Daniel. I really loved being with you in Vienna the other day, and I must admit I was very tempted simply to stay in bed, instead of rushing back. But now I'm counting the days.

DAN: Believe me, so am I. Take good care. Big kiss, sweetie.

JANNA: Yes. You too. And thanks again. Please try to call me again. I know it's hard to get through, but try. I love you! *She hangs up and smiles at Milas, but then looks at him, hesitating.* Milas. What's wrong? You look completely gone.

MILAS: I went to Biljana's parents' place, and they told me
    that she had fled town. She left you a note.
JANNA: Let's read it together, I can hardly read her writing.

Dear Janna. I'm fleeing S. This morning I found a dead rat in my
bed and a note attached 'you have 1 hour to get out'. I threw the
rat out of the window, grabbed a bag with my belongings and
jumped out of the window myself, as I was too scared to use the
front door. I ran to my parents. Janna, I am sorry, I cannot come
by to say farewell. Either I'll go into hiding or I'll bolt. If I reach
the hills, I'm free. How cynical that is. I'm free once I reach those
people on the hills who try to kill you and everyone in Sarajevo.
I'll send you a note as soon as I reach Belgrade or Zagreb. Love to
you & your family. Biljana

MILAS *looking at Janna*: Arseholes.
JANNA *looking shattered*: Oh God, Milas, who were they?
    What's wrong with our people? She is the most lovely,
    wonderful person. Most of her friends are Muslims.
    She's got zero interest in politics and stuff. *She looks
    sidelong at Milas*. Milas. Is there something you haven't
    told me...I mean, did you and she...?
MILAS *smiling vaguely*: Yes, of course, you fool. You never
    noticed? And now I hope to see her in Zagreb. I don't
    think they'll ever let me into Belgrade.

Calm steel – a soothing weight

Janna's parents' house. Living room. Int.

Janna is alone with her father. They are sitting in the room in darkness. Outside there is sunshine, but they keep their curtains drawn. Her father is drinking wine.

JANNA: How much wine have you got left?

DJEMAL: At this rate, the war can last another year and a half. At the moment I'm drinking some Rothschild of the sixties and seventies, which is quite decent. I haven't started the Burgundy yet.

JANNA: Why don't you sell the stuff to the UN? There are plenty of French officers who'd pay a fortune.

DJEMAL: Why should I? This is all we've left of culture. *Furious:* Our humanistic culture. *Silence. He walks over to Janna and embraces her.* But it's not all the Serbs. Most of our friends are Serbs. Or Croats. *After a pause, in which he looks at his feet, he adds quietly*: Biljana was a Serb.

JANNA *alerted*: What do you mean, 'was'? What happened?

DJEMAL: I couldn't…I, I just didn't know how to tell you. You know she tried to flee Sarajevo. And some of our guys got her. Just there, up in the hills. And she was of course known to be a Serb. *Even more quietly*: So they raped her and then someone from town came and simply killed her. *Tears are running down Janna's cheeks. She does not say anything.* And I thought we, our troops, had moral values. But our ethics are dead. Nothing is left. Der Verlust des Menschlichen, as you always say so wisely. *Janna is crying quietly. She puts her head on her arms, leaning on the table.*

JANNA: Oh god, what swine! What bastards! *Jumping up*: What fucking swine. *She walks towards the window, moves the curtain and looks out, fists clenched.*
Djemal gets up and walks over to a chest of drawers. He opens a drawer and takes out a small Uzi submachine gun. He carefully assembles it, checking details. Janna looks at him startled, wiping away her tears.

JANNA: Dad, what are you doing?

DJEMAL *going over to her and handing her the gun*: It's an Uzi. It's fast, efficient and deadly. Take it. It's yours. *He reads the wording on the side of the gun and smiles ironically*: It's made in Israel.

JANNA: I can't. I cannot kill.

DJEMAL: You need not kill. It's just for deterrence. To protect you. Do you want to end up like Biljana? If someone knows you have a gun, they're less likely to shoot. *She shakes her head and refuses to take the gun, turning away, sitting down at the other end of the room. Djemal picks up a chair and places it right in front of her, sitting down opposite her, looking straight into her eyes.*
Janna. Daniel's brother would probably be alive had he carried an Uzi. Biljana would be in safety now had she carried an Uzi. Sarajevo would probably be free by now if we all had weapons to stand up to the aggressors. We don't. But you have to have one. What happened to Biljana... *Janna looks down...* shouldn't happen to you. *He pauses and shows her how to operate it, how to load it.* OK. Let's go to Mandic's place and practise in their garden. Aim at the gnomes. *He smiles at her, but she cannot return the smile.*
Cut.

Mandic's garden. Ext.

*Janna and Djemal are in the garden of a large private
house. In the background, Sirius is running around. It is
twilight, late afternoon, a grey day, no sunshine, but heavy
clouds block the view of the surrounding hills. Her father
shows her how to load the gun. He has taken a number of
empty wine bottles along, which he puts down on a sawn-
off tree trunk at a distance. He aims briefly.*

DJEMAL: The first three will have to go. *He fires three shots
and smashes the first three bottles.* Your turn. *He hands
her the gun. She aims for a long time. Djemal laughs and
takes her into his arms:* Shoot! You have to be faster or
you'll be dead meat! *Janna steps forward and instantly
shoots from the hip. The bottles shatter. Sirius starts
barking loudly.* That's better. Now the tree over there.
*Janna shoots at the tree, without much aiming. The bark
splinters.*

JANNA: Well, that's easy. It's like watering a lawn. *They
prepare to return and walk out of the garden gate up to the
street, which is deserted. They walk back, slowly, side by
side, Janna carrying the gun with Sirius at their heels.*

DJEMAL: Shoot first. And ask later. Otherwise you're dead.
Shoot to wound and not to kill. Unless you want to
kill – or need to kill. And forget about Moses. *He stops
and looks at her.* Commandments are bullshit in war.
Religious hype! And God is always on the side of the
winners! Never on the side of the victims.

JANNA *grave, resting her arms on Djemal's shoulders so that
she can look straight into his eyes:* Dad, there's no God in
Sarajevo.
Cut.

Sarajevo hospital room. Int.

Milas is waiting. He looks grim, unshaven and not very clean. Janna enters the room and, seeing him, takes him into her arms. She holds him for a long time and then looks into his face, which is sad and serious.

JANNA: Milas, I don't know what to say. It's so dreadful. I'm so sorry.

MILAS: Don't say anything Janna. Please. I can't talk about it...But we need to talk about your container.

JANNA: You're great, Milas. *She takes a step back.* So you've got it. I can't believe it. How on earth did you manage to get a whole container into town without anyone noticing? More importantly: where is it?

MILAS: Sorry. We got the container from London. So we got it into town. But it's being held by...er...you know the characters: Ardo and Bojan.

JANNA *shouting*: What? Our bloody Mafia?

MILAS: Hush...please...

JANNA: I can shout as much as I want in my hospital. They can't be serious. They don't know what's inside, do they?

MILAS: I'm afraid they do.

JANNA *shouting, outraged*: Fucking bastards! What do they want? *She starts raving*: Those bloody swine. What do they want? It's medicine. I can't believe it!

MILAS: It's not my fault. I got it here. But they stopped the truck. They want to speak to you.

JANNA: OK. Let's go. *Milas leaves and Janna, with determination, crosses to a chest of drawers and takes out a sports bag. She opens it and looks at the contents, bundles of deutschmark notes. She grabs her Uzi, checks it, stuffs more money into her bag, and follows Milas out of the door. Cut.*

Garage. Int.

The truck is standing in the middle of a big garage. Milas and Janna enter. Sirius stays outside as they close the door. Next to the truck are two men in army fatigues, Ardo and Bojan, in Ray-Bans and gold chains, smoking – the men she had seen trying to enter the café in her first month in Sarajevo.

ARDO: So you're the doctor! *He smiles at her with contempt.* And pregnant too. What a pity. I thought I had a nice price for this truck. And now it's just cash. Sod it!

JANNA: OK. Shut the fuck up. This is my truck. Hand it over.

BOJAN: Hold it, sweetie. Not so fast. What's it worth for you? Want to take your blouse off?

JANNA *in utter fury*: Piss off, you thieves. This is medicine for children. There's no room for parasites like you. Give me the fucking truck.

ARDO: Not so fast, sweetie, what's it worth to you?

JANNA: Piss off. *She walks closer to him, looking with hatred into his eyes.* I've had enough of you foul shits. *She turns round and walks away, fumbling with her bag. She pulls out her gun. A single shot is heard, fired by Bojan, aimed not to hit her but to stop her. The bullet is heard flying past her.*

MILAS: Stop! Janna!

BOJAN *unnerved*: Steady. Just drop that gun. *Shaken, she drops the Uzi.* Let's make a deal. Fifteen thousand deutschmarks. In cash. Now. And the truck is yours. And that's cheap. We normally take thirty per cent of the value.

JANNA *pale, shaking but undeterred*: Nothing, you spineless creep.

ARDO: OK. Bye-bye then. That's it. We'll sell the container to the Croats and your kids are gonna die. Because of you! Nice doctor, Miss!

BOJAN: Don't forget, we got your last WHO shipment too. And we sold it.

JANNA: So you shits were responsible for that? *Shouting.* Are you aware that people died because of this? Because of you?

ARDO: Steady! We get the cash, you get the truck.

MILAS *walking over to Janna, putting his hand on her arm and whispering into her ear*: Be reasonable, Janna. Give him the cash. What's fifteen thousand marks to you? It's nothing. *To the men:* seven thousand.

ARDO *is just shaking his head and moves away*: You must be joking!

JANNA: Ten thousand. That's all I have on me.

BOJAN: OK. Done. But only because I can't be bothered to wait another day.

JANNA: Oh God, you are spineless crooks. Just wait until all of this is over.

The men just smile arrogantly. She takes bundles of notes out of her pockets and out of a bag and hands them the cash. They count the money, put it in a bag and disappear through the door.

MILAS *turning to Janna, wiping his forehead*: Holy smoke, you were lucky! They could have raped you. Slaughtered you. Like Biljana. Right here. God, you're naïve. Promise: don't ever do that again. If you have a gun, beware what you're doing.

JANNA: I don't care any more. *She picks up her Uzi and climbs into the driving seat. Milas opens the front doors of the garage and also climbs into the truck after Sirius jumps in.*

MILAS *annoyed*: You should care. What use are you to your kids in hospital if you're dead?

Cut.

Janna's hospital. Int.

In the hospital corridor nurses are carrying in loads of boxes from the truck. Janna is standing by, watching, laughing. She puts her arm around Milas.

JANNA: I guess I owe you a lot. How much do you ask for that trip?

MILAS: Nothing. But we have to drink a bottle of your father's Château Margaux.

JANNA *smiling at him*: So your cut is just as high as Ardo and Bojan's. You know the price of a bottle of Margaux? *Milas laughs but then turns silent, thinking.*

MILAS: I've got some news about your brother. I think I now know where he is.

JANNA *excited*: Where, Milas?

MILAS: He's a prisoner, but we can get him out, I think. Unfortunately, we'll have to rely on similarly unsavoury types to get him out.

JANNA: Milas! This is amazing. You have to get him out! Don't worry about dealing with those types. That end justifies the means.

MILAS: I may need a lot of money though to buy him out.

JANNA: Shit. Milas. I have hardly any left. Oh shit.

MILAS: Don't worry, I think I can get the cash.

JANNA *looking at her watch*: Damn. I've got to rush. I'm going to my parents, and need to drop those antibiotics at Braco Bobar's house. *Milas frowns.* Yes, I know it's in no-man's-land. But he's so sick he can't move, and I'll take care. Don't worry.
Cut.

Sarajevo road. Ext.

Janna is walking briskly down the road in the shadow of the houses. Sirius is following, sniffing at the rubbish lining the street. Janna is looking nervously around, eyeing the buildings with searching glances. She arrives at a house and knocks at the door. Braco Bobar opens and greets Janna.

JANNA: Here you are. As promised. Don't take them all in one go, though.

BRACO: Thanks, Janna. It's pathetic, but I can hardly get out of bed, I'm so weak.

JANNA *looking down the street*: This has become a bit of a rough neighbourhood. You shouldn't stay here, Braco.

BRACO: Don't worry, Janna. I'm safe. But I need to lie down again. Thanks again.

They shake hands, and Janna turns around and starts walking back home, Sirius running behind her. After she has been walking for about fifty metres an army truck suddenly appears out of a side street in the distance. Janna ducks instinctively inside the entrance to a house. The truck turns and stops in front of another house about seventy-five metres away from her. Six men jump out. They shout, wait, and then kick down the door of the house. Janna grasps her Uzi, grabs the dog's collar and moves closer to the next entrance, where she hides again. The men fire their automatic weapons inside the house, and screaming can be heard from inside. The men reappear, dragging a woman and a child. Both are struggling and shouting, screaming. They beat them and throw them onto the truck. Two men are dragged out of the house. They are kicked in the back so that they fall face-down on the pavement. They struggle to get up again and the soldiers step back and then fire at them. Both men collapse. The soldiers move closer and fire at them at close range, killing them.

Janna's face is agonised. She grabs her gun, standing paralysed, fear on her face. The soldiers light a cigarette in

*a leisurely way and get into the truck. The engine roars as
they pull up the road. Janna suddenly lets go of Sirius and
starts running towards the scene. But the truck is already
too far away. She holds her Uzi ready to fire, aims, but then
drops it without firing and runs towards the men who are
lying on the ground, turning their bodies over, checking
their arteries, their eyes. She breaks down in the middle of
the street on her knees, crying.*

JANNA: Oh my God! Why didn't I shoot? Oh God! Oh,
damn me! *She remains kneeling, banging her fists onto the
road and then throws up, shouting in spasms*: Oh shit!
Shit! God, help! *She collapses and turns on her side,
pulling her legs up, lying in a foetal position.* Oh shit!
Fucking goddamn shit!
Fading.

Janna's parents' home. Int.

*In the living room, Janna is sitting on the sofa, a bucket at
her feet. Her father is sitting next to her, his arm around
her shoulder. She is completely depressed, looking down at
the ground, her head covered by her hands.*

DJEMAL: I've also seen it. Sometimes you can do something.
Then, at other times, nothing. Often it's better not to do
anything. Like this, you can save the children. And the
women. I've got many free afterwards.

JANNA *shaking her head, looking up, her face swollen and
tearful*: But the men are dead. Butchered. Like fucking
sheep. I saw their brains on the asphalt. *She is shaken
by convulsions and throws up again.* Oh shit! Oh
goddamn shit!

DJEMAL: And I still can't convince Braco to leave the
neighbourhood.
Cut.

Thou shalt not kill

A long end of March

I am sitting at my desk, looking through the cold window onto the city I once loved and which I now loathe because of its cruelty, its treacherous streets. Today I saw killing, and could not help. I have been staring into death's ugly face every day, and have seen many pass away. But today I saw it happening. Saw death, and the bringers of death. And almost killed the killers myself. I am appalled by the fact that I did not act, did not shoot those who killed. And I am even more appalled by the fact that I can even think this way. I should not. Killing causes even more killing. I try to remind myself:

Thou shalt not kill.   Thou shalt not kill.

I need to write it again, though I have written it before. I need to write it twice, once for each eye, so that I cannot miss it. Oh Dan, what would you have done? I cannot tell you how much I miss you, miss your thoughts, your heartbeat.

Thou shalt not kill. But what then? I decide that I have to stop all of this. I am a doctor. I have helped both sides. I don't differentiate. I don't care which side someone is on. A human being is a human being.

How can I help? Go and speak to both sides? Try to mediate and bring peace? Shuttle like Kissinger? Nobody dares to do this. It's naïve. But someone has to start, and I seem to be the only one who wants to start, who wants to start the beginning of the end of the war.

I sit for a long time, looking out of the window and at Dan's picture, which gives me strength. Should I decide to throw away my Uzi and walk the streets of Sarajevo with my head held high? No one is going to shoot me. Should I start the peace movement tomorrow?

How? I have no idea yet. Other women like me must have the same thoughts. Women like me came together from both sides to stop the slaughter in Northern Ireland. Why can we not stop the war in Bosnia? Free Sarajevo? I remember the graffiti I once read on a wall in London: 'What if there were a war and nobody went?' I remember laughing about it together with Dan. But how true it is! Most mothers are fed up with war, about seeing their sons and husbands die. We have to start the end together. I imagine a demonstration of all the women of Sarajevo against the war. I imagine us all in white dresses. White, our colour of peace. But my mind wanders and cannot concentrate on the idea of peace. Instead I think, when did I last wear a white dress, or any dress for that matter. When did I last have long hair, flowing in the wind? When did I last use perfume? I do not even remember where I left my favourite bottle, in London or in Lujeron, near the big mirror, where I used to look at myself, admiring the slightest visible curvature which has now become so round, kicking from the inside.

I pray to God to give me and others strength to fight the evil with love. But my prayers are too weak: at the same time as I am writing these idealistic thoughts, I feel hatred inside me. And I feel the reassuring touch of the cold metal of my Uzi at my side. God is always on the side of the winners. I do remember Dad's words. No, I think, I will not be the stupid martyr, not even to bring peace. Snipers are not interested in peace – they kill the innocent first. The innocent and the naïve who'd march around town in their white dresses for peace, dreaming of perfume when the town stinks of shit and death. Reading my own words I realise: Sarajevo has become a mixture of shit and death!

Five hours later. I am awake, thinking, wishing to feel warm summer air, thinking of Lujeron. Should I call Milas now and leave straight away? The thought is tempting. I am so torn. I have become tougher and less idealistic. I cannot wear white and demonstrate for peace if there are men on the hills not interested in peace. I decide to wear my hidden Uzi with hidden pride until there is peace. And use it if I need to use it.

Oh God! Why have you created us with such contradictions?

Eight hours later, I still smell the smell of death that floated through the air and hear the piercing cries of the women and the children, the moaning of the men hit by bullets, the thump of the bullets when they hit the bodies. I feel the bitterness of my stomach's acids as I choked and threw up on the asphalt. The self-disgust that manifested itself in my vomit spreading on the street.

I feel a wave of disgust coming over me: disgust at Sarajevo and disgust at myself. I realise now I would have shot had things not been moving so fast. I would have killed in order to stop killing. No, maybe even in order to avenge killing, not only to prevent killing. I walk over to look into my mirror, and see two deep black eyes, that do not recognise me any more. Are these the same eyes that looked at you, Daniel, in the Orangerie the second day we met, not understanding your militancy? Are these the same eyes that spring with tears when they see children lose their limbs? I doubt and look and search. I shake my head and see my eyes moving in their sockets, trying to keep contact with their counterparts in the mirror. I hate this mirror that tells me the truth I do not want to know. This is a million times worse than losing your virginity. Will I ever be innocent again? Is this now me? Grown up? Does growing up mean a readiness to fight? To murder when it's necessary? I do not want to lose the God in me that keeps me going. The God I feel every morning deep inside me, pushing me to do what I am doing.

And yet this God is telling me it is all right to kill, when justice is in your hands only. I promise myself never to kill just in order to kill. But always to fight for justice.

I look into the mirror again and see my eyes, and find a light, a tiny sparkle in the black that tells me I am right. I am not sure when I will talk with Daniel about this day. I am not sure whether he will ever understand or walk away, saddened by my change. I think of him, and his picture smiles back at me from my chest of drawers, giving me hope and strength. A few more days, not even weeks.

As I am reading these lines now in the garden of Lujeron, I realise that for some reason I had feared this transformation that was happening, which I had noticed when we were having dinner in Vienna. Back then I was glad, as pacifism in the middle of a war zone is dangerously naïve. But at the same time I was worried, scared, since I loved her absolute pacifism, which I felt was part of her personality, unchangeable, like her black eyes. What would she be like once she lost these ideals? What would be her Leitmotiv in life without them?

Alea iacta est

5 April 1993

I cracked! I cracked! The shelling was successful.

I'm back. It's getting bright. I took advantage of the early hours of the morning, the break in the shelling, when the cowards on the hills are falling asleep after a night of heavy drinking, to run back with Sirius to Mum and Dad. To my surprise they were up, sipping coffee.

Alea iacta est.

At three o'clock I decided it was time to go. Enough is enough. I do not want to kill. I do not need to lose my sanity. I'm leaving Sarajevo for good. I had feared the wrath of my parents, the anger for abandoning them in the middle of the war, but received only kindness and understanding. I cried in their arms, realising that I may not see them for a long time, not until this war is over. Our neighbour went to get Milas, and we decided to go in four days' time, with the next UN plane to Split, if they are flying. At the moment, they are shooting at UN planes again, so the UN has stopped flying. Four days, Dan, and I'll be in London, home. Four days.

I need to close my book, to go back into theatre. Three more days of operations. And yet, my heart feels heavy when I think of all my friends here at the hospital. My colleagues. My patients. Am I a spineless coward, leaving them? Maybe, but then four days, four days. I cannot wait...the shelling really worked on me. Anyhow. I'm getting called: another wounded person. How many more will I stitch up?

Those swine. They shot at Sirius and wounded him. A man picked him up and brought him back to hospital – the whole town knew whose dog he is. Instead of shooting me, they – whoever it was – shot Sirius. He was still alive, but crippled. Dogs have such sad sad eyes. Sirius looked at me full of hope that I would help him. I anaesthetised him and operated on him. In his leg I found a bullet. I thought about putting him to sleep, about ending his life. I am sad, this is so pathetic – here I am surrounded by dying children and adults, and I am sad because a dog, whom I could not have given a hoot about a few months ago, is wounded. But he has become such a loyal friend, and his growling kept me safe.

Milutin

I was still in bed when Milas called early in the morning. He was speaking in a hushed voice, and said he needed a hundred thousand deutschmarks, as soon as possible, to get Milutin out. Milutin – Janna's brother. I jumped up.

'Where is he?'

'Not too far from Sarajevo, Dan.'

'But how the heck are we going to get him out of there?'

'We need to buy him out. Do you think you can get the money?'

I paused to think. I had never heard such garbage, but this was Milas, and the war in Bosnia is not like war in normal situations.

'Where are you now, Milas?'

'Hungary.'

'Call me back in one hour,' I said. Milas hung up.

How do you get a hundred thousand marks into Bosnia? I rushed to the office and asked Tom, who simply suggested we deliver the money ourselves.

'But how?'

'Let's just get the cash and fly to Budapest and try to meet up with Milas over there.'

'Give Milas the money? They'll just take the dosh and shoot him. They'll never let Milutin out.'

'Look, you arrange the logistics with Milas, and tell him we'll see him wherever when he's ready.'

Milas gave us four hours to get organised. I got the cash and put on my roughest clothes, an old army anorak, boots. We were off. I almost did not recognise Tom at the airport, and feared they would never let him onto the plane.

Tom laughed: 'Bankers playing Rambo.'

It was in the late afternoon when we arrived in Budapest. Milas was waiting in the arrivals hall, and grinned when he saw me. We gave him the bag containing the cash.

'We're coming with you,' Tom told him.

He looked at us incredulously.

'You must be joking. Milutin is in a war zone. Combat zone. This is not for bankers. You won't survive a minute.'

'Actually, Milas, Tom was in the army before he became lazy. He was a Marine in the States.'

'Good joke!'

'Well,' Tom said with a wry smile, 'it's actually true. Not that I saw a lot of combat, but…'

'Holy shit!' Milas interrupted. 'But don't kid yourselves. War in Bosnia is different. It's not like in Kuwait.'

'Look Milas,' interjected Tom, 'we worry about ourselves. We're not naïve. But I know that if we let you walk into their trap with all that dosh, you wouldn't see much of it, Milutin wouldn't see you, and probably neither you nor he would see Janna in Sarajevo again.'

'You get us in and out of wherever Milu is at the moment. And we'll be with you and take Milu back with us. Or you take him to Sarajevo, whatever he prefers to do.'

Milas stared at the ground for a long time, and then turned round, beckoning us to follow him. At the end of the arrivals hall he walked out to a black BMW that was waiting for him. We got in, and the driver sped us away. He stopped half an hour later at a small airstrip near a hangar, and we saw a small plane waiting. It was old and rusty, painted grey. To my surprise, Milas unlocked the doors and climbed into the pilot's seat.

'Can you fly this sucker?' Tom asked.

'Well, I've flown it a couple of times now. But I still prefer the UN planes. This thing is pretty unstable.'

'But do you have a licence?'

Milas roared with laughter. 'Who do you think will check my licence?' We climbed in and he took off, flying low, following the contours of the landscape, over rivers and hills in the evening twilight. The thing was fast. We had no idea where he was taking us.

'We have to cross Croatia and make sure not to stray into Serbia by mistake!' Milas shouted over the droning of the engine. At last he went even lower and landed on a road in what looked to me like a valley. A normal road, no airstrip. We could have hit anything, and would have been killed instantly if there had been any debris or cows on that road.

'I know this place pretty well. We used to come here as kids. My grandparents lived over there.' Milas pointed at the distance where we saw nothing. We nodded.

'Here, take this.' He handed each of us a gun and ammunition. Tom loaded it professionally. I looked at mine blankly.

'An AK-47,' Tom said. 'That's pretty cool.' Milas urged us to hurry. Behind the barn, into which we pushed the plane, a jeep was hidden. We squeezed in, and Milas drove off at high speed. In the car, Tom showed me the basics, like how to pull the trigger. At last we came to what looked like a farm. We saw a light in one of the houses. Milas ordered us to stay in the background, not to be seen. He knocked. The door opened, and two guys walked out, dressed in army fatigues. We could not hear what they were saying. But the men disappeared again into the house, and from behind it we heard a gate opening and a jeep manoeuvring out onto the road. It sped away. Milas came back and explained that the two were going to get Milutin, and should be back in less than twenty minutes.

'Are they Serbs?' Tom asked.

'No. Probably just criminals. They'll come back with which-ever criminals are holding Milutin now.'

'So it's not them?'

'No, they are just middlemen.'

'And take a cut?'

'Probably. Anything and everything is tradable, including Bosnian fighters and their girlfriends.' Milas paused. 'When they are back, we need to hand them the money and exchange it for Milutin. Same ceremony as if we exchanged prisoners. They think they are surrounded by ten to twenty Bosniak fighters.' We could see him grinning.

'But how will they know whether the money is real?'

'Someone else will check it, of course.'

Just as he was saying this, the door opened and a woman came out. We stepped into the background, and Milas went up to her.

She shone her torch into the bag and started examining the money, counting the bundles. It took her a long time to count the full hundred thousand deutschmarks. Satisfied, she shuffled back to the house. A short while later the jeep reappeared, together with a black Mercedes limousine, which stopped at some distance from the house in the middle of the road, having done a U-turn. One of the men got out of the jeep and went into the house. When he came out, he beckoned to Milas.

'OK. You stay here with the money next to the stone, till they come out. And make sure no one does anything stupid. Tell your guys to go easy. And both of them will be OK.'

He went over to the Merc and we heard muffled voices. Milutin and his girlfriend Alma were dragged out of the car and started walking towards us, their hands and feet tied together so that they could only walk slowly. They were held by a soldier whose face was covered by a balaclava. Milas held the bag of money in his left hand, approaching the couple. He handed the bag to the hooded soldier and grabbed the couple, quickly cutting their ropes, and pulled them towards his jeep. The hooded soldier turned round and headed quickly back to his Mercedes.

All of a sudden there were shots, smashing into the other men's jeep and the Mercedes. Then from the side, from the field, the headlights of a car were switched on and shone onto the hooded soldier, who was frantically trying to open the front door of his Mercedes. From inside the Merc, someone returned fire, and an anti-tank gun appeared through the window. It destroyed the car in the field. We jumped into the ditch next to us as bullets came flying through the grass, hitting the mud on the other side of the ditch. The headlights of yet another car were turned on, and shone at us, but there was a burst of machine-gun fire at my side and the car was hit and exploded in a ball of fire. The Mercedes revved up and sped away. Tom aimed and pulled the trigger. The Mercedes, hit, swerved off the road and crashed into the ditch.

'Gotcha!' I heard Tom shouting.

I could see two soldiers getting out of the Mercedes, shooting at whoever was in the field. They were instantly hit and collapsed.

I looked around in terror. Who were they? How many? How long had they been watching us? I realised that we were in the middle of a two-front battle. From the top of the house someone now opened fire, and I could hear voices in the field. Tom fired again, and someone in the field returned the fire. Tom got hit. I aimed and shot at where I had seen the silhouette of a person in the field, but did not see whether I hit him. Instead, bullets were flying low over my head. I ducked. From nearby someone else was firing at the people in the field. I did not look around, but shot at wherever I suspected the fire might be coming from. We needed to get out of here. I moved backwards through the ditch towards our car, which had miraculously not been hit, and stumbled.

'Fuck! Ouch!' It was Tom, who was lying on his back, gripping his arm.

'I'm hit. My shoulder. Chest! Where is Milas?'

'I don't know. He must be somewhere near the car.'

Again bullets skimmed the grass above our heads. I held my gun over the ditch, and fired without aiming. The person on top of the house fired too, until a bullet hit him. Then there was silence. I looked up and saw in the light of the burning car a figure in the field crawling towards us. From nearby a single shot was fired. I heard the thud as the bullet hit his body, piercing his jacket. The figure fell over and remained motionless. Next to me on the left I heard moaning, and on my right just silence. I looked around. Milutin came crawling towards us, carrying Tom's gun. He was the only one with real experience, and had probably saved us killing the people in the field. He grabbed Alma, who was shivering in panic. We saw Milas...was he dead? He had blood all over him, but he seemed to be breathing.

'We've got to get out of here,' Milutin hissed. We picked up Milas and dragged him towards the car, heaving him onto the back seat. Alma climbed onto the seat next to him. Then we rushed back to get Tom. He was unconscious and heavy. We dragged him with all our force through the ditch and heaved him into the back. Suddenly, as I was about to climb in, I heard a voice shouting from the distance in English: 'Leave the car. Get away. We need it.'

I could not see who it was.

'No way!' I shouted back. He was at least fifty metres away. Milutin started the engine.

'Get in!' He hissed. 'And shut up!'

I was about to get in when a shot caught my shoulder. I dived into the car, feeling the pain and smelling my blood. A second shot hit the door. Alma pulled me in, when a third shot shattered the back window and ripped through Tom's body. Alma slammed the door shut as the engine roared and Milutin accelerated the jeep up the road, turning into the forest. Strangely, there were no more shots, and I was hoping that he had run out of ammunition. I figured he would not use an anti-tank gun if he still wanted the car. But the seconds were terrifying.

I touched my shoulder and felt the warm blood. But the bullet seemed to have just scraped my arm, ripping off skin and flesh, without getting stuck in the muscle.

Milutin drove fast through the night. Alma had regained her composure, and managed to bandage us by tearing up her shirt. Milas and Tom were in bad shape.

'I fear he won't make it. His heartbeat and breathing are really faint,' she observed from the back, crouching over Milas.

'Where are we going?' I asked Milutin.

'We need to get into Sarajevo. There's no other way out of here, unless we fly. But I can't fly Milas's plane, so we have to risk it and run. If they get us at the barricades, they'll probably shoot us. If we get through, we're OK.'

'What? Risk what? Going into Sarajevo? That's crazy!' I shouted. 'No one gets in by jeep, Milu.'

'At three in the morning there's no one around. Don't worry. Besides it's the only option, otherwise I fear the two in the back will be dead.' He smiled for the first time. 'And I know my way. I've been there more often than I would have liked.'

'Yes, but the last time you got caught,' I said.

'Not in Sarajevo, though.'

'How do you want to get across the airport? We can't just crawl over the runway with those two on our backs,' I objected.

'It's because of those two that they'll let us through. Honestly, don't worry. They'll give us a Humvee for the last stretch.'

All of a sudden he looked at me. 'And who are you, by the way?'

'I'm your sister's boyfriend. Daniel. And the guy in the back is Tom, a good friend of mine.' I managed to smile vaguely.

'Daniel. Amazing. I've heard about you. What an absurd way to meet my future brother-in-law! Definitely in his element here in the middle of nowhere in Bosnia!'

He added after a while, 'Thanks for getting Alma and me out.' He looked at me and smiled. 'I assume it was you who paid the ransom, wasn't it?'

I nodded and closed my eyes, and wished that we could get to Sarajevo quickly, or rather to any hospital other than one in Sarajevo quickly, before it was too late for Milas and Tom. Sarajevo really was the last place I wanted to go to now, but Milutin was adamant that it was the only place where we'd have any chance of getting them operated on. Thank God it was still early spring and the morning would not come for some hours.

Janna's hospital. Int.

The children's ward. Janna is seen leaving the ward, coming out into the corridor. A clock on the corridor wall shows 5.45. Voices can be heard from downstairs. She walks down the staircase to the entrance. A nurse is looking at Braco Bobar, who is sitting slumped on a bench, his shoulder and arm covered in blood.

JANNA *rushing towards him*: Braco! Shit! What happened?
BRACO: The same thing you saw in our street the other day. *He breathes heavily.* Except that I was alone and managed to escape through the garden.
JANNA: Oh shit. Those bastards... You've lost a lot of blood. Where are you hit?

BRACO: They got me in the shoulder. *Janna gently takes off his jacket.*

JANNA: Damn! I'll have a look, take out the bullet and stitch you up again. *She turns to the nurses.* Please take him to the theatre in the basement. I'll be right there, Braco. Do they know you were there… and escaped?

BRACO: Of course. *He starts coughing.*

JANNA: OK. Right back. *She goes back into her room and grabs her stuff, taking her bag, and goes to the chest of drawers, taking her Uzi, checking it. She grabs a green towel, wraps it around the Uzi, and leaves.*
Cut.

Reunion

Janna's hospital. Makeshift theatre. Int.

Braco is on the operating table. Janna is operating. She is assisted by Dr Halim, and one nurse. A clock on the wall shows the time: 6.30.

JANNA: OK. That's it. Just the one bullet. He needs to stay the night and then he'll be all right. *She pauses.* God, I'm tired. I'm going back upstairs.

DR HALIM: Don't worry, Janna, we'll take care of him.
Janna takes her bag and walks up the stairs. When she reaches the entrance hall, the noise of a jeep is heard, stopping with screeching brakes in front of the hospital. Footsteps are heard. Heavy army boots. She freezes and listens and takes her Uzi out of the bag, covering it with the towel. A soldier in army fatigues, wielding a gun, enters.

JANNA *shouting panic-stricken*: Stop! What do you want? Get out of here! This is a hospital. *The soldier stops and waves his gun, indicating that she should get out of the way.*

SOLDIER: Where is Braco Bobar. He must be here. *He moves threateningly towards her, getting dangerously close. Janna doesn't flinch.*

JANNA *hissing at him*: Get out of here!
The soldier starts shooting, aiming away from her. A window and a door splinter. From underneath the towel, Janna fires too and kills the soldier. He collapses, his face in complete surprise. A second soldier approaches, firing. Janna tries to hide behind a desk, returning the fire and misses him. The wood splinters as he shoots at her. Janna shoots at him from underneath the desk, hitting him. He slumps forwards, dead. Then silence. The two dead bodies are lying in puddles of blood. One can hear Janna moaning.

She is hit, crouching against the wall. Slowly she gets up, clutching the desk, then her chest and shoulder. There is blood everywhere on her clothes. Her face is determined.

JANNA: Oh fuck. Fuck! *She gathers her strength, covers her Uzi underneath the towel again, and moves slowly, stepping out onto the street, where she sees the jeep standing some thirty metres away. Ardo, the Mafioso, is approaching her, gun in his hand, anxiously looking around. He sees her.*

ARDO *shouting*: Wait!

JANNA: What are you doing here?

ARDO: We got nothing to do with this. We just drove them here. *Janna levels her Uzi.*

JANNA: Liar! Scum! *She fires and Ardo falls backwards, clutching his chest.*

JANNA: Finally I get you! You shit. *A shot bursts through the Jeep's window, missing Janna. Janna looks up and sees Bojan sitting in the driver's seat, aiming his pistol at Janna. She empties her gun into the jeep, which explodes.*

JANNA: Goodbye to you too, you scum! *The picture blurs while Janna continues shooting, so that only the red of the fire is seen as Janna faints. The picture slowly fades away, the shooting echoing, as in a wide valley. The screen turns black.*

Cut.

Sarajevo. Outside Janna's hospital. Ext.

An armoured UN vehicle arrives at breakneck speed, drives past the burnt-out jeep and comes to a screeching halt outside the hospital. Milutin and Dan jump out, and Milutin runs into the hospital. Out of the building two nurses and Milutin come with a stretcher and rush up to the vehicle. The driver jumps out, puts his blue helmet on and helps Milutin and Dan open the back door and put Milas onto the stretcher. As Milas is carried into the

SARABANDE

hospital another nurse appears with a second stretcher, and she and Dan carry Tom into the hospital. Alma follows them into the building. Milutin embraces the driver, patting him on the back.

MILUTIN: Eh, merci Jacques. Grand merci. Hasta luego.

DRIVER: Nada, amigo. A bientôt. Mais plus jamais a l'aéroport.

He laughs and waves goodbye, gets into his armoured vehicle and drives off. Milutin walks into the hospital.

Janna's hospital. Room. Int.

In the hospital. Janna is in bed, in agony. Djemal is standing next to her, leaning over her. Janna is in a kind of delirium, half waking and then dreaming on. She finally wakes up. Her face is determined.

JANNA *seeing her father*: Daddy! I killed them all! I just shot them all. Scum! *Silence. Her father bows over her, smiling, stroking her head.* Dad, how is my baby? Please tell them to save my baby. *She touches her belly and her face is in agony.*

DJEMAL: You'll be all right and baby will be fine. You've been patched up. You're OK now, and they'll do a caesarean, in a few minutes.

JANNA: Daddy, just save my baby. Please tell them to be careful. Where am I hit? I don't even know where I'm hit. Oh God! Have you told Dan?

DJEMAL: I tried to reach Dan, but he's not at home, and at his office nobody knows where he is at the moment. Milas is not around, and I don't know where he is either. *A nurse enters and beckons.* Janna, I'll be right back. *He leaves, but the door to the corridor is left open.*

NURSE: Milas is downstairs. He just came out of theatre.

DJEMAL: What?

NURSE: He was wounded. But it looks as if he's OK. And
there are two other people too. One guy is dead but
the other one's just lightly wounded. They don't look
as if they are from here. They look really rough –
maybe they are mercenaries. I can't understand what
they are saying.

DJEMAL: I'm coming down with you. *He goes back to Janna.*
Janna, I'll be back in a minute. It looks as if Milas was
brought in wounded. He is downstairs. *Janna turns her
head as he leaves.*
Cut.

Janna's hospital. Room. Int.

*A spacious room, with white walls and a bed in one corner,
in which Milas is lying, unconscious and attached to drips.
On the other side of the room, Milutin, Alma and Dan are
sitting around Tom's bed. Dan gets up and walks over to the
window. His face is ashen. Through the open door people
can be seen walking past. Milutin is looking up as Djemal
walks past the door. He jumps up and runs to the door.*

MILUTIN: Dad! Dad! *His father stops and turns round. He sees
Milutin, who runs up to him with open arms, which he
throws around his father. They embrace for a long time.*

DJEMAL: Oh Milu! Milu! This is amazing! *He looks Milutin
in the face and caresses his head.* Milu, I'm stunned.
How come you're here? I was looking for Milas.

MILUTIN: He's right in here. But unconscious. *Both men re-
enter the room. Dan and Alma look up. Djemal looks at
Milas and tries to lift the cover to see the extent of his
wounds, but drops it again. He glances briefly at Tom and
Dan and then turns to Milutin.*

DJEMAL *hushed*: Milu. I have horrible news for you. Janna
is really badly hurt upstairs.

MILUTIN: Janna?

DAN *looking up*: Janna? What are you saying about Janna?

DJEMAL *turning round to look at Dan*: Yes. *He looks Dan up and down.* I think I recognise you, but, this cannot be…

DAN *interrupts*: I'm Dan. Janna's…

DJEMAL: Oh my God! *He walks up to Dan and shakes his hand with both hands.* I'm Djemal, her father. Janna got hurt in a shootout, and things are really bad. They are operating on her right now. Caesarean.

DAN: Oh shit!

DJEMAL: Her baby looks like being OK, though. *He sighs.* What a time to meet in Sarajevo! *He looks at Dan's shoulder.* What happened to you?

DAN: Nothing. I just got strafed by a bullet. But Milas is in bad shape and…my friend Tom is dead.

DJEMAL *looking down*: I'm sorry. That's terrible. I'm really sorry.

MILUTIN: They are the guys who got us out, together with Milas.

DJEMAL: Oh God…

MILUTIN: Dad. Alma is here too. *Alma gets up and joins them. Djemal embraces her. The door opens and a nurse comes in and whispers something into Djemal's ear. She leaves again. Djemal turns towards the door.*

DJEMAL: They are starting the caesarean. Let's go upstairs. *Milutin, Dan and Alma follow him out of the room.* *Cut.*

I looked at Tom and left the room, only to re-enter a minute later as there was nowhere else to wait. Tom's face was grey and distorted. The last bullet had hit him in the lower back, and he had probably died in the car before reaching the hospital. And now Janna. We were all incredibly tense. Milas should have been in intensive care, but he was just lying next to Tom, unconscious, though I was not sure whether that was because of the anaesthetics or because he was close to giving up life too. A nurse came by every ten minutes to check, but there were no heart monitors or any other technical equipment. He could easily have died without anyone noticing. So we took his pulse every few minutes and checked his breathing.

I wanted to see Janna and our baby. Milu, Alma and I walked outside, where the air hung grey over Sarajevo. In the distance we could hear the thunder of artillery fire, but not the thud of landing grenades. Away from the entrance stood a Jeep, burned out, still smoking. The pool of blood on the floor indicated that someone had been hit here within the last few hours. The air smelled of burning rubber, rather than nature. Spring had not yet arrived, even though the grass was turning greener and the wind was not as icy as I had felt it in Budapest. The nurse joined us. Milutin offered us all cigarettes, which we smoked to fill our anxious wait.

'It's probably only another fifteen minutes, then Janna will be out. She'll come round.' I nodded, looking at the destroyed jeep and the pool of blood. I felt disgust, and the bitterness of stomach acids in my mouth. I was glad to have a cigarette.

'So what happened? Do you know?' I asked, turning towards the nurse, who was pale and shivering. She did not look into my eyes, but stared at her cigarette.

'Not really.' She replied. 'I wasn't there. I only witnessed the end from the window up there.' She pointed up at the windows on the top floor.

Alma turned to her, as she remained silent. 'And?'

'I just saw Janna coming out of the hospital, seeing this guy next to his jeep, and she shot him.'

'Janna shot him?' I asked.

'She just mowed him down.' The nurse looked at us as if she was surprised that we found that unusual.

'And then?' I asked, still in disbelief.

'Then she blew up the jeep.'

'Holy shit! I can't believe it.'

Alma took my arm. 'Don't hold it against her,' she said. 'This is war, and you don't know what those guys were up to outside the hospital.'

At that moment the door opened and Djemal came out of the hospital. Despite everything, he managed to smile at us.

'What are you doing here? Milas has woken up, and Janna has come out of theatre, and you're smoking.'

We rushed upstairs. Djemal went back to Milas, and the nurse took me a floor higher to Janna.

At Janna's bed. Int.

The camera focuses from above on Janna's bed. She is now on white linen, in fever and pain. She is rolling her head in agony. Her face is very pale. The bump of her belly is gone. She holds her baby, clutching her to her chest. The door opens and Janna turns her head. Dan enters, looking exhausted and worried. Janna smiles, overjoyed. Dan walks up to her and kisses her tenderly.

JANNA: This is a miracle. How did you get here? I can't believe you're here. I wake up and you're here, in Sarajevo. *She looks around.* We are still in Sarajevo, aren't we? *She smiles at him but he cannot return her smile. She shows him the baby.* Here, this is her. A girl. Take her. She's yours. Isn't she wonderful? *She smiles, as Dan takes his daughter into his arms, overcome by emotion. The door opens and Djemal, Alma and Milutin enter.*

JANNA *looking at them in disbelief*: Milu! I can't believe it! Oh Milu, I'm so glad you're alive. Did Milas get you out? And Alma! *Milutin goes up to Janna, caressing her gently, holding her hand. Janna closes her eyes in exhaustion.*

DJEMAL: I think we'll leave you two alone for a while. *Djemal, Milutin and Alma leave.*

JANNA *looking at Dan and their baby*: Look at her. She's absolutely fine. We had a caesarean. She wasn't hit. *She*

smiles and looks at her baby. Can we call her Camille?
Dan smiles at her. I don't want to give her a Bosnian
name. I don't want to attach her to this place. Camille
sounds so beautiful. The name reminds me so much of
our time in France. *She pauses to breathe, closing her
eyes, her face tenses in agony.* I'll be all right, the doctors
said. They think I'll be OK. *Dan caresses her head,
wiping sweat from her forehead. He gives Camille back to
her. The baby is sleeping, sucking her little hand. Janna
cries silently because of the pain, tears streaming down her
face. She clenches her fist and rolls her head, eyes closed.*

DAN: Did you get any painkillers?

JANNA *between clenched teeth with her eyes shut*: I don't
know. It feels as if I didn't. But no, I'm sure they gave
me plenty. *She pauses and opens her eyes and tries to
smile at Dan.* It's the stuff your mother sent. But I don't
want to be completely dopey while you're here. *Dan
caresses her head again and attempts to smile. Janna looks
up, clenching her teeth*: I've been hit by a bullet. By
bullets. But they are all out. I'll be OK. *Angry*: We
operated on Braco, one of Dad's friends, and they came
to kill him. But I killed them all instead. All four of
them. Oh God! Those bastards. *She closes her eyes and
sweat appears on her forehead.* 'Thou shalt not kill' is
what I preached to you. Remember? *She tries to look at
him, tries to smile, her speech slows down.* The first
discussion we had? And here I am. 'Thou shalt not kill'
is a commandment. *She breathes heavily and pauses.*
From God. But there's no God in Sarajevo. *She is very
still, just tears streaming from her eyes; her teeth are
clenched and so is her free fist, her other hand holding her
baby gently. She slowly moves her head in agony.*

DAN: Oh Janna! Please! Oh God, please!

She opens her eyes again, looking determined.

JANNA: No. Don't worry. *She caresses his arm with a warm
smile.* I'll make it. We'll fly out of here in two or three

days' time. Milas will get us out. He's promised. He has. Please help me make it.

She closes her eyes and dozes off. Dan takes the baby and lays her into the cot next to Janna's bed. He then rushes to the door to look for a doctor. Dr Halim enters the room and checks Janna's pulse.

DR HALIM: She was badly hit. Much worse than we thought before the operation. She had massive internal bleeding. She never wore her bulletproof vest in hospital. How could we know they would shoot inside? It had never happened before. *She pauses, looking at Janna with anguish.* If she makes it tonight, she'll make it. Tonight is crucial. I don't know. I just don't know. *Smiling vaguely*: The baby is fine, though. Sweet and healthy. Absolutely healthy. *Silence. Dr Halim looks at Janna with a sad and desperate expression.* I just don't know. Why did she get hit? *Dr Halim starts crying, holding on to Dan's shoulder.* She helped so many. She saved so many lives. So many adults and all the children. Serbs, Croats, Muslims. It didn't make a difference to her. And then they shoot her. *Silence.* We wouldn't have made it without her. *Dr Halim turns to leave.*

DR HALIM: Please call me if you need me. I'm either outside or in the room on the right next door. *Dan sits again beside Janna at her bed, gazing at her. He takes Camille into his arms, rocking her gently, examining her with a smile. He puts her back into the cot and studies Janna's face. She is white, but breathing. She opens her eyes and smiles at Dan, vaguely.*

JANNA: Daniel? *He draws nearer.* Daniel, please take care of our baby. *He caresses her, smiling. She looks at him, smiling too, very pale, white. She tries to lift her head but does not succeed, and falls back onto her pillow. She looks at him with distant eyes, whispering*: Daniel, I…I…I feel…I'm not going to make it. Please, please take care of Camille. Please take care of yourself too. *He clutches her hand. She smiles and tries to say something. But her eyes become empty. Dan looks at her.*

DAN: Janna? *She does not respond or move. He shouts*: Janna! JANNA! *No response. He turns her head.* JANNA? HELP! *He rushes to the door and shouts into the corridor.* Help! HELP! *Dr Halim and a nurse come rushing in, look into her eyes and feel her pulse, check her breathing. Dan waits impatiently. At last they sit down on a chair, Dr Halim covering her eyes with her hands.*

DR HALIM: She … she's dead.

DAN *screams, looking at her*: Janna. JANNA! *But she just stares at him, motionless, with blank eyes. He sobs more and more quietly*: Janna. No! No! Don't go! Oh, God. Oh, my God! Oh no!

He looks at Janna for a long time, then closes her eyes and sobs in silence. Finally he walks over to the window and stares into the distance, his face motionless, his eyes staring, his cheeks wet from his tears, his fists clenched. The door opens and Djemal, Milutin and Alma re-enter. They look at Dan and Dr Halim, and realise what has happened. Djemal leans against the wall, covering his head with his hands. Alma sits down and sobs quietly. Milutin turns to Dan and puts his arm around his shoulder. Djemal walks over to them and hugs both of them.
Cut.

Janna's parents' place. Int.

In the living room. Leila is pacing up and down. The room is quiet. Jasminka is sitting at the table, her head in her hands. Someone knocks on the door. Leila opens it. Dan, Djemal, Milutin and Alma enter the room. Dan is carrying Camille, wrapped in an old blanket. He is still as dark and unwashed as he was in hospital. Leila looks at Milutin and smiles for a second as she rushes to embrace him.

LEILA: Milu! Oh Milu! Milu! I…I thought…*She turns silent and suddenly lets go and looks at Dan. Dan abruptly looks down. She turns to Djemal, who is also looking to the ground.*

LEILA: What…what's the matter? *Djemal takes two brisk steps over to her, his mouth tense, tears flooding down his face. He sobs loudly and embraces Leila.*

DJEMAL: They killed her. She…she is dead.

Leila remains silent and looks with a vacant stare at the wall. Milutin walks over to Jasminka and takes her hand, sitting down next to her. Also Alma sits down, burying her head in her hands. Dan stands alone, rocking his daughter in silence.

Fading.

Janna's funeral. Cemetery. Ext.

A barren piece of land in the middle of Sarajevo that used to be a park and has been converted to a cemetery. It is a cold, grey day; the wind sweeps through the grass, clouds hang low and cover the sun. About thirty people are huddled around a grave. All are dressed in black, their clothes worn, their faces expressionless, many silently crying. Everyone Janna knew is present: the doctors, the nurses, friends, Djemal, Leila, Milutin, Jasminka, Alma, Braco and Dan. Her coffin is slowly lowered into the ground. Earth is thrown down. No speech. People just say farewell individually, silently hugging each other. Djemal holds his wife. Jasminka stands with Alma and Milutin, crying. The last guest passes the coffin and the funeral is over. The grave is filled in with a shovel. There are no flowers. Dan stays behind as people are leaving. Djemal turns round, sees Dan standing alone and walks back towards him, taking him by the arm.

DJEMAL: You should come along too. This is not safe, you're too easy a target for a sniper. *Dan looks at Djemal and shakes his head.*

DAN: If there was a sniper he would have probably shot every one of us already.

DJEMAL *smiling vaguely*: Dan, don't trust the logic of Sarajevo…

Everyone is leaving together, except for Dan. He stays with his daughter, who is in a big black pram. He is all in black. He takes a cello out of its case and walks over to the pram and looks at his daughter, who is sleeping. He sits down. Slowly he starts playing the Sarabande of Bach's Suite No 2 in D minor.

He continues playing until the camera withdraws, widening the shot, leaving him alone in the cemetery with the pram beside him.

Epilogue

Today it is just over seventeen months since we escaped from Sarajevo. As soon as Camille was old enough to travel, we got on a UN flight to Budapest. It was hard to leave Milas, Milu, Alma, Jasminka and her parents behind. Jasminka could not obtain a visa to get out – it was hard to believe that people, her own people, could be so cruel as to prevent a child from leaving a war zone. Milu was gone, back to the army, a few days after we arrived in Sarajevo. His sister's death had strengthened his resolve to defend Sarajevo. Djemal and Leila wanted to stay where they said they belonged. I wanted to leave the place where I knew I did not belong and which I hoped my daughter would nonetheless feel some longing for. Outside the hospital I discovered Sirius. He was limping badly, but his wound was healing. I decided to take him with me.

We buried Tom in London. Tania was playing a Mazurka by Chopin. I held Camille in my arms, crying silently, feeling responsible for his death.

The same evening I flew back to Lujeron.

I want Camille to be a true child of Sarajevo, not adhering to any single religion, but still it took some persuasion to get her blessed in a ceremony in London by three clerics, representing Sarajevo's three religions: a Muslim, a Christian and a Jew. Milas and Tania are her godparents. It was the first time I had seen Milas wearing a suit. He looked like an English gentleman, and behaved like one.

So now it is September 1994. Lord Owen and Cyrus Vance's peace plan for Bosnia is dead. But NATO has taken the initiative and has threatened bombing. Miraculously, the Bosnian Serbs stopped shelling Sarajevo in February. By March the trams were running again and there are signs that finally Sarajevo may find a more permanent peace. I often speak with Leila and Djemal. Milas is back in business, running his local FedEx courier services. I noticed that Tania had started going on trips to Vienna and Zagreb on a regular basis.

Becks has bought more medicine, which Milas is shipping to Sarajevo – though he never managed to get his plane back. Jasminka has gone back to school, and Alma is preparing to study medicine in Zagreb once the war is over. She has Croatian family. So full post-war normality will soon be setting in. They now drink Burgundy of the 1980s.

Sirius has become as French as a dog can become. He happily barks along with the local dogs and chases local cats. Instead of eating rubbish and excrement he is now on to sausages, and absolutely adores foie gras. Still, he will never forget the war, as he still limps and hates fireworks.

Once we arrived in Lujeron, I spent months just taking care of Camille. I resigned from our partnership, even though my colleagues persuaded me to finish what I had started. Somewhat listlessly I worked on my transaction in Milan until it was completed, always flying back as often as possible to Toulouse to drive down to Lujeron. I gave my flat in London to Tania as a present, as I could not stand living surrounded by art and money anymore. I kept Janna's studenty place, though, but moved to Lujeron, which had become my new home. I love the peace, the solitude, the mountain air, the poverty of Ariège and the house that is slowly falling apart. My parents spent months in New York, leaving Camille, Sirius and me alone in the big house. But they came back, looking after Camille so that I could withdraw and write.

I play the cello in the garden or, in the evenings, near the fireplace. Camille sits listening intently.

For me it is like a miracle to see Camille growing up, smiling, crawling around the floor, her interest in everything she can put in her mouth. Once, when I returned to London for two weeks to take care of the flat, and close the Milan transaction, I felt the urge in the afternoons to spend time at the Tate, and took Camille with me, carrying her in my arms. I was surprised at her curiosity, her awe when she was soaking in the bright and melancholy colours of the Rothkos – or was she just reflecting my melancholy feelings as I was overpowered by the serene monotony of his colours? Would she love the same paintings that Janna used to love?

At night I have been sitting next to her bed to read and write. Most nights she is restless, so I take her into my arms. Looking at her, I walk around the room.

Camille has the same tanned skin, the same sweet mouth, but most strikingly the same dark eyes, conveying a sense of urgency at an age when time should not matter, deep and thoughtful, and yet sparkling, full of mischievous laughter.

When finally Camille could stand she treated it as a major achievement, on which she congratulated herself by clapping her hands, falling down on her bum as a result. She still needed her hands to hold herself up. Soon after, she could reach the piano, and 'played', once again applauding herself, delighted with her more abstract Mozart imitations.

Most mornings Camille wakes me now by gently pulling on my blanket. How she manages to climb out of bed is an enigma, probably to both of us. She loves taking showers, the spraying of warm water, playing with shampoo. We always shower the way the Japanese do: sitting on tiny stools, showering and pouring buckets of water over our heads. I wash her hair. She shrieks and laughs.

One day, Camille returned from a toy shop with my mother. She came walking into my room – I had not heard them coming back. My mother had wanted to buy her a little doll. They had spent barely five minutes in the shop, as Camille knew what she wanted the moment she saw it. She handed the doll to me with a questioning smile. It was a little doctor, with a white cap and a big red cross on her chest. I was stunned and speechless. Why? I grabbed her and held her in my arms, looking for a long time into her eyes, black, serious, tense. Like Janna's.